The Truth about Jacob

Sherry Long

PublishAmerica
Baltimore

© 2005 by Sherry Long.
All rights reserved. No part of this book may be reproduced, stored in a retrieval system or transmitted in any form or by any means without the prior written permission of the publishers, except by a reviewer who may quote brief passages in a review to be printed in a newspaper, magazine or journal.

First printing

ISBN: 1-4137-8690-1
PUBLISHED BY PUBLISHAMERICA, LLLP
www.publishamerica.com
Baltimore

Printed in the United States of America

To my brother Mike, who was born with a book in his hand, and my mom-in-law, Mattie Davis, both of whom had they lived long enough to see this book in print, would have been my two most loyal fans.

Acknowledgments

This book would not have come about without the help and encouragement of many family members and friends. I would like to thank my husband, children and grandchildren for making my life so thrillingly busy and complete.

A special thanks goes out to Louise Hering, Claire High and Lori Curran. They are my editors, mentors and friends. Without their help, this book would still be hidden on my computer.

Last, but not least, my heartfelt gratitude goes out to Randy Fowler for his endless hours of typing, editing and administrative assistance. Also, I would like to thank Byron Campbell, Don Freemyers, Donna Pero, Ellen Babb and Ramona Sannar. You all know the role you played in the formation of this project.

Chapter 1

It is late spring, 1879. The man stands alone remembering that day many years ago as if it was yesterday. As a boy, he had stood at this very spot, the highest point of Wild Cat Ridge, with a furry black cat in its full prime tucked securely under his scrawny arm. Looking out now, just as he had done that day, he scans the gigantic wall of rock spreading below him. From his precious perch where he stands, he studies the hundreds of feet of solid rock angling down to the river with layer of layer of craggy boulders jutting out and spilling into the ribbon of water far below.

He was only eight years old at the time, although sometimes it doesn't seem that long ago. He vividly remembers how he had calculated his every move. Before he had set the cat ablaze, he had briefly stood staring down over the ledge, his mind's eye picturing what the hairy fireball would look like burning intensely all the way to the bottom of the gorge. At that very moment, he could almost sniff the rancid odor of burning hair consumed with flames and visualize its charred flesh; so black it was beyond recognition. He remembered being excited to hear the blood curdling cries of the cat as it fell swiftly to its death, spilling its guts on the jagged rocks below. His final act being a fulfilled satisfaction to a fantasy he had held for so long.

That was thirteen years ago, and other than a few worthless rodents he had dissected merely to see what they looked like on the inside, it was his first real taste of death. He had felt no remorse or regrets for killing that cat. If anything, in his eagerness to satisfy his own curiosity, he had felt such a titillating thrill of gratification as he doused the cat with coal oil. From the very instant he sparked the flames, he was consumed by the addictive surge of power that rushed through him as he had listened intently above the busy whisper of the wind to the fading screams of the cat all the way to the bottom.

Still reminiscing, his thoughts go back to about a year prior to the day he had killed the cat. That's when Jacob's family first came into town. Unfortunately, every time he thinks about that day, he can still feel the sting of his father's razor strop across his bare bottom. He had bellered like a bull during that beating, and swore to himself at that time that one day he'd be big enough to stand up to that drunken old fool. When that day arrived, he would never again allow his father to lay another hand on him.

That particular whipping was uncalled for, he thought bitterly, standing here again all these years later. *It wasn't my fault the Fowlers were run out of town.* He sure as hell didn't have anything to do with their mysterious disappearance the very next day. When six-year-old Jacob came wandering back into town all alone and confused, it was Jacob's own stupidity that had caused him to crawl into a hog pen attempting to hide from two local men that were merely trying to help him.

To his surprise and dismay, no matter what he claimed to the contrary, it turned out to be his word against the local gossipers. Gossiping was not frowned upon in Johnson's Flat and of course the rumors were flying. His innocence began a steady decline and from that day forward he was pegged a troublemaker.

Above the pounding pressure in his head he was reminded of what galled him the most, the fact that Jacob had ended up living on the Baxter ranch enjoying a life of luxury. He, on the other hand, was forced to live with a worthless, drunken father who got his kicks out of making his own son's life absolutely miserable.

It was no wonder my heart was filled with envy, he thought, as his hate for Jacob sent the adrenaline roaring through his entire body. "Two men chasing the same rainbow," he said to himself with a strangled whisper. "That's where the real problem lies."

His throat began to tighten. He could feel and hear the blood pounding in his ears as he fantasized about what Jacob's broken body would look like sprawled across the rocks at the bottom of the ravine. *Worse things have happened to other men who got in his way*, he quietly justified. He felt the familiar surge of pleasure as in envisioned the many different ways there were to eliminate that man who was a nagging thorn in his side. "Oh, the accidents that could happen, especially on a working ranch," he muttered softly as his mind feasted on all the possibilities

The next day, nineteen miles southwest of Johnson's Flat, California, a slight breeze fanned the barren terrain with a weak wind that barely brought a breath of relief from the rising ninety-degree temperature. The hot sun blazed down in long streams of golden fire throughout the foothills and valley floor surrounding the Baxter ranch. Thin veiled clouds sliced through the pale blue sky, bonding the two into a physical intimacy. The warm season had just begun.

This particular Saturday morning found Billy, or, Bragging Billy Bronco as the locals preferred to call him, mounted on a horse as black as the ace of spades. He took little notice of the sweltering heat. He was much too busy savoring the flattering swell of all the attention he drew. His unyielding determination to break the will of the wild horse undulating beneath his body enabled him to ignore the stifling forces of Mother Nature. He craved the emotional charge he felt from being in control of something so large and powerful. Nothing else seemed worth fussing over, including the sun blazing straight through his backbone or the sweat washing over his entire body.

Rachel grunted as her pretty face puckered into a sneer. "You know, Father, other than his ability to break these horses, Billy's absolutely worthless on this ranch. He's lazy when it comes to some of the chores and repair work around here. He just puts in his time only trying to look busy."

"He's good at working the cattle drives," her father replied.

She rolled her eyes and ignored his remark. "Just look at him. You'd never guess a man like Billy would step within one foot of a wild horse, much less ride one without fear of getting hurt. He's so skinny and pale looking. In fact, if I didn't witness it for myself time and time again I wouldn't believe you, even if you swore on a stack of Bibles that he really is this good at breaking horses."

"I'll admit he doesn't exactly fit the image of your run-of-the mill bronco rider, but he does seem to possess a level of pure strength and willpower that stands above most other men. That young man can handle a wild bronc like many other men only wish they could. Of course, that's with the exception of Jacob," Baxter confirmed.

He then turned and faced his daughter. With a raised brow he drew a curious breath. "A whole stack of Bibles and you still wouldn't believe me?" he asked with a frown.

Looking back at him she just smirked with a silly grin on her face. Raising her chin upwards and standing on her toes she kissed her father with a dainty peck against his unshaven cheek and shrugged her shoulders.

Rachel and her father, Byron Baxter, the wealthiest rancher north of Sacramento, had just approached the corral a few minutes earlier. They were leaning up against the railing, totally involved in what was taking place.

Rachel's face reflected her disgust in Billy. She watched him for a few moments without another word as he rode the horse with methodical efficiency. His spindly legs and arms carved

The Truth about Jacob

the air with swift slices. The sunlight reflected on his pocked face revealed an infestation of lumpy acne scars along with what seemed like three thousand plus freckles. He had a mop of red wiry hair that had gathered a thick coat of dust.

Billy broke all the rules of gravity riding the bronc. Rachel reluctantly admired his expertise with the horse. How could she see it any other way? But everything else about him turned her stomach sour. He was arrogant, conceited, obnoxious and condescending. The list went on and on.

"He also smells worse than a dead skunk," she muttered out of the blue.

"So do most of the other cowboys on this ranch," her father clarified as he raised a stern brow. "Now you know he's not totally opposed to a bath once in a while. And you also know the ropes around here well enough to understand that it's tough for all of these men to take care of their basic needs with so very few daylight hours to work with. These cowboys come back to the ranch, after spending all day out in the fields with barely enough time to grab a square meal before its time to turn in. They do get up with the chickens you know, unlike someone else I know, who manages to get more than enough of her beauty sleep," he said with a wink.

"Yeah, well I'm beginning to believe Billy sleeps with the chickens. You can stick up for him all you want, but as far as I'm concerned he acts like he was born in a barn," she retorted.

"Some things have to be sacrificed for the sake of getting all the chores done in the small amount of daylight hours we have to work with."

"Maybe so, but he sure manages to find the time to spruce up a bit for his big hoot in town every Saturday night."

"You're much too hard on Billy, my dear." He replied protectively with an edge to his voice.

"And you're much too partial to him, Father. I'm waiting for the day you take those blinders off your eyes and see Billy for the troublemaker he really is. He plays by his own rules and you just let him get away with it whether it's fair to the other men or not."

"Now you listen here, young lady, if its one thing I make sure of around here is that every man on this ranch gets his dues fair and square. You're talking with a biased tongue and you know it," he accused.

She had the grace to blush. "I'm sorry. I know you do your best," she responded in a small voice.

"You need to learn to ignore his crazy antics. Don't take him so seriously all the time. That's just his way. He doesn't really mean any harm by it."

Her mind whirled with her father's words, she looked again into his face and said measuredly, "I can't say as that I believe he's perfectly harmless. You know darn well there's been many times when his outspokenness has provoked dissension among some of the other hands. His tendency to think he can call the shots on this ranch when you're not around certainly doesn't set well with any of these men, especially those who have worked for you a lot longer than Billy has. Seniority is important to the older men and I've heard a few of them openly complain about his high-handedness."

Baxter gave his daughter a hard look. "Rachel, you know I have never shied away from my responsibilities on this ranch. If there is any man in my employ that has a grievance with Billy, he sure hasn't come to me to complain about it. And I don't see any point in stirring up dust over matters that aren't important enough to bring to my attention. I've always reassured my men that if there is any kind of trouble around here they can feel free to come to me about it," snarling at the thought that his authority might be in question.

"And furthermore, young lady, if someone were to claim I was partial to anyone on this ranch, other than my little girl, it would be Jacob. From the first day Doc brought him here I've treated him as if he were my own son. I didn't pamper him none, I admit, but I've watched over him like he was my very own

The Truth about Jacob

flesh and blood. Isn't that true?" he challenged, looking at her intently.

Rachel smiled coyly up at her father as he gave her a stern look. "No, I don't deny that. You've been good to Jacob, and for that I'm very proud of you. I know you helped in the search for his missing family, and for that I'm sure he'll be eternally grateful. I certainly appreciate the fact that you gave him a place to call home after his family practically vanished into thin air," she said blushing pink with pride at her father's generosity.

"You and me both, my dear," he said without hesitation. "It's a terrible thing for a child that young to be abandoned like that. I've not regretted my decision to take him in and I've tried my best to live up to my promise to old Doc to take good care of him."

Baxter leaned over and kissed his daughter on the forehead with a gleam in his eye and added, "That young man has proved to be worth his weight in gold and I don't say that lightly. Kindhearted, too. The boy would give any man the shirt off his back without asking anything in return. Never have known Jacob to say or do anything to hurt a living soul."

She nodded in agreement and then mentally compared Jacob to Billy. "Unlike someone else we know who set a cat on fire and tossed it off a cliff just to hear it squeal."

"That was just a rumor, Rachel. You know very well no one witnessed that incident. We all suspected that that was just an eight-year-old's way of trying to get attention. Billy always has stretched the truth a bit just to shock people."

"Maybe he did make up that story, but it's no rumor that Billy's killed before. Doesn't it bother you that he has put more than one man in his grave?" she boldly asked.

"It's called self-defense, my dear, when two men draw against one another."

"Maybe so, but I heard from a very good source that the last fellow was barely old enough to use a razor," she informed him with her hands on her hips.

"Well, its rough times were living in. When men get to playing cards and drinking too much just about anything can happen. I don't say as I approve of any of it, but it's not my place to pass judgment on something I didn't see with my own eyes. As long as Billy doesn't go slinging his gun in the air around here, then I have no cause to stick my nose in his business."

Rachel slipped her right arm around her father's back, which because of his large size barely reached his backbone. He was built like a bull with a barrel-shaped chest and seemed to stand as tall as the trees. He had a grayish brown wooly looking mustache and a dark birthmark that shrouded nearly the whole left side of his right ear lobe. He garnered a broad friendly smile and was surprisingly soft spoken. There were a few sprigs of nappy brown hair sticking straight out from his square shaped heavy head that were wedged in-between his big ears and his hat.

Baxter and Rachel watched for a little while longer as Billy poured his guts into the final phase of the battle to prove his dominance over the horse. The animal was no longer whirling with frenzied kicks in the air as it danced around making awkward patterns on the dry choppy ground.

Rachel finally decided she'd had enough of Billy for one day, so she strolled along the railing to the adjacent corral where Jacob was also breaking a wild horse. Soon after she arrived a small group of other hired hands gathered around as well.

She tried hard to ignore all the other men close by even though she could feel their eyes upon her. The thought that some of these men were in competition with one another to win her affection was somewhat flattering, but the rivalry between them was totally unnecessary. She had long since refused to give any suitors the time of day, especially Billy.

She already had a beau, her mind whispered. Their relationship hadn't been consummated with a ring or a spoken promise, but Rachel knew Jacob had feelings for her. There was no secret that he certainly knew how she felt about him, since

The Truth about Jacob

she wasn't one bit shy about flirting with him when no one was around.

Just looking at him right now emptied her mind of all other thoughts except what it might feel like to kiss such a perfectly formed mouth. Unfortunately, she had yet to experience that pleasure.

"May I ask what is it that makes my little girl smile so big," Baxter teased.

"Oh! You startled me," she said, blushing furiously.

"I can see that. Kind of sweet on the boy aren't ya? I know that look very well. Felt that way a couple of times myself way back in my younger days." A faint smile playing on his lips and a gleam in his eyes were plainly visible.

Rachel blushed again and turned her face away from her father's probing eyes. "Don't be nosey. You already know how special I think Jacob is and I certainly prefer his company to Billy's."

There was a brief moment of silence between them. Even at seventeen, she was well aware that the merest spoken implication that she had come into her own would be met with resistance from her father. Rachel was near certain he looked upon her and Jacob's relationship as nothing more than a passing fancy. It bothered her more than she let on that he still tried to treat her like a little girl, but she understood his reluctance to let go of the child and see the woman she was becoming. She was all he had since the death of her mother, so of course he was going to be slightly overly-protective of her.

She was afraid by now her love for Jacob had to be obvious to everyone except her father. By the way he talked about the matter, he thought being sweet on Jacob was a far cry from being in love with him. Out of respect for her father, who was still living in denial, she'd have to continue to hide her feelings as best she could, which wasn't as well as she had hoped.

At this very moment Jacob was meticulously working on a horse that he had caught up on Wild Cat Ridge. Rachel could tell he was aware of her presence because every so often he'd glance quickly over in her direction.

"Now, Father, that's how a man should look whether he's working horses or not working at all," she confirmed. There was a short silence as her mind considered all the other pleasant things about him. "He always smells good, too," she added.

"Yes, Rachel," Baxter replied. "I can see his rugged looks have won your favor. I don't know one man on this ranch, other than Jacob, that bothers to put Bay Rum on before he starts his day. But then most men around these parts don't look as if they just stepped off the last train from Sacramento, either," he chided.

"Oh, never mind. You're just being silly now," she blurted.

Baxter let out a hearty laugh, patted Rachel on the shoulder, and then turned towards the house where he had piles of paperwork to tend to.

Rachel's mind was racing as she watched her father walk towards their stately two-story white house that commanded a view over a vast expanse of plush grazing fields. During the summer months it was shaded by tall trees full with leaves bigger than Tahitian fans. The many large windows placed evenly every few feet were opened wide to capture any wisp of air that might waft through. The cobblestone path in front of the house led all the way up to a beautifully crafted wraparound porch with a ten-foot overhang.

Kate's familiar face stood in the open doorway sweeping the dirt from inside the house out into the quiet afternoon breeze. Rachel continued to watch her father. She noticed that he acknowledged Kate with a tip of his big-brimmed hat as he passed by her on his way into the house. She was their hired cook, housekeeper and most important, the best friend Rachel had ever known. Rachel was extremely grateful for her friendship. She was the closest thing to a mother figure that she could remember. She had always been there to give her the best of female nurturing all little girls should have while growing up.

The Truth about Jacob

She was pretty, with plain brown hair graying at the temples. It was neatly pulled back in a bun the size of a large donut. She was a bit hefty in size, having filled out her clothes on the tight side. Her pale yellow apron caught the glow of the sunlight adding a dressed up look to the drab gray skirt and plain white button down blouse she wore.

Rachel had secretly hoped that Kate and her father would eventually marry one day. Even as a young girl, she was aware that they were extremely fond of each other simply because of the way they spoke so highly of one another. After all, he'd been a widower since her birth and Kate had never married. She often wondered what possible reason there could be to keep them apart.

Her eyes left Kate and suddenly drifted back over towards Jacob. She couldn't help but notice how he dressed to please a woman's eye. His jet-black hair was always washed each day and combed the first thing in the morning. He was tall like her father with an even tan on his high cheekbones. There was never a night that she didn't dream about him and walk upon unknown paths filled with pure pleasure.

Doogan Westmore limped up beside Rachel with a big grin on his face. "Mornin' to you, Missy Rachel. How's the day been treatin' ya so far?"

"I'm just fine, Doogy, thanks for asking," she said. "How are you doing?"

"As well as expected. Can't do much better till this durn leg of mine decides to heal. It's just not meant for a man like me to set on his haunches and do nothing all day long while everyone else is pullin' his weight aroun' here."

"Now, now, Doogy. I'm sure everyone understands you have to take it easy until that bone is completely healed. We don't want another infection to set in now do we?"

"I s'pose you're right, but I could help that pretty little Kate in the kitchen if she'd jes' let me," he sighed. She won't hear of it though. Don' rightly know why. I promised I wouldn't spit no t'bacca in the food. She's kinda sweet wouldn't you say?" Doogy asked with a sly grin.

Rachel tried to swallow her giggles. "Don't take it personal, Doogy, Kate just prefers to work alone."

Rachel knew firsthand the real reason he wasn't allowed anywhere around her food. Kate had pointed that out many times. She'd say, "That skinny little runt makes my scalp prickle and my skin crawl. If I wanted the room to smell like piss ants, I'd hang the filthy little man in the breezeway by his suspenders."

Rachel had to admit his hands did look a might crusty most of the time. However, some of the brownish coloring was an accumulation of age spots. After all, he was closing in on seventy-two, if she remembered correctly. His shabby clothes, along with his unkempt body, were also in bad need of a good scrubbing.

Looking back towards the corral, she asked, "Is Billy finished breaking that black horse?"

"Yeah, that ornery little cuss is just about done working old blacky, but not done struttin' around with a pumped up chest like a cocky banty rooster. He'll spend another two hours showing off. That pip-squeak's so durned sure of himself his chest is about to pop. He's too full of hot air, that one is."

Rachel laughed hard. "Yeah, I know what you mean."

"Every man on this ranch knows he's out here for only one reason. Durn fool is following some crazy notion that all this, and you too, is gonna be his one day. Why, he's half convinced some of those new siderods your father hired last spring that he's just sittin' on a pot of gold that's his for the takin'. Course, the older geezers like me don't buy into all his big talk. Without your hand in marriage there ain't no way Mr. Baxter's gonna hand this ranch over to that scallywag." Doogy raised a brow and asked Rachel in a whisper, "You ain't aimin' to marry that good for nothing now are you, Missy Rachel?"

The Truth about Jacob

Rachel's jaw dropped and she nearly choked hearing his words. "Not even if he was the last man on earth! Is that really what he's claiming? Is he talking as if there is really something going on between us?"

"Well, not in those same words, but that's what he's gettin' at."

"Doogan Westmore, I'm surprised at you! You of all people know me better than that," she scolded. "Now you can just set the record straight around here with the rest of these ignorant galoots who fall for all of Billy's big lies. There is nothing between Billy and me and there never will be," she confirmed indignantly.

"I kinda thought that's the way it was," he said looking down at his boots, ashamed at his ever doubting her good sense.

Rachel and Doogin exchanged disgusted glances while shaking their heads.

After a moment, she added, "There's only one reason why Billy's still on this ranch. Father believes his skills in breaking horses more than makes up for his laziness in other areas. Billy's here for no other reason than that, but if I had my way about it he wouldn't be here at all. The fact that he rubs everyone else on this ranch the wrong way doesn't seem to matter to my father. You know as well as I do that Jacob can work circles around Billy and does a much better job at breaking horses. Why else do you think father gave Jacob the foreman position? He's well rounded in all his ranching capabilities and he's been here working faithfully for father a lot longer than most others," she declared.

Rachel then turned an angry eye on Billy. "I can see that Billy and I are going to lock horns one of these days and he's not going to like what I have to say. I'm sick and tired of his crazy notions, especially when they involve me. I don't care if we've known each other since we were kids, if he doesn't learn to watch what he says about me I'm going to give him more than a piece of my mind."

"Mums the word, Missy. I won't warn the little worm he's ruffled your feathers." Doogin spit his mouthful of tobacco on the dust below his feet and hobbled off towards the barn smiling to himself.

Rachel again turned her attention back to Jacob. His approach to breaking horses was quite different from what most other men practiced, which was simply to engage the trust of the horse. His style was as soundless as the air above his head. His techniques had been widely used among the Indian nations, but virtually unheard of in these parts. His procedure was accomplished entirely with hands and quiet words. His soft whispers to the horse seemed to invite the animal's full attention and curiosity. Long, smooth, tender strokes over every inch of its lean muscled frame achieved results that were nothing short of uncanny.

Jacob had learned this extremely disciplined method when he was twelve from a full-blooded Maidu Indian by the name of Eagle Eye Joe. He was an eighty-year-old headman for his tribe that had passed through this territory on their way to the northern tip of the California border. The whole process usually took less than three days. Billy's brutal methods produced an efficient animal, but Jacob's horses gained something extra, a willingness that made his animal more desirable to ride.

The Indian, who was a respected elder in his tribe, had explained it all carefully to Jacob. He had said, "When a man first comes upon a wild horse, the horse sees him in the same way as any other predator that represents potential danger. His finely tuned defense mechanisms are immediately activated and so the animal's instinctive reaction is to flee. By using a technique that introduces a non-threatening creature, it automatically creates an intense curiosity within the horse. Once a man establishes a non-threatening relationship, dominance is also established. It's the same type of fraternizing as if the association were with another horse. This builds a good working camaraderie that allows a man to control and tell the

The Truth about Jacob

animal what to do. The horse is more willing and actually applies itself better to the task at hand."

Incredible as it may seem, those lessons taught to him by the old Indian he still remembered word for word.

The Palomino Jacob was working was a tall horse, standing nearly sixteen hands. Rachel watched him as he stroked his calloused hands carefully across every inch of the stallion. She couldn't help but notice that those movements caused his own muscles to flex and strain against the thin blue cotton shirt he wore.

A gradual calmness was beginning to show on the horse even as he touched the horse's most sensitive areas. The animal's bright bulging eyes darted back and forth in his sockets showing a little concern as Jacob's hands explored untouched areas. No loud hooplas were spoken, only soft quiet whispers that no one else could hear except the horse and the man who uttered them.

After repeating this same procedure for more times than she could count, Jacob gradually eased in closer to the horse, leaning heavily against him. He then cautiously inched his way up onto the horse's back, which by now accepted his weight with complete confidence. He rode slowly around in circles for a good half-hour and then quietly slipped away from the crowd riding off alone across the back pasture toward the low-lying edges of the foothills.

Jacob always did this, but offered little information as to why. It was highly suspected that he merely removed the horse from the noisy environment, giving the animal the opportunity to understand additional structured conduct that would be expected of him in the near future.

Everyone on this ranch knew Jacob's rule. No one was to follow, not even Rachel. Although deeply disappointed, she had always respected his wishes. After all, it was old news how he chose to handle his horses with no one around and she certainly wasn't about to question his motives at this late date.

Later on, after enjoying a pleasant dinner with her father, Rachel returned to the corral and hung around the rest of the afternoon watching Billy and a few of the other cowpokes break more horses. She kept a watchful eye in hopes that Jacob would return at any time, although she was a little stymied as to why he hadn't yet.

Her thoughts were conspiratorial in nature as she contemplated the advantages of seeing him return first before anyone else. Then, maybe, she would be fortunate enough to whisk him away from all the curious eyes if only for a few minutes. But she wouldn't hold her breath waiting for that wonderful idea to come about.

As the last layers of light lingered across the horizon, the sun's face gradually began to dip further from view, bringing Billy and his horse down from midair for the final time. He was panting heavier than the animal beneath him. He allowed the horse to waltz around in quick jerky movements scraping the dirt to dust. After a few minutes of prancing he was able to slow the animal down, bringing it into further submission.

His triumphant spirit was emphasized by a broad grin moving across his face as he advanced in Rachel's direction. She knew he expected praise for his accomplishments. She had learned only too well how to interpret his facial expressions while she was growing up with Billy.

Sure enough, before she even had the chance to think about what was happening, he was off his horse and at her side. She gasped in alarm as he pulled her close with remarkable quickness and pressed his dirty lips over her mouth. Her eyes opened wider when he pulled her even closer with both hands planted firmly on her shoulders. She struggled to break free and turned her head away for one brief moment when an offensive odor drifted up from underneath his wet armpits. Repulsion shivered through her entire body when she saw how his sweat soaked shirt had soiled the front of her tan cotton blouse. Her knees nearly buckled beneath her in a vain effort to fight against

The Truth about Jacob

his unwarranted advances. She squirmed away the best she could.

With only a fraction of an inch between them Billy squeezed her up even closer, forcibly pressing another unwanted kiss against her quivering lips. Then he backed up slightly, dropped his hands to her waist and hoisted her onto the horse he'd just broken.

Rachel's face was blood red as she glared at Billy with murder in her eyes. She used her sleeve to wipe away the gritty, salty sweat he left on her mouth. "Don't you ever do that again!" she snapped.

Billy's smile left his face, but not his squinty eyes. Mocking her, he said, "What, you mean, that harmless little kiss?" he asked defensively. At the same time he glanced boyishly at the other men standing close by just to show them he thought the whole incident was very amusing.

The air was alive with muted snickering.

Rachel was irritated even more by his roguish display in front of the others at her expense. "These are my lips, Billy, and I'll be the one to choose who kisses them!"

"I'll bet you wouldn't have said that to old Scarface if he had kissed you!"

"I'll bet that's none of your business!" she retorted. Rachel abruptly ended their argument mainly because she knew she'd be wasting her time anyway. Generally, every word that came out of Billy's mouth was utterly meaningless. He would argue with a tree about how tall it should grow if he had a mind to.

By now she was madder than a hornet, so she leaned over and snatched up the reins and rode off in the same direction Jacob had gone, leaving Billy behind nursing his bruised ego. Rachel knew her intentions were downright crazy and even though it occurred to her that Jacob might frown on her for breaking his rule, she rode after him nevertheless.

Billy squirmed a little in his boots, humiliated to no end. He wasn't one bit fooled about where she was headed. Infuriated, he gave the rocky ground a high kick with his boot, scattering dirt in every direction. He held his eyes glued to Rachel's image until it gradually faded away in the distance.

All he could think about was her beautiful face and dark eyes like liquid oil. Her waist was so tiny any man could easily surround it with both hands and touch his fingertips. She had exquisitely large breasts for a short woman, but every other feature on her five-foot frame was perfectly proportioned. Yet all that beauty was out of his reach only because Jacob stood in his way.

Jealousy swarmed around him as he stood watching her ride out of sight in search of Jacob. He was very aware of the budding romance going on between the two and it gnawed at his gut, the fact that she preferred Jacob's company to his. It was a painful blow to his pride because everyone else on the ranch knew it as well.

His brow knitted into an ugly scowl as he watched Rachel vanish completely from his sight. He had never shot a man before just because of jealousy, but he was seriously thinking of making an exception in Jacob's case.

Rachel rode around in circles for at least twenty minutes or so looking for Jacob. Unfortunately her efforts were cut short by the pending death of the sun. The huge mass of orange light was beginning to ease down over the horizon pulling a darkening sky behind it. She couldn't hide her disappointment as she rode on, a definite slump in her posture. With the rolling gait of a good horse beneath her, she was forced to return home without the reward of at least one brief moment alone with Jacob.

She'd known all along in the back of her mind that it wasn't going to be that easy, no matter how hard she tried to find him. Whenever Jacob Fowler disappeared into the wilderness it wasn't meant for anyone to find and disrupt his training process, and that included her.

Rachel hurried back to the corral hoping to catch him if by chance he had already returned. In order to avoid running into

The Truth about Jacob

Billy she sneaked in the back way going through the barn. Her hopes however were short lived. She always seemed to be an easy target when it came to Billy's eagle eyes.

When he saw her trail of dust off in the distance he hid himself from her view. She wasn't but fifteen feet away when he sped over like a whirlwind to her side; it was obvious that he had been lying in wait for her return. His eyes were all over her like a hot iron. No matter how hard she tried to rein up and swing down on her own Billy refused to take no for an answer.

He held her rein and his position just a breath away from her left leg while insisting on helping her down. Billy stood there with his arms reaching up leaving her no other choice but to let him slide his dirty hands up under each of her arms. His eyes continued to crawl down over every curve on her supple body as he slowly lowered her to the ground. He pressed his chest closer than necessary against her cotton blouse, making her skin crawl again for the second time in less than an hour.

Rachel could see the hunger in his eyes and felt undressed and dirty in his presence. He leaned closer, leaving little more than air between them. She could smell the stench of day old whiskey on his breath. His pleasure seemed to heighten when she drew her head backwards in order to prevent him from pressing his puckered lips against hers. When he spoke she could see traces of chew packed just under his lower lip allowing the sticky muck to ooze in-between his brownish teeth.

Her stomach began to turn. It was absolutely distasteful being so near him and having to listen to him going on about how beautiful she was. Rachel definitely didn't care to hear sweet talk from a mouth that reminded her of a cow's afterbirth, nor did she have any intentions of allowing him to get the upper hand again.

She quickly diverted their conversation to the horse she had just dismounted as she cleverly ducked under his arm and scooted five feet away. "This horse performs very well. He moves quite nicely under the saddle and handles real light," she said, attempting to put their relationship back on a professional level.

"He doesn't handle nearly as well as you," he teased.

She glared at him. "I'm not in the mood for word games, Billy."

"I don't play games when it comes to you Rachel, you know that."

Rachel rolled her eyes and quickly excused herself before he had the chance to catch her off guard again. She immediately headed in the direction of the house, paying no attention to Billy's reaction. She did, however, take the time to pet Weckles, Jacob's black and white mongrel.

The dog stood at her feet wagging his tail with his tongue flapping down the side of his mouth. He was the only remaining mutt left from the last batch of puppies her own dog, Happy Jack, had birthed. That old dog and all the rest of her offspring had long since joined their ancestors in a permanent bed of dirt out in the south forty where the small family pet cemetery was placed by her father when she was a child.

Weckles presence revealed to Rachel that Jacob, too, must have already returned. The dog never left his side no matter what unless Jacob was retired indoors. The shaggy little dog rolled on his side as usual and stretched out his neck just begging for some frisky scratches on his belly. Rachel eagerly obliged the friendly little pooch, happy for the distraction from Billy. She decided this display of affection deserved some mushy baby talk. "You sweet wittle, Weckles," she said. "Mama loves you, you silly old goose."

As Rachel was stooped over, stroking the dog, she could see Billy out of the corner of her eye trying to ease his way in closer to her. She had little doubt that he was just itching to touch her again. Knowing another encounter was inevitable, she quickly straightened up and swiftly backed away from Weckles.

"What, no good night kiss?" Billy teased, simply to pester her some more. "I figure a little smooch from me now is worth more to you than the ones you'll have when you dream about me tonight. As close as we are, Rachel, practically family and all, I reckon I've earned the right to a kiss or two once in a while! I know you didn't get the chance to waste those pretty lips on old Scarface, so you ought to be able to spare me one more!" He patronized sarcastically.

"Well, you figured wrong," she blurted angrily. There was a momentary silence and then Rachel sneered at him and shook her head not able to think of an appropriate thing to say at this moment. She finally found her voice and said, "Now I want you to quit calling Jacob 'Scarface.' You know how that irritates me. You of all people should know better than to make fun of someone else's misfortunes. That was a horrible accident and he doesn't need to be reminded of it every time he's in your presence."

He gave a scornful snort. "Oh, you're makin' me cry. It's his own darned fault for climbing into a pen with a hog sportin' piglets. He ought to feel down right lucky she didn't chew his whole head off," he blurted, irritated at how quickly the conversation turned back to Jacob.

Rachel rolled her eyes again and shook her head in utter disgust as she stormed in the direction of her house. She had no patience for his ill-mannered comments.

It had always been a mystery to her where Billy got any of his crazy ideas about some sort of romantic involvement going on between them that simply never existed. Even more worrisome was the fear of what outlandish whim was going to pop into his head next. *Billy may be hungry for love*, she thought, but as far as she was concerned, he had better start looking in someone else's back yard for companionship.

Lately she was feeling more and more boxed in by his aggressive actions. She had come to realize that his imagination had taken over. Now more than ever, she knew she needed to get Jacob to make some sort of commitment to her. Then maybe

Billy would back off and leave her be. If that didn't happen soon, then she'd be forced to ask her Father to have a word with him.

With a lopsided grin on his face, Billy's pulsating eyes followed his ladylove until she disappeared inside her house. *Rachel could dole out all the resistance she wanted*, he thought defiantly. That wasn't going to stop him from trying to win her affections, and it sure wouldn't make any difference in the way he felt about her. He wasn't about to give up that easily. He always managed somehow to get whatever he wanted, whether from a horse or a woman. Why should she be any different?

Chapter 2

It was early Sunday morning and everything lay quiet except Jacob. He had lain awake most of the night with eyes open and a mind much too active to allow him any sleep. It wasn't the cool evening breeze rustling the leaves against the roof or even the cacophony of crickets that had kept him awake. It was excitement that had caused him to spend the better part of the evening staring at the monotonous grooves in-between the rough-hewn rafters above his head. He finally gave up in the wee hours of the morning trying to grab a decent amount of shut-eye.

At four a.m. Jacob gave up his battle, rose and downed three cups of piping hot coffee as he mentally prepared himself for the day ahead. All he could think about was what he'd been itching to do for weeks now. He wasn't interested in joining some of the other ranch workers who planned to spend this Sunday morning catching up on their rest while the Baxters were attending church. Nor did he have any desire to waste a perfectly good day at Packy Pete's Saloon hitting the sauce as Billy and his crowd would be doing at about the time the clock struck noon.

He was going hunting. Jacob had eyes in the back of his head when it came to spotting any signs of wild horses on the move and that's exactly what happened yesterday to prompt today's hunt. He'd stumbled across numerous hoof prints when he was out in the far northeast section of the ranch searching for strays. The prints indicated a good size herd of horses. The first thing he aimed to do at daybreak was to follow those very prints and hope that they wouldn't lead him down an empty trail of false hopes.

Jacob was pretty much packed and adequately prepared, eager to spend his entire day tramping through the canyon and valley floor, if need be, to reel in a few of those horses for his own keeping. One horse in particular was the one he'd had his mind on all night. Jacob reckoned that if the first group of tracks led him to an empty nest, then he'd head straight for that wise old owl's favorite watering hole because that was his next best bet. *Either way he felt good about today because it had all the earmarks of a perfect time to hunt down the wild stallion*, he thought smugly.

Jacob was well aware that the stallion was not only smart, but also extremely spirited. He was as white as the snowcaps in December and wild as the south wind. Jacob, along with every other siderod around here, thought about getting their hot little hands on that horse. So far, neither he nor anyone else had been able to get within one hundred yards of him—much less near enough to snag a rope around his neck. He hoped today that he could cut short the horse's long string of good luck.

Within the past three weeks, more than one cowpoke had reported spotting him hanging around the Canyon Creek Bridge that crossed over Morgan's Gulch road, just ten miles south of town. Better yet, he was seen in the company of a fine group of healthy mares. That particular site was a popular watering hole for many wild horses. Of course, there was no way of knowing with true accuracy the exact whereabouts of the stallion today, however, he knew this area well and would begin his search somewhere in that vicinity. It was an easy two-hour or so ride from the ranch. He'd also keep a good eye on every grassy slope along the foothills. There might be a chance the herd was grazing close to one of the many mountain streams that trailed through the hollers lined with rocks and brush.

Jacob found a great deal of satisfaction in another thought. The mares that were usually in the company of the stallion would be quite a bonus if he were able to capture at least a few of them. *In all probability that's exactly the way things would go since it was customary for the mares to follow the stallion wherever he went.* There seemed to be no give in those ladies' favoritism and Jacob was counting on the assumption that they hadn't changed their habits. But if for some odd reason they weren't in his company, he'd be plenty tickled just to snag the main prize.

Jacob grabbed his coat even though the day looked to be a warm one. The month of April was known for being a real teaser weather wise. If, by chance, there were any nasty conditions lurking around out there bringing with it a sudden change in the temperature, he was going to be prepared because looks were often deceiving. Early spring in these parts at times managed to sneak in a late storm or two like a bolt out of the blue. On rare occasions these unexpected surprises had been known to suddenly appear out of nowhere, packing with it forceful winds saturated with enough rain to flood even the small water veins stretched sporadically throughout the valley floor. These cloudbursts could easily cause flash flooding in some of the larger creek beds that were already gorged to capacity left from the rains of the now-fading winter. These afterthoughts from Mother Nature kept the valley alive with fresh greenery and splashes of many brilliant colors.

Growing up around here you learned to stay alert and expect the unexpected.

For Jacob it felt good just to slip off into the clear crisp air all alone without a care in the world. This was especially true when he was doing what he loved to do best. He knew he'd be surrounded by nothing but isolation when he dove head first into the fresh day ahead of him. He would skillfully pound the dirt to dust in search of the elusive stallion while going over every trail left behind by the wild herds that freely roamed the foothills.

Jacob felt the wind in his face and was reminded of how much this sort of peaceful solitude soothed his weary soul. It was at times like this that he understood what it meant to be free. That's what he wanted most of all. Freedom without feeling the chains of obligations to any other man! Even as fair a man as Baxter had been to Jacob, it was time to spread his own wings without feeling hogtied by loyalty. As long as he worked for Baxter he was obligated to Baxter and he in some ways controlled his time. One day soon he would walk out his own front door and know that the whole day belonged entirely to him. He had lived on the Baxter ranch without a total range of freedom long enough. The time had come to change all that once and for all.

Building a sizeable herd of horses was exactly how he was going to do it. His pockets weren't bulging yet, but that wouldn't be the story for long. He'd saved every penny he'd earned over the past thirteen years working on the Baxter Ranch, so his blueprint for the future had already begun to take shape. He had also accumulated a large number of horses, which enabled him to make a few economically substantial transactions here and there. He was already planning the next advancement move. Jacob had his eye on a small section of land just north of town owned by Baxter himself. A few conversations on the subject with the old man two weeks back had the ball already rolling on a sure deal.

After his affairs were signed and sealed, he'd build a log cabin with his own hands, keeping just enough horses to work the land. Eventually, he would slowly start to sell off the surplus stock for a profit. That was easy enough for one good reason. He knew in the larger cities horses were in big demand. The progression of a horse's value had spread not only on the North American continent, but on the south as well.

The Truth about Jacob

Only when all of this was accomplished, and only then, could he seriously think about taking a wife and settling down. That thought, of course, struck a nerve and Jacob's mind immediately turned to Rachel. She gave his life a sense of stability. She was the primary purpose for his whole existence. She taught him how to look at everything as if he'd never seen it before. No one had made such a difference in the way he viewed the world around him. Even a flower seemed more colorful and alive when she was around.

It took his breath away when Rachel looked at him with such longing. Those big brown eyes framed by long auburn hair were an image that stayed in his mind as detailed as a photograph. He had fallen in love with her when he was only seven and was nearly certain by the way she talked she too had experienced the same exact phenomenon. Judging by the way she had been acting lately, a might more flirtatious than usual, they both seemed to share a vision along the same lines.

Jacob readied his buckskin and mounted her at daybreak. He called her Uno. She was the offspring of the very first horse he had captured for his own at the age of twelve. "Come on, girl'" he said. "Today it's just you and me and good old Lady Luck. "

His favorite baby perked up her ears and threw her head back prancing in one spot with excitement long before he poked spurs to her flanks. With full steam they rode hard on a steady course. They spoke the same language when together. Their ride was smooth, free and graceful. There was no need to answer a bit since she already knew where to go, so Jacob just gave her the head.

After a good two and a half hours of tracking, he finally spotted the stallion lurking near the water's edge along with about nine mares and several good-sized colts. They were feeding on small patches of new grass that lined the river. Jacob sat perfectly still, watching his prey like a hawk. He studied both sides of the river and carefully plotted his next move.

As he and Uno slowly began to ease forward, the wind suddenly shifted. With a raised head and flamed nostrils the stallion sniffed the scent of man. As soon as his ears caught the sound of the hunter's prowl he began driving his herd down the canyon with their colts following close behind.

Jacob, knowing he would loose his prize on open ground, quickly applied his spurs and hightailed it back downstream in hot pursuit. He hoped to cut them off at the mouth of the canyon. He was fully aware that it was at that particular bend in the river that they could easily escape. His luck held out.

Even though he was on the opposite side of the river, Jacob had managed to make it there just ahead of the herd and he was able to start driving them back upstream. He knew he could corner the horses between the bluffs and the boulders behind the waterfall that brought this portion of the river to an abrupt end to the horizontal linear flow.

As the horses advanced, they slipped and stumbled over the rocks as they waded up through the swirling current. At times, when they strayed further away from the banks of the river, most of their lower legs seemingly disappeared under the rushing water. Their speed of retreat varied, always changing in order to keep a minimum distance between themselves and this predator that pursued them.

Jacob's loud bellows echoed through the canyon as he continued to move the horses straight up the river. He raced just a step behind, giving them no leeway whatsoever. He'd lose his advantage if he allowed them even the slightest opportunity to circle around him and change their direction. Jacob angled off just a smidgeon to the right and then to the left every once in a while working his way over the entire bed of water.

He felt positively explosive. His heart raced as he tried to maintain his speed. He had a good feeling. His luck was going to hold out this time. No horse could get by him now, at least not without a good struggle.

The Truth about Jacob

Although he felt confident, Jacob wasn't one to get too sure of himself. *That's when a man makes mistakes*, he thought decisively. No man ever called him foolish or too quick to pat himself on the back until the goods were bagged. So, with eyes wide open and focused, he paced himself no faster and no slower with only one thought in mind—*he had to have that horse.*

Jacob could feel the cool splashes of water against his face. The dozens of pounding hooves had sent the normally tranquil river into a wild disturbance. He was feeling not only the thrill of the chase, but an excitement in anticipation of what could come from this if he was successful. These were magnificent animals.

From a very early age he acknowledged the exhilaration of being in the presence of such a noble creature; nothing fearful or startling, just something satisfying and out of the ordinary. His love for horses went beyond just a mere fascination of their beauty. He strived to achieve an in-depth knowledge about their breeds and styles whether in the wild or already domesticated. He wanted to learn as much as he could about their history, physical statistics, health and management. He was well aware that this was more than the average man would care to do and felt that it lent to his ability to produce a willing work animal, one that wasn't "broken" into submission.

Jacob wasn't taking any chances. Each man out in the wilds was on his own. Since no one was aware of his comings and goings today he wasn't counting on help from someone else to gather up these mares along with the stallion. Besides, a man throws his own rope in this territory when it comes to padding your own pocket book.

It was to his satisfaction that the mares looked to be a fairly healthy group. A little scruffy, still wearing their heavy winter coat, but a fine bunch nonetheless. Jacob was sharp-eyed when it came to horses and didn't limit himself to selecting strictly high-quality animals. Every variety of horse or pony served some sort of useful purpose on a ranch providing it had a man's expert direction. One way or the other they were all still money in his pocket.

Jacob was still keeping a pretty good pace with the horses, actually within the space of their shadows. The horses were headed right where he wanted them to go. Once they realized there was nowhere else to turn he was certain most would give up without much of a fight, except the stallion of course. He expected a good deal of trouble from that fellow. He'd given him a hard chase twice before so knew what he was in for. It was no surprise that even now he still had the glare of fire in his eyes.

Barely ten minutes into his chase, as he was closing in on the last bend in the river, the glory of the world suddenly opened up to Jacob. He was awestruck at the beauty that lay just ahead. Each time he returned to this very spot it was like seeing this particular magnificence of nature for the first time.

The rocky bluffs were well in his sights. The rushing waterfall was violent in the background, spraying water ten feet outwards in every direction. The current of the water moving from the foot of the falls flowed into an infinite horizon to the valley beneath its strength. The roar of the water crashing against the rocks grew louder. The closer he came the more it sounded like thunder.

The small herd of horses stopped abruptly, shying away from the speeding bullets of water. Jacob leaned forward grabbing his lasso as he trotted within throwing range of the stallion. Bringing his rope to bear, he slowly approached the cornered herd twirling it high above his head. The stallion stood challengingly between the man and his mares. Jacob's stomach squeezed with excitement. He knew his dreams were within his reach as the loop fell cleanly over the stallion's head. Then all hell broke loose. Just as soon as the rope tightened around the animal's neck, he bolted into midair. Jacob drew a tight rein and then allowed his mare to lurch forward with the beast. He tugged on his reins every so often just to keep the stallion off balance as he reared backwards.

The Truth about Jacob

Uno stopped abruptly and then began to dance slowly in reverse. This was exactly what was expected of her. However, the stallion began to dominate the struggle. This was something that Jacob was expecting and he was prepared with a change in strategy. With the rope tightly wound around his saddle horn, he carefully maneuvered the battle towards a lone pine tree along the water's edge. He knew the stallion had twice the strength of his mare, especially when his adrenalin was pumping like a steam engine. A hard jerk on his reins, moving Uno away briefly, managed to unbalance the stallion just long enough to tug him closer to the tree.

Angered more than ever, the stallion snorted and reared, jumping five feet in the air trying to break free. Jacob had a good solid hold on him as he closed in on the tree, circling it twice before stopping to watch the horse's fierce tug-of-war. The stallion was an unquestionably sturdier opponent, but the tree put the odds in the lady's favor. At first the stallion just seemed to work harder and aim his kicks higher. Obviously he was not ready to admit defeat because his strength did not wane. His powerful legs and sharp hooves crested the cold water as if it wasn't there and crunched against the large stones like they were mere pebbles.

There was a wild and crazy spirit in his nature, and until he decided to completely surrender to Jacob, there would be no release of tension on the rope. That's when Jacob would feel confident that the horse was his for the keeping. Until that time he would take every precaution necessary to make sure he had secured his hard earned prize.

The battle raged on for another five minutes or so. Finally, the stallion grew less aggressive with his kicking, although Jacob couldn't be certain just how much his own struggles had worn him down. He knew that eventually the strength would vanish from the stallion's legs and he'd be forced to resign himself to the fact he was no longer in charge and would now have to answer to a master. Of course, Jacob knew the beast hadn't completely given up yet, as he was still wild. So he and Uno would just sit tight until the stallion's muscles were so fatigued that all the horse could think about was rest instead of freedom.

Fierce sounds of snorting still filled the air and Jacob understood the horse's lingering resistance and fight. He knew very well the feelings of freedom lost. Jacob himself was not a free man, yet, that's why he played these games of chance. By selectively breeding this horse to high quality mares, he would be assured of getting top dollar for his product. With all that money he could buy his own freedom and then be at liberty to marry Rachel.

Even though the stallion was equipped with a strong defense mechanism, the half-hearted manner in which he kicked his hind legs and pawed the water indicated the fight was winding down. With his muscles quivering, the proud stallion stumbled over a few more rocks and then finally stood, head down, wheezing, and drenched with sweat and water. His was the stance that a defeated horse often took. He was snorting and fighting to catch his breath, yet it was plainly visible that the fire was still alive in his eyes. There was nothing more for Jacob to do but continue to wait for the struggle to end.

He was in hopes that the water would add just enough resistance to discourage any last efforts on the horse's part to snap his bonds. No sooner had he settled on that thought then the stallion proved him wrong. He had underestimated the courageous beast's resurgent survival instincts as he tempered one last valiant attempt to break free. Shifting his balance on all fours, he scrambled around like crazy for a few seconds more, moving belly deep over layers of rocks.

Jacob again sat patiently watching. He was in no hurry so he'd wait him out. The stallion gave it his all; pulling and tugging every which way except to get free. After another minute or so the stallion once again gave into exhaustion. With dignity so fitting the gallant steed he held his head high, staring his new master in the eyes without the look or obvious presence of fear. Although the horse was now standing three legged and appeared totally worn out, Jacob knew he dared not let his guard down. This animal was far too crafty and he highly suspected still had enough pepper left in him to jump at the first opportunity to break free.

Jacob smiled with great satisfaction, refusing to allow pessimistic thoughts to dampen his spirits or change his happy frame of mind. This day had turned out just as he had hoped and nothing was going to spoil it. Suddenly out of nowhere, a shot rang out, then another volley. The third discharge ripped through the stallion's left ear, severing the upper tip.

Jacob was forced to make a difficult decision and make it quickly. Obviously someone was trying to sabotage his hunt. Either he would have to stand his ground with the risk of losing the horse for good to a stray bullet or simply set it free. The urgency involved in this matter added weight to his decision. Whether he liked it or not the horse's welfare prevailed.

Within seconds Jacob jumped from his horse. He ran up within three feet of the stud with bullets whizzing by his head, leaned over as far as he could and cut the rope at the shortest point within reaching distance. That would hopefully prevent any chance of the horse tripping on it and possibly breaking his neck. It was a pretty close shave, but Jacob managed to duck for cover behind a large boulder just as the stallion dashed on past him down the river. It wasn't long before the rest of the herd followed suit.

Jacob shaded his eyes with his hand and looked up to see who was doing all the fancy shooting. Unfortunately, he was somewhat handicapped as far as a clear sight to the top of the bluff because the jagged rocks obscured his point of view.

Despite the serious fix he was in, his anger took control. Using some pretty slick maneuvering, he darted back and forth from boulder to boulder, until he drew near to his mare. He quickly mounted her and rode off full chisel to try and apprehend the hard case that had hornswoggled him out of what was rightfully his.

By the time Jacob managed to tackle the rocky riverbed again and ride up to the bluff, whoever had been there was long gone. He carefully examined the ground from where he sat to see if there was any sign of the culprit's hoof prints. Unable to tell for sure from where he sat he got off his horse. He poked around long enough to confirm that the sharpshooter's trail would actually be a fairly easy one to follow because the rider's horse at some time or other had thrown a shoe.

A greenhorn could follow a trail as easy as this one, he thought smugly to himself. Tracking was second nature to him since he'd spent much of his time over the years tracking the whereabouts of stray livestock and predatory mountain lions.

He followed the horse and its rider for nearly six hours, having to stop every so often to pick up the trail again after losing it amongst the rocks. It was of no great surprise to Jacob that all his tedious tracking took him right back to the Baxter Ranch.

He headed straight to the corral and quickly patrolled the immediate area. There wasn't a soul in sight but he did happen to notice that Billy's sorrel was wringing wet and there was a considerable amount of white lather collected around the edges of its mouth.

This was ample enough proof to convict the scoundrel in any cowboy's court of law. Just to make doubly sure he decided to poke around some more. He lifted the left hind leg of the horse only to find it was missing a shoe. Jacob could feel his jaw tighten and his eyes narrowed as he stood there alone studying the situation in the dark.

He reckoned he had proof enough, but when push came to shove, facing Billy, even with this kind of evidence, would only amuse him. He'd just argue his way out of it anyway or dig up one of his subservient cronies to lie through his teeth to give him

The Truth about Jacob

a perfect alibi. He decided against bringing this matter to anyone's attention.

This injustice carried out by Billy was a serious matter to Jacob, but it most likely wouldn't mean as much to anyone else around here. Some of the men would probably admit to themselves that Billy was a salty dog for pulling one over on Jacob, but wouldn't say a word out of fear of reprisals from him. The rest would just laugh it off as a silly prank whenever Billy was around.

Despite his misgivings he would have to sheath his claws and hold his anger as he had so many other times when Billy pulled stunts like this just to get a rise out of him. *Besides,* the thought occurred to him, *a man like Billy would slip up on a much larger scale sometime or another anyway.* Jacob was a patient man. He'd put aside his desire to make Billy face the music tonight. The smartest thing he could do was to just bide his time. A lot could happen between now and Billy's next foray.

There would be another day, another opportunity to capture the stallion, he decided. Only next time he'd make darn well sure nobody knew what he was up to or where he was going. Jacob wasn't in the habit of playing mind games, but was almighty sure of trying to beat Billy at his, especially after today's hard lesson learned.

Billy would one day have to pay his dues for every cheap shot he'd taken and gotten away with. A sureness of that fact would have to carry Jacob for a spell. One day he'd nail his ornery hide to the side of the barn. Jacob relied heavily on that thought. It helped to take his mind off what he was looking for right now, vindication.

Of course Jacob wisely reasoned that vindication is satisfactory only if you live long enough to witness it. Billy had a tendency to talk with his gun, and with that being the rule of the day, Jacob would definitely never act on impulse. Endeavoring to square accounts with Billy would have to wait, no matter how torturous.

Chapter 3

The darkness of the night was alive with movement. The stars danced around like tiny ballerinas and comets streaked across the heavens as if excited to reach their unknown destination. There was just enough light cast from the quarter moon's glow for Rachel to see well beyond the front yard. She gazed into the distance from her bedroom window looking at the heavens and thinking about Jacob. When her eyes dropped momentarily, she caught a glimpse through the shadows of someone standing alone alongside the edge of the wooden railings of the corral. She realized, to her surprise, it was Jacob.

That seemed a bit odd because he was never known to be a night owl. He usually went to bed with the chickens and was up before the first rooster's cackle. *This was just too good to be true, and too good an opportunity to pass up,* she thought decisively. Rachel tiptoed from her room, crept down the stairs and stopped only long enough to make sure the coast was clear before stepping out into the cool night air.

She sneaked across the porch, quietly inched her way down the steps and headed straight for Jacob. Within seconds she was standing so close to him an inchworm wouldn't have breathing

The Truth about Jacob

room. They both just stood there and stared at one another for a long time.

Jacob was genuinely surprised to see her out and alone at this late hour. He was instantly pleased by her presence and welcomed the strange sensations sweeping through his body.

Finally Rachel broke the silence. "Beautiful night isn't it?" she said, trying desperately to knock down the barrier of his shyness.

"Uh-huh," he returned, self-consciously, after turning his head back around and pretending to gaze at the blinking sky instead of her beautiful eyes, ones that could melt any man's heart. All the while he fiddled with his fingers nervously because he was no hand with women folk. He shifted from one foot to the other with his eyes still firmly fixed on the heavens.

As a result of her many years spent closely observing Jacob she was all too familiar with his state of uneasiness when it came to intimacy. She feared pushing him too hard, because he might run the other way. Forwardness on her part could possibly do more harm than good. So in order to make him feel more comfortable she, too, pretended to stare at the twinkling specks in the sky. Rachel decided right then and there that she would spend a lifetime watching stars if that's what it took to eventually capture this man's heart.

Her dark brown eyes opened wide with greedy pleasure and she blinked sweetly at Jacob whenever she felt his stare upon her. As she stood next to him formulating her next move, she was not embarrassed by the fact that he knew she was examining him for the longest time. His broad shoulders bulged with ridges of muscles tightened the natural way. *His many years of lifting heavy bales of hay had worked wonders on his entire body*, she thought. Jacob's narrow hips were well developed. Her eyes couldn't make out the telltale scars on his face in the dark, even this close. Her heart told her it really didn't matter anyway.

Despite her determination to control her emotions, Rachel could already feel the blood run to her face. It was difficult to suppress her yearning desire to just reach out and touch him. Knowing she dare not left her feeling frustrated. She had more courage in her little finger than the average young woman when it came to the man she loved, but she also had good common sense. Being too forward right now could undo all she had worked so hard to achieve.

Rachel silently scolded herself for entertaining a few other shameful thoughts that also entered her head.

They continued to stare into the sky for a good minute or so with little more than an inch of cool night air between them. And still, Jacob was unable to offer anything in the line of casual conversation. Rachel pulled her shawl up over her shoulders as a wisp of wind brushed across her neck. Listening to the quiet that followed she pondered over what favorite topics most men preferred to engage in. Since she had spent the better part of her growing years in the presence of menfolk, it wasn't difficult to settle on some small talk that she felt Jacob would feel quite comfortable with. She knew by now that it was up to her to initiate his interest in some sort of conversation just so the entire evening wouldn't be a total waste.

Of course Rachel would never take his silence personally. Jacob's quiet behavior was his way of handling his shyness. She knew early on he was simply a man of few words except when working the horses. It would have to be she that opened the conversation and she could only hope that it would eventually lead to something more personal as well as rewarding.

After another long pause between her thoughts, Rachel finally spoke. "If money were no object Jacob what would you want most in life?"

"To find my family, of course," he said without much thought.

She dropped her jaw when he mentioned his family. Up to this point in time, that had always been an untouchable subject to speak about. It was as if his family had never existed and he had no past. His silence on the matter simply let everyone know from the start that he would never offer any additional information beyond what they already knew, that he had been abandoned by his family as a young child.

It had been that way from the very first day he came to live at the ranch. She couldn't believe he mentioned it now however, it pleased her to think she was the one he chose to confide in.

"So where were you born?"

"A small settlement somewhere further up north. I'm no mountaineer, mind you, but I'm gonna ride up that way one of these days just to satisfy my own curiosity. Maybe I've still got some kin living up there somewhere. Although I don't suppose there's much chance of that happening."

"Why do you say that?"

"Well, because my family was pretty small to begin with. My Papa Peter, who was my mother's father, died just a short time before we left our home. He was a widower. He only had two other children besides my mother. My Uncle Clem never was quite right in the head. Had an accident when he was a boy which sort of left him, well you know, not exactly sharp in the thinking department. He was more like a big, overgrown kid after that old mule of theirs kicked him in the head. As far as Uncle Brad, well, he kind of liked the ladies of the evening and hung around the local saloon a lot. Guess he had a little problem with the sauce too. I can distinctly remember my father saying time and time again, "Why, that boy won't live to see his twenty-first birthday. If the whiskey don't kill him, then some drunken, jealous cowboy will.""

"What about poor Clem? I can't imagine your folks leaving him behind to fend for himself."

"Oh, they tried real hard to persuade him to come along with us, but he wouldn't hear of it. He flatly refused to leave the only home he'd ever known. He had enough sense about him to understand what was going on. Besides, Uncle Brad gave my father his word he'd take good care of him."

Rachel continued to pry with interest. She really felt they were making some headway and certainly didn't want to stop the momentum now. "Was it a very large community?"

Jacob's face took on a perplexed look. It had been a long time since he'd pictured Indian Valley in his mind. At five years old he hadn't really thought in terms of large or small.

"Don't rightly recall," he said. "I was pretty young at the time. I'm not quite sure about the exact number of people, but to the best of my recollection it seemed like there were quite a few dwellings scattered about and the streets of town were always busy. There were a lot of farms spread out across the valley. A couple of times a year most of the folks would flock into town all at once for a barn dance or the annual harvest parade. But for the most part it was just dire necessities that brought the valley population trickling in at different times."

It was at this point that a pleasant expression grew across his face and Rachel waited patiently for Jacob to speak again.

"I'm hoping there's still someone up there that might remember me. Maybe they could even shed some light on what happened to my folks. Maybe Mrs. McAndrews is still alive. We lived in a small cabin behind her ranch house. She was a real nice lady, and if my family were to contact anyone, it sure would be her. Like I said, it won't be long before I venture up that way to find out for myself."

"Surely there's someone up there that's wondering about you, too, Jacob," she said. A long silence followed as Rachel stood there still sizing up the situation. "How long will you go on looking for your family if no one up there has heard anything about them."

"As long as it takes." He paused briefly, looking upwards at the stars as if they had something to tell him. "It troubles me that I remember so little about them. Pressing a little boy's memory doesn't always pay off. I just seem to come up on the dry side when I try to picture even the smallest of details on their faces."

The Truth about Jacob

Right about this time his mind began to wander elsewhere. This was because Rachel had a tendency to brush up against him every so often. He was never any hand with women and really didn't know what to do at a time like this. But this much he did know, Rachel knew exactly what she was doing. She was causing a mighty peculiar stir in the pit of his stomach that gave him a strong urge to pull her close. He was downright uneasy with that desire without knowing if it were too presumptuous on his part. He decided to wait, hoping she would make the first move.

Even in the darkness Jacob could still picture Rachel's shapely figure. That caused him to sweat a little. He supposed that just came natural to any man who stood this close to a pretty woman. Since he happened to be in love with this particular one, that was even more understandable.

Jacob didn't know he could love anyone so much. In that respect, how could he? He had never been particularly interested in any other girl, nor had he ever remembered actually mingling with one other than Rachel.

As he stood there worrying about his backward insecurities and thinking about Rachel's pretty dark eyes, something of profound importance come to mind. That importance prompted him to speak of it now.

"If I could just remember the color of her eyes. I don't know why, but at times it just drives me crazy trying to picture her eyes." Jacob's face grew remarkably somber as he continued to stare deep into Rachel's eyes almost as if he had traveled back in time.

"Whose eyes?" she asked puzzled.

"My mother's, of course," he returned, astonished that she didn't know who he was talking about. *Surely*, he thought, *she would wish the same for herself, to know what her mother's eyes looked like.*

"Why is that so important to you?" she asked, genuinely interested.

Jacob paused for a moment, surprised that she didn't immediately understand why this matter would be so important to him. With her being such a sensitive woman and all, he figured that of all people she would. But then again, after a little thought, he reasoned, why should he expect Rachel to understand such a loss such as his? After all, how could their two situations be compared? At least she knew where her mother was and what had happened to her, so there was certainly no way for his fair lady to feel the same emotions he felt, nor could she even remotely understand why he tortured himself over not recollecting something as simple as the color of his mother's eyes.

"One should at least remember the color of his own mother's eyes, don't you think?" he asked.

"You were only six years old, Jacob. That's not something a child of that age would pay close attention to. You're being much too hard on yourself."

No sooner had she spoken those words she suddenly found her mind wandering off to a ghost in her own backyard.

"My mother died giving me life. There are times when I wonder what her voice sounded like or if she enjoyed the same splendors of nature as I do. But I most assuredly don't let it tear me to pieces."

But as soon as those words left her mouth, Rachel again became caught up in her own past and for a moment did what came natural. She tried to picture her mother through her father's words.

"My father tells me she could sing like an angel. Obviously I wasn't blessed with that talent." Rachel let out a girlish giggle. "Actually, when you get right down to it, my mother and I look absolutely nothing alike. That has always puzzled me somewhat." With lukewarm confidence she added, "I suppose there's a likeness somewhere that I'm just not aware of."

Rachel again looked at Jacob's face and sensed a real commitment on his part regarding this matter. Though she had

The Truth about Jacob

to admit that this strong quality in him was partially why she loved him so much, she at the same time believed that this was Jacob's race. A race that he was suggesting he'd run forever and that was all well and good. Over the course of time she would be more than happy to help him all she could.

But that promise didn't include tonight. She hadn't sneaked down here this evening to use up what little time they had reminiscing about the saddest times in both their lives. There was no doubt in her mind why she was here. This was her opportunity to find out if he truly loved her—and she had no intentions of letting it slip away.

So with that thought heavy on her mind Rachel looked around quickly and carefully. There was no one to stop her. She took a long deep breath of fresh air and boldly moved forward towards Jacob. Without even the slightest hesitation she wrapped her arms around his shoulders and lifted her head up, staring at him through the vague half-lit darkness.

They both stared a moment longer, then their lips finally came together for the very first time. Their kiss was a little hesitant at first, and then it became passionate once the knowledge of each other's feelings were realized. Their chests molded tightly with a suffocating closeness. Time seemed to stand still during the duration of the kiss. There was no need to say another word and certainly no need to hold back emotions that had been held back for far too long already.

Rachel felt the pounding of his heart and the tightness of his muscles. Jacob felt the fullness of her breasts pressing against his chest. He stroked her hair, surprised at how soft it was, his fingers slithered through hundreds of silky brown strands. They held onto one another, too afraid to let go. His sweet breath tickled her tiny nose while his manly scent reached within and touched the very essence of her soul. She couldn't resist the temptation to taste his sensuous mouth again.

Rachel lifted her face so they could share another hard kiss. She knew that up until now they had been no more than casual, loose connections with a strong undercurrent of attraction for one another. But after just this one kiss she felt she could claim him for her own.

They had discovered a mutual desire to break the silent distance between them.

Jacob's skin was crawling with goose bumps. He'd wanted to kiss that girl awful bad and sure was pleased to think she was bold enough to make it happen. Rachel loved him. A man just knows when it's love. He had scarcely formed that thought in his mind when their hungry lips firmly pressed together once more. The sweetness of the moment soon gave way to a deeper passion.

Just when they were lost in each other, having given into exploring the passions between them and forgetting everything and everyone else, they were rudely reminded that the fresh night air did not strictly belong to them.

Voices approaching in their direction broke the couple's tight embrace. A sigh of resignation escaped them as they stepped apart. The silhouettes of two men appeared on the scene poking their heads out from around the north side of the bunkhouse. They were evidently there to answer nature's call before retiring for the night. One last smoke would keep them out there long enough to threaten the romantic mood of this evening's rendezvous.

Jacob instinctively pulled further away from Rachel as though he'd been caught doing something wrong. It was obvious to her that he didn't want to be seen just by the way he hovered close to the corner post of the corral.

A hush fell over them as they both watched from afar. There was a definite cool down in the air around the pair as they stood perfectly still in the dark with too much distance between them now. Hiding like thieves in the night behind the flat boards, the lovers patiently waited in hopes the men wouldn't take too long to finish their business.

The Truth about Jacob

But once both men had watered the dust below their feet, a conversation soon erupted thereafter between Luke and Bradford that complicated matters even more for Jacob and Rachel.

The two tired cowboys began to chew the fat about Billy. Their faces were grim and unsmiling. They stood barely thirty feet away, so the young lovers could clearly hear every word they were saying along with the sweeping view from where they were crouched.

The shortcomings of Billy Roberts was the last thing they wanted to hear right now. Unfortunately, being stuck in the awkward position they were in, they had no other choice than to wait out the two men.

Luke was leaning up against the water trough, puffing like a smokestack on a hand rolled cigarette of his own making. He spit bits and pieces of loose tobacco out into the dirt in between each word he spoke. After bringing his fingers to his lips for the tenth time and blowing the excess smoke out his nose, he extended the conversation further beyond Billy's continual escapades on the ranch. He moved their discussion onto an episode that had taken place in town the night before.

"Guess old Doc Stone will be able to save a little of Hank's one-eyed lizard after all," Luke confirmed with a disgusted look on his face.

"Why, what's wrong with his lizard?" Bradford instinctively asked.

"Didn't you hear what happened in town last night?"

"How was I supposed to hear anything about anything if I'm camped out at Two Forks Ridge? You know there's not a soul around for miles way up there. Told you last week I was gonna sleep out under the stars and get an early start on that fencing before it got too hot. Now spit it out. What happened to Hank?" he asked, his patience wearing thin.

"Billy stabbed him right between the legs. Divided the north from the south."

"Damned you say. What the hell for?"

"Seems he and Billy got into a little dispute over who was gonna sport Lu Lu first, so Billy settled the argument."

"Damned you say."

"Guess Hank can count his lucky stars though. After all, look what happened to poor old Maurice last year just for cheatin' at poker." He looked around at Bradford and whispered," Remember, Billy shot him right between the eyes." Luke dropped his chin and stood there shaking his head in disgust.

"Better keep this little matter under your hat, though, I don't know yet how much of this episode Billy wants told since it's kind of a sensitive subject and all. I just can't figure what gets into that cowboy's head sometimes. It's one thing to defend yourself, but maiming a man like that for no more reason than that, why it just don't make any sense to me. A man's gotta be awful darn coldhearted inside to go around doin' things like that just for the hell of it. Guess for a man like Billy, any reason is reason enough," Luke declared, shaking his head.

"Why, you know yourself old Hank never hurt a soul in his life. Worst thing he's ever done is waste his weekly dollar to sport little Lu Lu. He don't have nobody to answer to at home but his Pa, and his Pa don't care who Hank rides as long as it ain't his favorite horse, Bucky."

Luke shook his head again like a dog with a foxtail in his ears. "Well, ain't nothin' can be done about it now. Hank won't be sneakin' a ride on his Pa's favorite horse for a long time to come. And Lu Lu better not hold her breath waitin' on him either. Talk is, poor old Hank doesn't have enough left between his legs to shake a stick at much less make that old gal howl."

"How long you s'posen the folks around these parts are gonna keep puttin' up with Billy? Ain't no man, woman, or kid can live in peace without worrying about what he's gonna up and do next. He don't put no value on no man's life," Bradford testified.

The Truth about Jacob

"Like I said, you just keep a lid on what I told ya, unless you wanna go around lookin' over your shoulder all the time, wonderin' if he's gonna shut you up for good. You know how he feels about anyone nosing around in his affairs."

Billy remained the bud of their conversation for another five minutes or so as they worked their way back towards the bunkhouse. Once they reached the entrance, they paused only long enough to take one last puff on their smokes before deciding they'd had enough of Billy for one night.

In the shadowed coolness of what was left of the evening, Jacob and Rachel watched closely as the two cowboys gradually disappeared back inside the bunkhouse.

"Well, he's right in one respect. Billy wouldn't take kindly to anyone spreading that story around," Jacob confirmed.

"They all need to be horse whipped for hanging around that saloon and that ancient strumpet with her tarnished reputation, as far as I'm concerned," she added.

Rachel stood flat-footed, feeling irritable and very restless. She didn't want to think about Billy or even hear one more word about that sore subject. She still had plenty of excitement stored up inside her and was more than ready to carry on where she and Jacob had left off. They were alone once again and she couldn't imagine anything nicer or any other place she'd rather be than alone with Jacob. She naturally assumed he would also feel the same as she did so she waited patiently for him to make a move towards her.

After more than thirty slow seconds dragged by she realized to her deep disappointment that Jacob obviously didn't see things her way since he made no effort to take even one tiny step her way. He remained standing three feet away with too much silence between them. It was as if a cool wind had chilled his fire. They stood quietly for thirty more seconds listening to the soft breath of the sleeping horses.

Rachel felt the pressure building in her temples. It was apparent that their evening of romance was spoiled after all. It was pretty plain to see that Jacob was still rather hesitant when it came to being bold about their involvement. It aggravated her to think that he allowed two hot-winded old cowpokes to ruin their evening. The realization of that thought hurt her deeply. She had so hoped that after tonight's unveiling he would now be brave enough to shout their newfound love to the whole world as if he were proud to be her man. Instead, for some reason he appeared to still be afraid of the dangers of discovery.

Rachel was saddened by his cowardly reaction, even though she was well aware that he was possibly more concerned over what her father might say about his daughter out sneaking around in the dark, rather than what any of his fellow comrades might think about them being out late together. In her mind that didn't seem to make a difference in how angry she felt right now.

She was downright furious at Luke and Bradford for ruining her evening, and even more exasperated at Jacob for showing such weakness. She didn't care if her father did know the truth or if talk about them spread up and down the streets in town. *That surely was bound to happen sooner or later anyway*, she reasoned.

Rachel's anger allowed her to step out of her usual understanding and considerate character. She looked sharply at Jacob unafraid to speak her mind. "What are you worrying about? For crying out loud, Jacob, they didn't even see us. Besides, we weren't doing anything wrong! We're both of age you know!" she clarified with a girlish enthusiasm between her angered words.

Her eyes were still filled with desire. She was as much as begging Jacob to do something to bring their brief moments of pleasure back to life. No telling how long it would take before they would be able to meet again. Rachel held her breath in anticipation of his first response to her pleas. After all, she wasn't asking for that much.

The Truth about Jacob

It had been only an impossible dream of Jacob's for so long to hold Rachel as close as he had just done tonight. Revealing that fact to her before now was unthinkable. He was more than pleased to think that she had jumped in headfirst and dragged it out of him. His face felt hot toying with the idea of just touching her one more time. It was such an intense emotional rush that the mere experience of it was enough to sink any normal man's resistance to fall in love. And deep in love he was.

He tried to say something a couple of times, but he just couldn't get up the courage. Instead, he kept his silence, looked at his boots and kept changing the weight of his body from one foot to the other. Jacob kept thinking about the possibility of her father finding out that they were sneaking around behind his back. The thought of that happening scared the life right out of him.

Besides, there was another problem to consider. Tonight he discovered he was a hungry man. He needed some cooling off time. That wasn't an easy thing to do, especially standing next to the most beautiful creature he'd ever laid eyes on. Even with modesty so befitting him he feared he would be tempted to break the rules of propriety. He was embarrassed over the intimate desires that were dancing around inside his head and elsewhere. He could feel the flush in his cheeks wondering if she could read his mind. He prayed that she couldn't.

Though the desire was still there he feared he lacked the resistance to stop something once he started. Jacob kept his head hung down and began to blubber all over himself. "Guess we better call it a night, Rachel. Your father will be sending the troops out after us next the way our luck is going."

Her eyes searched his face. There was a deceptive sound in his voice. He was a man that normally feared nothing. She got the impression there was something else he was hiding from her. Deeply hurt over his less than courageous perspective on the entire situation, she didn't waste anytime letting him know just how she felt about his lily-livered attitude.

Because he was going to run like a scared dog, the smile disappeared from her face and she barked back at him, mad with disgust, "What exactly are your feelings for me, Jacob? I really think I've been patient long enough! Am I just some sort of social friend you might exchange a kiss or two with occasionally when the mood strikes you? Or do you care for me the same way I care for you?"

Jacob couldn't have been more pleased with what took place here tonight. The unexpected interruption was a bitter disappointment to him, too. Unfortunately, he had other things to consider that were of an embarrassing nature. It's not as if he was turning his back on her, but it was much too soon in their relationship to share such intimate thoughts with her, no matter how much he loved her.

Jacob knew he wasn't very good at this new game of love and cursed his own inability to be bolder. Why couldn't he just say the words, "Marry me, Rachel." For heaven's sake, how hard could that be? But her direct question caught him off guard. He sure didn't expect her to be so blunt and put him on the spot like this.

Unable to think quickly enough, his hands began to tremble as he awkwardly stammered his words, "I'm...I'm not sure! I guess I just need some more time to think."

Rachel jerked her head back with a shocked look on her face.

Even in the darkness of the night Jacob could see the anger grow in her eyes. He knew immediately that he hadn't said the right thing. If anything, he laid their awkward relationship wide open for more confusing question about their future together.

He felt like slapping himself for his vague answer. *What stupidity*, he thought to himself. Again he cursed his unworldly ways in the art of courting. When he thought further about what he should have said, he realized his short reply confirmed that he just didn't have a clue as to how to properly respond to woman's emotional needs. His response wasn't enough to

The Truth about Jacob

suggest even a casual interest in her, much less a promise of 'till death do us part.

Jacob's hands began to tremble more and his throat felt dry. Telling Rachel the truth about how much he really loved her seemed much too difficult for a man like him. He felt bad about it because he sure did love this girl.

Blood rushed into his cheeks, but Rachel couldn't see the flush of color nor would she have cared. Right now she was seeing red because his empty words were still caught in her throat like a jagged bone. Choosing not to shelter her anger, she swallowed her pride and then let him know exactly how she felt about his sheepish response.

"Suit yourself, Jacob Fowler!" she blurted with a rough edge to her voice. "Whenever you decide to get your head out of the sand you know where you can find me! But you just remember this," she warned as her eyes brimmed with tears, "Good things don't always wait forever, so don't think for one minute I will!"

That was a joke, she thought to herself without cracking a smile. *She'd wait forever if she had to, but she certainly wasn't about to let him know that.*

"I'm sorry, Rachel. I didn't mean to hurt your feelings," Jacob pleaded.

Rachel stepped back, trying desperately to compose herself. She walked away in a huff, wiping the tears from her eyes, ignoring his meaningless words.

However, his words did make her only too aware that she was doing what she swore she wouldn't; rush his heart. She just couldn't help herself.

Her head was spinning, her stomach was tied in knots and she was overcome with a sickening sense of failure. Annoyed by how this evening had turned out, she walked towards the house feeling that all her efforts tonight had been for nothing. She failed, in her anger, to hear Jacob say he loved her. The most frustrating thing of all was how she'd come up empty-handed as far as gaining some kind of commitment on his part.

But Rachel knew she wouldn't give up, no matter what kind of setbacks she encountered. Some people spend their entire lives looking for that one perfect person. This little gal was lucky. She had found hers right in her own backyard and sure wasn't about to let him get away. The chase had just begun she promised herself as she panted her way up the stairs to the front door.

Chapter 4

It was a blue Monday in midsummer. Lately, temperature highs had been teetering between 105 and 115. By noon, the sun was hotter than Hades, and by the time Billy finished fixing three measly posts he was drenched in sweat. The sweat trickled down the small of his back and beads of perspiration sparkled on his face in the sunlight. His shirt, colorless in the wash of the summer sun, showed signs of wet, dusty patches.

There was no shade along the many miles of fence that stretched out across Baxter's land. Mending fences wasn't exactly Billy's favorite part of ranching. In fact, he'd come to the conclusion that he didn't like it at all. But it was just one of the many chores that had to be taken care of to keep a ranch this size running the way it should.

Above all else, he'd rather be handling the horses. He could climb their backs better than any other man, and when all was said and done, he came away a master among amateurs. Bronco busting was the only area of ranching where no one questioned his know-how. Even Baxter gave him free rein with his horses.

This particular portion of fencing was in deep disarray. It needed a good deal of patching and it needed to get done before this day died. The south wind that usually carried heavy rains had done a real number on the battered posts. After the posts became waterlogged they were an open invitation to further abuse by wind or more savage rains. This was evidently the case here, even though last winter hadn't been what Billy considered to be a severe one. But that only led him to believe that Mother Nature may be storing up to spit out a nasty winter season this year.

The harsh winds that roared through the parched valley had picked up what was left of some of the more damaged posts and broken them into smaller pieces. Most of them were either slanting or completely lying down on their sides. The largest portion of Baxter's livestock would be housed within these borders for the better part of the winter months. For that very reason Billy was out here now with grim determination to get the fencing back into proper order.

Nothing much had changed around the ranch since he was a boy, with the exception that he now lived there full time. He'd taken up permanent residence in the bunkhouse right after his mother had passed away six years ago. He would have left home long before that, but didn't dare desert that dear woman.

It had been rough going for his mother to take care of a man who was pretty much spooney every day. His father couldn't manage a pleasant conversation, much less be good company for his wife. Despite Sam's shortcomings, Parilee was a faithful wife and refused to leave him in his time of need when he was strapped so tightly to the bottle.

It was beyond Billy's reasoning as to why his mother chose to live under such harsh conditions. It was a known fact that his father gave her nothing in return, despite all her years of sacrifice. She never had the modern conveniences most other women took for granted. Even though it wore her body down, she managed to take care of the worthless drunken nimshi right up to the very day she died.

The Truth about Jacob

Other than Billy, that man seemed to be her only purpose in life, despite the fact he was an embarrassment to them both. His barbershop folded up completely after he accidentally slit Jake Wilke's throat. This happened when he negligently cut a clean path, nearly severing his jugular vein, while trying to give him a shave when he was three sheets to the wind. Billy liked to drink with the best of them, but there was one big difference between him and his father. He knew when to call it quits.

Perhaps the townsfolk were fooled, but Billy wasn't. Most people believed his mother died of natural causes; he knew otherwise. During the course of his parent's miserable marriage she simply worked herself to death. A broken heart only quickened the destructive process.

Amazingly, she never stopped loving her husband despite the fact that he preferred a bottle of whiskey to her company. He'd broken every promise he'd ever made. He didn't quit drinking, he didn't support his family, and last but not least, Sam didn't partake in any of Billy's activities that were crucial to the proper growth of a young boy. The only contact Sam had with his son was to discipline him. As a boy, Billy was starving for love and encouragement from his father. He'd belly-crawl like a dog at his heels just for a pat of approval. But all he got was a handful of disappointments.

His mother worked overtime trying to fill both sets of parenting shoes. Parilee spent her days and nights lavishing all her affection on Billy, which helped to make the hard times easier to swallow. But no matter how hard she tried to meet her son's needs and fill his void, Billy still felt the absence of a strong father figure in his life. He'd never forgive his father for all the beatings he got or for treating his mother like a piece of dirt beneath his feet. Billy blamed his father for his mother's death and would hate the old man with every fiber in his soul until the day he took his last breath.

Billy and his father hadn't spoken to one another in over ten years. As far as Billy was concerned it would stay that way. The way things stood now, Billy didn't need anyone to fight his battles for him. He no longer had to depend on his mother to protect him from his father or anyone else. The only friend he needed was his Colt forty-five, strapped to his hip. His talents with a gun gave him an advantage over anyone who crossed him. Reluctant to let go of his tough guy image, he browbeat the underdog in order to satisfy a need deep inside, to blame others for his own misfortunes and to fill a void that couldn't be filled.

With the noon hour drawing near Billy could hear the call to lunch, so he begrudgingly drew away from his quiet thoughts about his mother. The faint clang of iron off in the distance was Kate's signal that the noon meal was ready.

From out of his watch pocket he removed a rusty old timepiece that he had stolen years ago from one of the local drunks his father had dragged home for the night. Billy drew it upwards and checked Kate for accuracy. "Right on time," he whispered lightly. Like clockwork that woman never missed a lick. Judging by the size of her backside and her undefined waistline he believed she ate her meals with as much vigor as she put into preparing them.

Although Kate was about the same size as his mother, it somehow looked quite different on her. To him, his sweet mother was just pleasantly plump. Kate, on the other hand, was an eyesore with rolls of flesh spilling over her hips and a derriere that was a harvest of plenty. *And oh my God,* he thought, those awful mountains of breasts that spread out across her chest like full moons were designed to keep a man's eyes busy.

Still, nobody in their right mind would argue the fact she could cook circles around any other woman in this valley. That had included his own mother, but he would die a thousand deaths before he'd ever admit that to another living soul. Billy didn't think much of the old gal, and of course she wouldn't scratch his back either. Seldom did they strike up a conversation on a friendly basis. For the most part, they pretty much tried to stay out of each other's way.

The Truth about Jacob

The men rode in from all sides of the ranch. Each came from a different direction, having tended to chores on other sections of the ranch that numbered in the thousands of acres. Billy rode in on the horse that should have been Jacob's pride and joy—the white stallion from Butte Creek Canyon. He named the horse Jacob's Loss out of pure orneriness.

After securing his favorite stud in the corral with fresh water and a little hay, he headed towards the ranch house. There was a large eating quarters on the east side of the house that was separated from the kitchen by a door and a narrow five-foot stretch of hallway. Billy hurried along to join the rest of the ranch hands. He could feel the saliva fill his mouth. The rich aroma of salt-cured ham was thick in the air and he could hardly wait to sink his teeth into some.

Byron Baxter stepped out from the north end of the house, blocking Billy's entrance to the chow room. The old man's face showed a deep concern over something that was obviously weighing heavily on his mind. Billy couldn't help but notice that he was hesitant at first to speak. After clearing his throat a couple of times he finally delivered the bad news that had pained him.

"Billy, I'm sorry to tell you this, but your father is not doing well." Baxter's gaze dropped to Billy's eyes as he spoke. There was a long stretch of silence between them.

"So what's new? He hasn't done well in years!" Billy returned sharply as if to say, "Who gives a damn?"

"No, I mean, he's very sick this time." Baxter blinked his folded lids that were lined with a few graying lashes. "He's not expected to live through the night, and well, he's been asking for you. Old Jake, who still looks in on him from time to time, told me just this morning on his mail run that he looked like death warmed over."

Jake and Sam shared a casual friendship that had survived over many years, despite the fact that Sam had nearly killed him with a sharp edge razor.

"Well, you can tell good old Jake to just give him another bottle. That's all he really needs!"

"You don't understand, Billy. Jake said he knew for certain he wouldn't pull out of this one."

"Well now, we all gotta go sooner or later, don't we?" Billy snapped with no pause in his words.

He shrugged his shoulders, not allowing the facts to sink in. *This had happened many times before*, he thought. It wasn't difficult to believe that this was just another one of his father's many sick spells. *Besides, he's too stubborn to die. He'd pull through this one just like he'd done a hundred times before*. He really didn't care one way or the other, so what did it matter?

Baxter wasn't sure what to make of Billy's lack of concern over his father's serious condition. His reaction to the news was disturbingly cold and insensitive. Baxter found this deeply troubling and just stood there dumbfounded.

Billy stared blankly at Baxter, well aware of his troubled thoughts. "Well now, just what did you expect? Did you think for one minute that drinking like a fish all these years wasn't gonna catch up with him someday? Does it really surprise you that much that he's in this kind of a fix?"

Baxter didn't answer. He stood there listening to the scorn in his voice.

Billy continued to point out a few other facts with his arms awkwardly swinging in the air. "What do you expect me to do? Fall down on my knees, all broke up over a man who made his own stupid choice to drink himself to death? Have you forgotten how he made my life miserable?" he asked as he leaned closer, unconsciously drilling a forefinger into Baxter's chest. "You've been more of a father to me than he's ever thought of being. He's done me no favors. He couldn't even sober up long enough to stand by my side when mother died! No, but you did. He didn't manage to drag himself away from his bottle long enough to pay his final respects to the woman

The Truth about Jacob

who took care of his sorry butt for over twenty years! So don't you go expectin' me to just drop everything and rush over to his bedside just because he wants me to. Where was he when I needed him? You know as well as I do where he was. Nowhere!" he blurted. "Now I've said enough about that old man and I don't have nothin' more to say about this whole matter! If you'll just step aside, I'll be on my way!"

"He's still your father, Billy, whether he acted like one or not. He made some real bad mistakes, I admit, but don't we all? You sure you want to let him die hatin' him like you do?"

Billy stared coldly at Baxter. He said nothing. He sidestepped Byron, walking with a purpose, towards the eating quarters as if they had just discussed nothing more important than the weather.

Baxter watched Billy's back until he disappeared from his sight. He had taken great pains to try and talk some sense into Billy. But he could tell by the way he stood his ground on the issue that he flatly refused to change his mind about his father. For that reason he felt saddened. This could have been the only opportunity for the two men to make amends. Tomorrow may be too late.

Baxter rubbed his hand over his forehead. He stood there wondering why these two men couldn't just sit down like mature adults and put their differences aside. He pitied old Sam because he most likely never would know how much he hurt his own son. As far as Billy was concerned, he had no hope of talking him into anything, especially forgiving his father. That young man had lived too long with a deep hatred in his heart and now his worst enemy was bitterness.

Billy was nowhere to be found after the day's work was done. It was a weekend, so most of the ranch hands suspected he had gotten an early start to town to hoot it up as he usually did.

On Billy's long ride into town he thought a lot about what Baxter had said. Once seated at the bar he thought a lot more.

After four straight shots of pure corn juice the prodigal son disappeared from the saloon full of rowdy drunks out into the cover of darkness. Not many steps placed him standing outside a cloudy, dirt-smudged window. He paused momentarily, allowing his eyes time to grow accustomed to the dim light.

Inside his father lay on his bed groaning in pain.

Billy's heart sank to the pit of his stomach staring at only a vague image of the man his father had been. He hardly recognized him with his deep, sunken, yellow eyes and a bluish mouth, barely able to capture enough breath to raise his chest. His bloated body was puffed up to three times its normal size. Even his fingers and toes had nowhere to go except stretched straight out webbed like a duck's foot. His luminous, mustard-colored skin looked so fragile and thin that even the slightest pressure placed upon it would surely cause the tissues to break and bleed.

Clenching his fists into sweaty balls, Billy felt torn over what to do. The large amount of whiskey he had consumed hadn't bolstered his courage enough to try and help this man he'd hated for so long. Was he a fool for even considering it? After all, it was his father who had killed their relationship. Billy only began to avoid his father after the bottle became more important than anything or anyone. Billy ruefully thought about these things and decided he didn't need him then and he sure as hell didn't want him now. As he turned to walk away he suddenly found himself fighting long suppressed emotions. The air was alive with his mother's presence. He could almost hear her pleading with him. *"Help your father, Billy! Please do it for me!"*

Despite his efforts to stop them, her plea was relentless and for a moment he fought against it. Her whispers seemed to grow louder and louder. He wasn't able to push her words out of his mind. How could he deny his mother anything? Why would he want to disappoint her when she had always been there for him?

Billy had absorbed every word she said. As if possessed, he quietly entered the door, creeping slowly over to his father's

The Truth about Jacob

bedside. Pitifully surrounded by his own filth, Sam was staring behind blank eyes at nothing. The stench in the room was overpowering. Billy was overcome by waves of nausea. He fought the bile coming up in his mouth as he crept up to the side of this man who had become a stranger to him.

After several seconds, Sam's eyes flickered over Billy, he was looking into the freckled face of the young man he knew to be his son. Nobody else around these parts had red hair as coarse as chicken wire that stuck straight out.

Billy was uncharacteristically seized by a sudden urge to cry. He hadn't felt this emotion since he had buried his mother. His mouth curled and he felt his breath choke in his throat as he gasped for air. He tried desperately to tell himself that he was doing this only for his mother's sake.

Sam could clearly see that Billy's eyes were misty. He was cut to the heart with his son's surprising show of emotion. "I made a mess of things, didn't I, son?" Sam rolled his sunken eyes once and then continued to force his whispers. "Yeah, I botched it up real good." The dying man coughed and gagged on something real thick before swallowing it and gurgled out another shallow breath.

The corners of Billy's mouth fell, but he didn't say a word. He couldn't think of anything to say. Quite frankly, he couldn't understand what had come over him. All he could do was look long and hard at this bloated shell of a man squirming and twitching in excruciating pain. Each breath Sam struggled to take, Billy feared would be his last.

Sam was looking at Billy. His eyes were glazed, almost immobile. He lifted his stinking hand and touched Billy's arm as he swallowed some more pride. "I need, need a drink, son. I need it real bad. Would you get me just one? I mean just a little one. Nobody else seems to think I do, but I need it real bad." Sam tried to lift his head as he repeated his plea, but couldn't budge no more than an inch or two. At that point he lost what little strength he had mustered and his head came plunging back down on the dingy gray pillow that looked as if it had been used to sweep the floor. His eyes grew glassy. He begged again, "Will you do that for your old man, Billy?"

Billy felt badly for his father. He turned his head away and dabbed at his eyes with a dirty, calloused finger. A huge sense of pity swept over him as he looked down at this weak man who once had worn the armor of a ruthless tyrant. Suddenly, he got all choked up. His shoulders drew back as he tried to sort things out in his mind. He had always resented his father so much that it had been literally impossible for him to overlook the fact that his father's daily consumption of whiskey had in part been responsible for his actions. Now, strange as it was it seemed so natural to want to help his old man despite their differences.

So a quick decision was made in order to honor his father's dying wish. *If one last drink is what he wanted, then that's what he was going to get.* His father was standing on death's front door and Billy knew it. In desperation at that point he stumbled out of the house of his youth and blindly ran back into the busy saloon. Unnoticed by others, he quietly bought the cheapest bottle of whiskey and literally barreled back to his father's bedside within minutes.

Billy pulled up a chair alongside his father. Twisting the cork several times, it unexpectedly popped out against the wall, making a loud snapping noise. He turned the bottle towards his father's mouth, lifting his head up at the same time allowing his open lips to embrace the bottle. It was much more difficult to lift his head than he had expected. *Why was his head so heavy?* he asked himself in a puzzlement. Billy studied his father's face with caution. His eyes were blank and his arm dangled limply off the side of the bed. Strings of mucus dripped out of the corner of his mouth and his bowels had emptied leaving small speckled spots on the front of his pants.

The Truth about Jacob

He laid the dead man's head back down on his filthy pillow. Billy felt numb. He slumped backwards against the flimsy chair. *Even in his final moments I hadn't lived up to his expectations*, he thought grimly. Billy's painful childhood raced through his head. He once again found himself back on a familiar plain. He again lost most of his self-confidence and felt inadequate as he always had in his father's presence.

Just as he had done so many times before, he tried to look for one good memory about his father to hold onto. He found none. It was then that he screamed out at the dead man in angered frustration because he felt like he had failed him yet again.

"You couldn't even wait to die, could you, old man?" Billy blurted. He talked as if the dead man could hear every word he spouted. "You had to prove to me one last time that I'm not good enough to do anything right!"

Billy dropped his eyes to examine his father more closely. His eyeballs were rolled back into his head with only the yellowish whites showing. His heavy gray beard and long, tangly hair hadn't been washed or trimmed in months. Billy was sickened by his smelly unkempt appearance. As a child his father had drilled into his head the importance of good personal hygiene. The obnoxious mouth that never shut up now lay wide-open waiting for its last request.

Beads of sweat crystallized above Billy's freckled hairy brows. He didn't understand what had come over him and felt confused by these feelings that were so foreign. Why did he feel the loss of a man who hadn't done one thing for him, but blame him for everything that went wrong in his life?

But then the thought occurred to him that, for once, his old man would have to listen to him without cutting his words short with a slap across the face, or screaming at him at the top of his lungs. For the first time in his life, he was in control of his father and he spoke accordingly: "Well, old man, I got what you wanted, and I ain't gonna disappoint you this time."

As a heavy flow of tears streamed down his cheeks, Billy did his father one last favor. He again lifted his stiff, heavy head. He propped his mouth open wider with the neck of the bottle and then forced it two inches further down his throat giving him one last drink for the road.

Only Billy, and a lone cockroach crawling across his boot, would ever know that this prodigal son actually had a soft, caring spot in his heart for his father who had given him nothing but grief in return.

Chapter 5

Rachel's annual birthday celebration was a casual affair. At her father's insistence, Billy's name was added to the short list of invited guests joining them for dinner. Throughout her childhood and adolescent years his invitation to the festive occasion was simply taken for granted, so her father felt it wasn't right to break tradition after all their years of a close friendship, that he believed they still shared.

Rachel did not savor the idea but would not go against her father's wishes. So a compromise was agreed upon, but not without her experiencing a lengthy, quiet dread. She moped around the house for two or three days, trying desperately to think of a legitimate excuse to rid herself of the little red-headed nuisance. She thought of a few tempting ideas; however, reality forced her to think better of them because it would most likely land her in trouble with the law.

She and Kate saw eye to eye when it came to Billy. Both were of the same opinion that everyone would be better off without him around. This evening, in particular, would be more enjoyable for Rachel without having to put up with his immature shenanigans, ones that coiled her nerves like a tightly wound spring. But with the burden of a promise to Baxter, both women gave their word to treat Billy as cordially as possible.

It would be hard to digest his crude remarks that demanded more nail biting self-control than Kate and Rachel cared to muster up. One thing for certain, Billy would live up to his reputation. He had never learned the art of knowing when, and when not, to speak his mind. Armed with a filthy mouth, using inappropriate language impossible to flour down, he'd eventually push at least one person in the room past their limit. That person was usually Rachel. Neither woman looked forward to the prospect of a full evening gazing upon his strange little face that sucked in and popped out in the most unusual places.

Rachel sighed, just thinking about what was in store. He always put on quite a spectacle for only her eyes to see. Which one of his disgusting habits would he pull on her first: picking his nose and wiping it on his shirttail, or rolling his eyelids up until they locked into place? Even though her displeasure would show on her face, he'd repeat these childish acts just as soon as no one else was looking, just to get a rise out of her.

Oh dear God, she thought, *if he does it again tonight I'll just jump over the table and choke him to death, right then and there, in front of God and everyone. If he knew what was good for him, he'd better not press his luck.* As long as this was her house, she believed it should be a safe haven from the only man who made her flesh crawl. But unfortunately, once a year, not even the privacy of her own home was far enough away. Deep down she knew this evening would prove no different than any other with Billy around. She'd be forced to just sit there and suffer in silence.

As Rachel stood from afar, watching Kate fussing over the napkins on the dining table, her mind drifted away from Billy and back to Jacob. She closed her eyes for a moment, lost in the sensations she felt their last encounter at the corral. She remembered well his soft kiss, and that thought warmed her all over. She knew in her heart that his presence was all she really needed tonight. She had grown tired of hiding her true feelings for him. Maybe she'd get brave while they were eating and announce her love for Jacob loud enough for everyone to hear. *That ought to cook those peas Billy uses for brains*, she figured. Then maybe he could channel his mind and energy on someone else other than her. But of course she knew she couldn't just blurt it out. That would embarrass Jacob to no end.

However, that didn't stop her from concocting an alternate plan. Somehow she'd find a way to shed this audience tonight. During the course of the evening she'd think of a good reason for she and Jacob to just slip away from the others and enjoy some time to themselves. Maybe Jacob would have something promising to say to her. Maybe even some deep inner secret thoughts he'd never shared with a living soul before. She would find such pleasure in any kind of closeness with him. Sharing a kiss or two would be even better.

Rachel could only imagine how gratifying it would be to experience the sweet taste of Jacob's mouth again. To cup his handsome face within her hands and linger in an intimate kiss. To be able to do precisely what she pleased with him would, of course, have to wait until after they were wed.

Rachel's mind was always busy with thoughts about Jacob. Telling herself to be more patient didn't seem to help matters any as one of her biggest worries was still her father. She hadn't quite figured out how to handle him yet. She somehow had to make him understand that what she felt for Jacob was the real thing. It was love. Honest to goodness love and they were meant to be together.

Forcing her mind back to the present, she fixed her attention on Kate. For such a large lady, she had the agility of a swan. Rachel couldn't help but notice how she breezed effortlessly around the exquisite dining quarters, putting every last minute touch together in less time than it took to make a lady out of Lizzy. The house was already in perfect order and the floors were as clean and slick as a whistle. Today she would work a double shift making sure Rachel's party was all and more than the birthday girl could want.

As for right now, Rachel would be denied even the slightest opportunity to lift one finger to help in any way with the preparation of the dinner. This day was exclusively for her leisure and enjoyment. Kate had made that point perfectly clear a week ago, therefore, she would perform Rachel's normal duties of after dinner clean up. As long as Rachel could remember that had been her chore in order for Kate to make her way back home before dark. Tonight the grand duchess of hard work would take the privilege of a sleepover.

Kate had a certain program she followed when putting together a celebration of this magnitude. Many of her fine techniques were those she had learned as a child, but the dining room itself was the epitome of Baxter's own ideas on the latest in fashionable entertaining.

In his young bachelor years, he had attended many so-called high society functions in the larger cities such as Sacramento and San Francisco. On invitation by Governor John McDougal himself, Baxter had actually spoken at the Governor's inauguration on January 9, 1851, and attended his Inaugural Ball that had followed. It was at that particular function he was introduced to his future wife, Maxine.

Baxter took great pride in this dining room. The room itself, while sparsely furnished, contained a beautifully crafted table with chairs that was absolutely matchless as far as the fine quality of the wood, and a piano seldom played. It could easily seat fifty or more people at one event with the addition of all the adjoining leaves. The long cedar table was always dressed in the finest linen. Tonight Kate decorated it with tall white candles burning at each end and a large bouquet of roses arranged in a busy floral vase that was placed in the center, which pulled the whole room together.

Kate knew her way around the stove better than any woman in these parts. No one would dispute the fact that she was worth

The Truth about Jacob

her salt when it came to preparing a hearty meal. Working nonstop all afternoon, Kate had cooked generous portions of braised chicken, and mashed potatoes and gravy, along with her own rendition of lemon peppered green beans. The exquisitely cut, sparkling crystal glasses would be filled with the best wine money could buy straight from The Beringer Vineyards of the Napa Valley. Tonight's occasion would be played out on a lavish scale for all to enjoy with the ambiance of a perfect summer's evening.

Earlier this morning Rachel tried hard to get her fingers in on some of the work that had to be done, but Kate wouldn't hear of it. Her face catalogued her disappointment because she'd taken a liking to tinkering with decorating and often helped Kate in the kitchen because she really wanted to learn how to cook just like her. Not sure of what else to do with her time, she dawdled about the room bored to no end.

As she poked along, Rachel's attention was drawn to a small oval picture of her mother, taken on the day she and her father were wed. Looking for some new light on an old question, she removed the old wooden frame from the mantle above the marble fireplace and dusted it carefully with her eyes for the umpteenth time. Curiously, she browsed the black and white image staring back at her scouting for any similarities she and her mother might share.

"She was very beautiful. Don't you agree, Kate?" Rachel inquired.

"Yes, dear, she was quite an elegant lady," she said, honestly trying to show some interest.

When Rachel turned her attention back onto the photo, Kate couldn't resist rolling her eyes in distaste. It was very difficult at times to keep up with the charade. She so wished she could for once quit skirting around the truth and voice her true opinion about Maxine Baxter.

Over the many years working for her, she had learned things that few people knew about the woman. To put it bluntly,

Rachel's mother had no scruples and was a sorry excuse for a wife for poor Mr. Baxter. She had somehow managed to charm her way into the hearts and minds of many men, but of course she settled on Byron Baxter because he was moneyed. Maxine wanted to be somebody with prestige. She had entertained a selfish attitude right from the time she first dug her claws into him.

She had grown to resent the fact that she ended up on a dusty ranch out in the middle of nowhere instead of living out her dreams of high society ballroom parties and political functions that were so common in the bigger cities. In the end, she turned to the bottle to deaden her regrets of failed expectations. Because her young husband refused to uproot to a larger populated area, she held a grudge against him that lasted until the day she died.

Throughout their thirteen-year marriage Maxine initiated numerous physical confrontations with poor Mr. Baxter, not to mention the daily verbal abuse that would drive any normal man insane. However, he remained a perfect gentleman at all times. Not once did he ever lay his hand on her, except to protect himself from her sudden outbursts that were always accompanied by physical blows.

Worst of all, she began to deny him any intimate contact whatsoever. The combination of all these problems caused such a grievance between them that his life turned out to be a living hell the entire time they were together. Kate hated to even start thinking about Maxine because when she did, she fell into such a dark mood that she found it hard to climb back out of it. There was no love lost between them, but Kate held her tongue out of respect for Rachel.

Rachel shot a curious glance at Kate and kept the conversation going. "Doesn't it strike you as odd that I look absolutely nothing like my mother? Just look at this picture," she pointed out, sliding her finger over the smooth surface of the photo. "She's so fair-skinned with curly blonde hair and a thin, streamlined nose. She's tall and slim, but I'm short and squatty and I have more dark hair than I know what to do with. And from whom in thunderation did I inherit this little pug nose of mine? It looks as if someone dropped me one too many times on my face when I was a baby." She winked and giggled at Kate. "Just kidding, I know you didn't let that happen."

Rachel ignored Kate's silence and went on with her curious inspection. "I did acquire some of my father's features, though. My dark complexion I'm thankful for, but these big ears of mine I wouldn't wish on a dog. Thank you, dear Lord, for long hair, that's all I can say."

She shook her head as the same thought rose in her again. "For the life of me, I see absolutely no resemblance between my mother and me at all. If you want to get right down to it, Kate, I look more like you than I do her." Rachel chuckled again teasingly. "Guess we've been hanging around one another too long, you're starting to rub off on me."

Kate's hands quivered, but her eyes never left the ivory colored napkin she was meticulously folding on the table. Nor did Rachel notice the involuntary wetness that suddenly developed in Kate's eyes.

Kate didn't think about Maxine because she didn't want to. In fact, it would be her fondest wish just to erase any memory of the evil little witch once and for all, but in eighteen some odd years she'd never been able to accomplish that.

Kate finally found her voice and muttered. "Maybe you just have a few peculiarities belonging to some of your distant relatives on your father's side of the family. That happens sometimes, you know."

Of course Kate as well as Rachel knew that that foregone conclusion would be impossible to substantiate. Baxter's family had originated in England and when his mother, Sara, had decided to run away, she made a clean break of it. She took no drawings, or any type of daguerreotype with her, to share with her only child.

Unfortunately, during her courageous struggles to make a whole new life for herself and her son in America, she died tragically of consumption just six months after her ship docked in the New York Harbor. This sudden turn of events placed her youngster in the care of two old spinster sisters who were extremely religious. They happened to live next door to Sara Baxter and had taken quite a liking to both mother and child. The two aged ladies did quite well by the boy right up until their deaths, which was a good many years after he was old enough to venture out on his own.

Rachel made a comment out of the blue, which sounded pretty silly as far as Kate was concerned. "Wish I were as pretty as you, Kate."

"Nonsense, child. You're as pretty as pretty gets and I'm afraid there's nothing cutsie about me now. Maybe at one time I could hold a candle to some of the other women folk around, but not these days. Too many miles behind this old girl and way too much baggage hanging off these hips."

Rachel gave her a sheepish look. "Father doesn't seem to think so. I've caught him admiring you often when you're not looking. Kate, you're a worthy woman for any man to call his own, and I know father shares those same feelings. I'm not the only one here that hoped you two would eventually get together. I know for a fact that he's willing, but it's you that holds back. Why is that, Kate? He's rich and still handsome for his age. You know yourself that any lady within twenty miles of here would give her eye teeth to be with a man like him. Why not you, Kate?"

Rachel looked at her dear friend straight in the eyes. The tears she saw flowing like a quiet river down her face troubled her. Rachel was dumbfounded. She rushed to her side, throwing her arms around Kate in a tight bear hug.

"What is it, Kate? What's wrong? Are you hiding something from me? Has Father offended you in some way?"

The Truth about Jacob

Kate gasped to catch her breath and tried her best to calm her trembling hands. She was thinking recklessly to herself. How could she tell this poor sweet girl the awful truth about her mother? That would break her heart. Despite the fact that, like herself, Rachel didn't bend easily, she knew the truth would haunt her forever. After all, there were times when that's all she could think about.

Kate had had plenty of other opportunities to fill Rachel in on all the dirt about her mother, but she couldn't bring herself to hurt her in such a way. Besides, it wasn't her place to tell the real story behind what had happened that fateful night, she thought to herself. That was strictly up to Rachel's father.

Out of respect for him she had made a vow years ago that she would never breathe a word of this matter to anyone. So far she had managed to keep that promise with a tug-of-war of emotions. She would take that ugly secret to her grave if she had to.

Kate quickly shook off her trip down memory lane. "Don't be absurd, young lady! Your father's always been a perfect gentleman and the only thing I'm hiding from you is your present. I was just caught up in my own silly thoughts, that's all." Kate felt her gut tighten and prayed that Rachel wouldn't see through her lies. "It's just sad that you're celebrating your eighteenth birthday without your mother's presence."

Rachel leaned down and kissed her cheek. "I think you've filled her shoes quite nicely. I couldn't have asked for a better mother than you," she said with admiration.

Kate blushed and tried to hide her pride. She squeezed Rachel's arm and with a sassy smile gave her a little pat on the bottom. "Now you scat and get yourself all gussied up for that beau of yours and quit worrying about me!"

"Shush, Kate. Don't say that so loud, someone might overhear you!"

"Well, it's the truth and it's about time everyone around here got used to the idea, and that includes your father. There's no reason to keep it such a secret that you two are absolutely smitten with one another. You'd think love was off-limits around this place. If everyone on this ranch hasn't noticed by now that you and Jacob look at one another with stars in your eyes, then they're all blind as bats."

Kate gave Rachel a gentle shove on the arm. "Now get on with you! Put on that pretty lavender satin dress with the puffy ruffles all along the bodice. That ought to catch Jacob's eye." She winked.

Kate's expression still remained somewhat solemn, but Rachel was now harvesting a broad grin. This was not unusual for her because just thinking about Jacob could light her eyes up like moonbeams. She liked the sound of what Kate had said. She seemed to hang on every word, feeling very moved by her simple truths.

Rachel knew that it was a rare gift that Kate had acquired through all her years of experience to have such an amazing insight concerning matters of the heart. It was deeply gratifying to hear that she had also recognized the strong likelihood of love in Jacob's eyes too and that it just wasn't puppy love, like her father suspected. This was a big relief to Rachel since she needed a little reassurance once in a while.

But again, Rachel began to feel a bit nervous and leery of who might be lurking beyond the open doorway and cracked windows listening to them talk. She quickly glanced around the room to make sure it was safe to relax and enjoy the moment without worrying about her father overhearing their conversation. For all she knew maybe he was within hearing distance. That wasn't a pleasant thought, since she was so uncertain of how he would react if he found out she was pursuing Jacob in such an obsessive manner.

At that point, Kate gave Rachel another whack on the bottom. It was a deliberate move to hurry her along towards the privacy of her own dressing room upstairs. It was getting late and the magic hour was quickly approaching. Rachel pranced hurriedly across the dining room floor and stopped only long enough at the doorway to blow Kate a kiss. And then, only after Rachel was completely out of her sight, did Kate breathe a sigh of relief. She silently prayed that she'd never come that close ever again to telling Rachel something that would turn her day as gray as a day could be.

Byron Baxter was standing just ten feet shy of the open doorway to the dining room when Rachel emerged. Oblivious to his presence, she breezed by him and then climbed up the wooden staircase with a smile on her face as broad as a western sky.

He quietly moved his feet a short distance to the doorway. Bending at the waist, he peered around the corner. In front of him was Kate, sitting at the table, staring at a napkin. She was obviously deep in thought.

It would take all the nerve he had in him to confront her now, but he couldn't wait one minute longer to find out why she had been avoiding him. He knew there was something troubling her, something so bad that she had kept her distance from him for well over three weeks.

As soon as he entered the room, she looked his way with teary, hazel eyes, and just as quickly turned away. He moved swiftly to her side. What's the matter, Kate?" he asked as he gently placed his hands on her shoulders.

"Nothing I can't handle on my own," she returned.

"Are you running from ghosts again?"

"I wouldn't call it running, maybe butting heads, but definitely not running."

Byron shook his head. "You're not alone, you know. Everything around here reminds me of her. But the important thing to remember is the fact that she's gone, and gone for good. She can't physically hurt us anymore. It's time we mentally put her out of the picture too. We owe that to ourselves, Kate. I know it's not easy, but we deserve to be happy. Why can't you just put all those unhappy years behind you and allow us the opportunity to move on with our lives? That is something we should have done long ago. Now, I've done my part by trying to hide the truth from Rachel just as you asked of me, but it makes things much more difficult when you avoid talking to me like you have been lately. What's that all about?" he asked with a serious face.

"I'm sorry. I know it's not fair to ask so much from you. Please be patient with me for a little while longer. It's just that this whole party thing has had me running around in circles. I get so worried about everything being so perfect for Rachel, that I tend to forget about other people that matter too."

"Kate, why should this birthday party be any different than all the rest we've given her? I know you well enough to trust that tonight will flow just as smoothly as any other celebration."

Byron thought quietly for a moment. He loved this woman more than words could express, and he knew she loved him as well. He also knew this was a good opportunity to make her face another important issue. "When can we address the important matter of our engagement? They always say the third time's a charm, but as you well know, I passed that mark fifteen years ago."

Kate suppressed a feeling of sadness about his last remark, hoping he didn't see the guilt written all over her face. She knew in her heart that putting him off all these years was no more fair to him than it was to herself. "I know it's not right to ask you to be patient with me for just a little longer. We must be sure that Rachel is mature enough to accept the truth." She hung her head sadly and added, "I'd understand if you decided to move on to greener pastures."

Although patience had been one of his strongest attributes, he smiled weakly and inwardly rebelled against the idea of even waiting one more minute to take this beautiful woman as his wife. But what other choice did he have? "There are no greener pastures, Kate," he confirmed. "You know my heart belongs to you and only you. That's the way it's been for nearly twenty

The Truth about Jacob

years and you know darned well it won't change until the day I take in my last breath."

"Thank you for understanding the heart of a stubborn old woman."

"Don't get me wrong, Kate. There's a condition that goes along with this promise. Just as soon as Jacob and Rachel decide to get married, then I'll expect to announce our engagement soon after."

Kate stood up, whirled around and looked into Baxter's brown eyes in amazement. Taking in a deep breath, she asked, "You mean, you do realize that Jacob and Rachel are in love?"

"C'mon," he said, reaching for her hand, "you don't really believe I'm that blind, do you?"

"Well, it's just that you've never openly spoken to me about it before."

"That road goes both ways, my dear. I just assumed you didn't want to talk about their relationship. After all, I can hardly curtail you long enough to talk about ours."

She was flushed by his comment. "I thought you felt as if Rachel was too young to be involved that deeply with Jacob. I also believed you hadn't reached that point in time when you could willingly let go of your baby girl, so to speak."

Baxter didn't bother to answer Kate. He knew what she had just said was true. It was only recently that he had accepted the inevitable, Rachel would marry soon and leave her childhood home for a home of her own. He smiled and softly kissed her on the forehead. There was a comfort in the knowing that one day soon Kate would finally become his wife, the kind of wife he had always dreamed about.

Kate closed her eyes feeling a tinge of guilt, knowing she hadn't been fair with Byron by asking him to wait for her even longer than he already had. But in her heart, she knew this was the way it had to be—for the sake of everyone's happiness.

After Baxter left the room Kate shook her head stubbornly, straightened her shoulders and got a grip on her emotions. "You aren't going to ruin this day for her or me, you old hay bag, if I have anything to say about it!" she snarled. "I won't give you that satisfaction."

Having made that vow for the hundredth time since Maxine's death, Kate went back to work, not giving it another thought. As far as she was concerned, even the dogs on this ranch knew the old witch wasn't worth it.

Party time had arrived. Baxter was seated at the north end of the table where he always sat looking like a real statesman. He was proudly thinking of several dozen reasons why he deserved a pat on the back for having raised such a fine beautiful young daughter like Rachel.

Rachel was sitting at the south end with Billy and Jacob filling in the sides. Kate was flying around the table, like a chicken with its head cut off, checking every last detail and filling each glass with a delicious clear, sparkling liquid

Although she appeared to be absorbed in her duties and quite content, Kate had unfortunately found that her thoughts about Maxine had returned. Old Maxine seemed to be more of a nagging nuisance today than normal, and so, in essence, she was still minding Kate's business. Therefore, Kate was having a hard time trying to devote her full attention to her guests, and at the same time keep a big bright smile on her face.

Rachel lifted her glass in the air. "Let's give a toast to good health, good company and good wine," she said. She took a large sip of her wine along with all the other party attendants. Her nose wrinkled immediately because of the tart flavor. She'd rather drink medicine, she thought quietly. But for appearance sake she'd make a wild story of some sort to protect her cover. "That's good stuff, alright." She coughed a couple of times and then cleverly held her breath until she had swallowed the last of the nasty stuff. Rachel then quickly watered down her throat with a big gulp of fresh lemon-water.

"Here, Rachel, hold up your glass and I'll fill it for you again," Billy purred.

The Truth about Jacob

"No, no, that's enough for me. Thank you."

"Why that's not enough to wet an ant's whistle."

"Let's not get carried away, Billy. I do mean I've had enough. Just because you enjoy getting wide eyed and tongue-tied before dinner, that doesn't mean I want to indulge in the fruits of the vine to that extent. Drinking myself unconscious really doesn't appeal to me, I'm afraid," she responded, trying out her new age and maturity that was supposed to go along with it.

That comment only fueled Billy's determination to irritate her some more. "Oh, not your cup of tea, my dear?" he teased.

"Now, now, you two! Let's change the subject before you start throwing things at one another across the table," Baxter gently chided.

A shiver of regret ran over Rachel as she stared daggers at Billy. She knew what he was up to. The years had changed the way she looked at him. Given enough time and the opportunity to know him as well as she did now, even a longtime childhood friendship can grow cold. And grow cold it had. Every time she turned around she found herself having to give him a piece of her mind. She was tired of banging her head against the wall when it came to him. Rachel had long since detached herself from the Billy she once knew, simply because he no longer existed.

This was supposed to be her special day, Rachel thought dimly. But she wasn't feeling quite so special right now with Billy eyeing her upper chest as if she didn't have a stitch of clothing on. If her father ever caught him looking at her in such a lewd way he'd pluck his little red head bald. But Billy was too sly at his game. He only stared when the coast was clear and her father was at the present time engaged in some small talk with Jacob. She'd give her right arm to see him slip up just once so she could witness her father scalp him alive.

Rachel was still a little hot under the collar and by now there wasn't a soul in the room who didn't know it. Before Billy could butt in again and say something irritating, she squared her shoulders placing a steady stare on Jacob.

"So Jacob, I hear you've acquired a fine new horse."

He glanced over at Rachel looking slightly puzzled. He couldn't quite catch the drift of what she meant since he hadn't had the chance to venture out to the canyon in weeks to snag any more wild horses.

"Your mare foaled yesterday, didn't she? Does the colt look like the mare or more like the Tobiano Stallion?"

"A little of both I'm pleased to say. He's got a good combination of colors and not badly distributed either. Come to think of it, he's shaping up to look a lot like the colt she foaled three years ago."

"So does that give you at least a hundred head now?"

Jacob hesitated, then answered in a low tone so it wouldn't seem like he was blowing his own horn. "About that."

"Keep it up. At this rate, before long, you'll have more horses than Father," she remarked.

Her sly smile showed her pride in his achievements. It also occurred to her that every horse he got his hands on put him that much closer to being in a better position to strike out on his own. That, of course, meant he could settle down and take a wife. She would no longer have to take a back seat to anyone or anything, especially his horses. That thought so appealed to her it caused her hands to sweat in anticipation.

Jacob could almost read Rachel's thoughts. He could see the gleam in her eyes. He, too, wanted nothing more than to live out the rest of his life with her by his side. He wasn't insensitive to her growing need for some sort of commitment from him, but she had to be patient and give his plan a chance to work. That day wasn't too far off. He could almost see it happening, but was reluctant to jump the gun before he was positive he had enough money saved and of course, most important, her father's blessing. Jacob blushed pink and lowered his head, pretending to eagerly stuff another spoonful of Kate's mashed potatoes into his mouth while he entertained the idea of popping the big question soon.

Billy was grating his teeth with jealousy. Without realizing it, he was twirling his glass of wine in a small circular motion spilling small amounts onto the tablecloth. He was irritated that they hadn't included him in the conversation. After all, he should be the one she was bragging about since he'd come up with the catch of the year, the white stallion! He was even more annoyed over her flirtatious mannerisms. She had sat there like some dumbstruck, lovesick teenager making goo-goo eyes at Jacob from the moment they all sat down.

Billy ignored their rudeness and let out a big, belly giggle. "Yeah, for all the good it's gonna do him, or anyone else around here, for that fact. You all know as well as I do, that if something were to happen to Kate here, we'd all be in for some pretty rough times. It's a known fact that she's sittin' on the only water vein that continues to feed this valley after the winter's run-off dries up. And if her place was to fall into the wrong hands, then what would we do?"

Kate's head whipped around with two shades of red on her face. She could feel her blood boil because he was speaking about things that were none of his concern. That subject was a hot bed of coals with Kate and everyone on this ranch knew it, including Billy.

Not bothering to conceal her anger, she let him have it with both barrels. "You know, Billy, even after you're dead they'll have to kill your mouth to shut you up. Frankly, every time you open yours, you bother me. But if you feel you must spread those flappin' lips, then at least talk about something that's your business and not mine. My ranch and the land it sits on is a personal matter that pertains to just Ma and me. So don't be stickin' your nose where it don't belong! Ain't none of your concern what does or doesn't happen with our land." She wanted to say more, but thought better of it.

To everyone's shock, despite Baxter's presence, Billy continued to spout off. "Yeah, well you ain't gonna live forever, Kate. What happens to the rest of us if something was to happen to you tomorrow and your place did fall into some greedy hands? That land is worth its weight in gold and you know it. Now if the new owner was to turn out to be a real money hungry sort of fellow, then he might just up and decide to charge us all top dollar for using the water we need."

"Now you're just talkin' off the top of your hat! Ma and I have never refused water to any man in this valley and don't plan on leaving it to no one that would! But there's one thing you can bank on. It won't fall into your hands, Billy, which might make matters even worse than what you're proposing. We've already made our minds up about who would be best suited to take over for us upon our passin', and nothin' you say here tonight is gonna change things."

The corner of Kate's mouth curled down. She knew what he was up to. Trouble usually followed in one way or another when Billy deliberately tried to provoke her. Recently it seemed that every time she was in his presence he was on a hunt for any reason to turn a normal conversation into a heated word game over her land and the water that obviously meant so much to him. He'd certainly questioned her enough times over the past three years about the matter.

It was none of his business why she chose to work for the Baxter's. She had her reasons. She also wasn't born yesterday and could see straight through Billy's not-so- honorable disguise. He, for sure, wasn't on some sort of community rescue mission here. She wouldn't put it past him to pull that very calculating money-grubbing stunt he was speaking of on the rest of the folks in the valley if he were to get his hands on her property.

Appearances were deceiving. Billy's talent for deception was far greater than most people gave him credit for. After all these years watching him with a hawk's eye, she knew him well enough to know that this whole scene he was acting out was in all probability staged for the benefit of the oldest gent sitting at this table whom he was obviously trying extra hard to impress.

"Now you just listen up here, young man," she warned with a stiff forefinger pointed at his puckered lips. "Mark my words, don't you dare set one foot on my place, and that goes for those worthless varmints you run with, too! I'm warning you, if you so much as pop your head up within two hundred feet of my ranch I'll use your ugly mug for target practice! Now, this conversation is over."

Silence around the table sifted down like wilted leaves. Billy could feel all eyes upon him as his temperature rose with the enormity of embarrassment he was feeling. Her words had reduced him to what felt like a childish state again, feeling as if he had just been scolded by his father in front of the whole town. Old Sam had been pretty good about giving him the what for with other folks looking on in disbelief. The swing back into his past made him that much madder and more determined to put Kate in her place once and for all. But he couldn't very well do anything about her outburst right now with everyone looking on: That outburst was totally uncalled for, as far as he was concerned, yet Baxter wouldn't hear of him talking back to Kate disrespectfully. Nevertheless, he couldn't allow her to have the last word either.

Billy gave a rich laugh. "Should have known better than to try to give you some helpful advice." His eyes narrowed as he fought hard to hold back the urge to jab the fat woman right in the kisser. *Payback would be slow, painful and extremely rewarding,* he thought contemplatively, while Kate stared daggers at him.

Baxter's forehead was damp with beads of sweat just listening to them argue back and forth. He knew he had to do something, and do it now, before Kate slammed Billy's head into his plate of potatoes. He had no intention of allowing his daughter's birthday dinner to be turned into a free-for-all and spoiled in such a way. As gracefully as he could, Baxter made himself smile and then made his own thoughts known, stopping shy of reprimanding Billy for his bad timing and tasteless manners. That would have to come about at a later date in privacy. Besides, Kate was like part of their family in more ways than one and he would protect her no matter what.

"Kate has every right to handle her personal affairs any way she sees fit. Let's just leave it at that and show a little respect for her wishes. Ma and Kate both know the value of their land, but you could never convince them that it's worth is more valuable than sharing with neighbors." And then he added, his smile looking rather serious, "But tonight is not the proper place or time to discuss such poignant viewpoints. This is an evening for celebration. So let's celebrate!"

At one point in time, Kate had considered saying more and quite possibly getting a little physical with him, but she quickly pushed that thought out of her head. It was more trouble than it was worth. Besides, arguing with Billy was like scrapping with a wall. Disgusted and still fuming inside, she groped her way back into the kitchen for some refills. She felt she needed a few moments alone and to catch a breath of fresh air.

Billy pouted his way through another bite of green beans with his temper still as crooked as a Virginia fence. He'd figure out a way to get back at Miss Fancy Pants for coming down on him so hard in front of the others. He'd also put some more thought into how he was going to get his hands on her land, all nice and legal-like.

After a few moments of awkward silence and a lot of uncomfortable glances, Kate returned with a fresh bottle of wine and a huge platter of chicken. However, it was obvious she was still carrying a grudge and a big chip on her shoulder.

Kate noticed that Billy had already polished off the rest of the wine. There were two empty bottles situated at the head of his plate, and by the way he tilted his glass in her direction she could tell he was ready for more. She could also see the deceptive stillness in his face and knew his evil little mind was up to something. She reluctantly filled his glass. As soon as every glass was filled, they stood and tipped them again in a toast to happiness.

Kate pulled up a chair between Baxter and Jacob, but not before giving Billy another dirty look. She'd hold her peace for now, but had already made up her mind that if Billy as much as breathed one more word about her land and that damn water, she was going to nail his hide to the wall.

The rest of the meal, punctuated with pleasant conversation, was uneventful. There was no more talk about land and water, Baxter had seen to that.

Jacob and Rachel slyly exchanged adoring looks during the course of the evening. Between the two of them, she of course, was the most obvious with her signs of affection. The very idea of them making such fools out of themselves made Billy want to gag. All Rachel's body language made him green with envy, but he quit expecting things to change just because he was there watching their every move.

Baxter felt exuberant over the fact that he had managed to keep the peace and save the party from certain ruin. He felt bad that tempers flew, but was thankful that the others seemed to be in short memory of what had taken place earlier this evening.

However, he did keep a close watch on his daughter making eyes at Jacob from the other end of the table. She seemed to be expending an enormous amount of energy trying to attract his attention. That's when the thought occurred to him that, quite possibly, he had underestimated the extent of affection she had for Jacob. Judging by the way Jacob was looking back at her in return, just maybe he would be gaining a son-in-law much sooner than he had expected.

Kate was still wearing the lingering effects of not only tonight's argument with Billy, but many others as well. Over the years they had failed to see eye to eye on much of anything. She knew his true colors at an early age and was convinced he was headed for trouble no matter how hard anyone else tried to steer him clear of it.

As for Billy, his embarrassment over Kate's insults was short-lived. He had misjudged his opponent and had already licked his wounds. He'd made up his mind that he didn't owe anyone an apology for what was said here tonight, having the right to his own opinion like any other man. At least he would be cordial to Kate in front of old man Baxter. Then if something awful were to happen to the fat woman no one would have reason to lay blame on him.

Chapter 6

Rachel felt her nerves hum beneath her skin as she quietly crept down the staircase. She tiptoed past the open doorway of her father's reading room, pausing only long enough to make sure he was still snoozing in his favorite easy chair. "Good," she whispered under her breath, hoping her luck would continue to hold out.

As usual for this time of the evening, he sat comfortably resting with his chin pressed firmly to his chest and his right leg loosely crossed over the left. The Bible he had been reading was teetering between his legs. A great sense of relief came over her. She certainly didn't want to answer any questions he may ask about where she was going, or what she had on her mind once she got there.

Rachel rubbed her sweaty palms on her dress before sneaking out the door like a paroled prisoner. She headed straight towards Jacob's private quarters. After the passing of Smiley Colfax three years ago, Jacob had easily slipped into his shoes as the ranch foreman. Because of his position, Jacob now occupied the only other single unit on the place, Smiley's former residence.

Private quarters were just part of the fringe benefits of the prestigious position he had accepted. A dollar increase in his monthly wage would normally cause any new foreman's head to swell, but Jacob had never entertained thoughts of being better than any other man on the ranch. He didn't throw his weight around in order to get what he wanted, nor did he take advantage of Baxter's obvious approval of his widespread capabilities of being second in command. Jacob strongly believed that a man had to work hard to earn the respect of others. So it was with humble pride that he had climbed his way up the pecking order to earn the foreman's position.

The tack shed had easily been extended out twenty more feet by including four of the adjacent stalls in the barn. With a little sprucing up, it had been converted into quite a homey living space. After Kate and Rachel got their hands on it you could hardly recognize it as the same crummy place Smiley had called home for so long.

Rachel stepped outside the door and breathed in the fresh night air mixed with the familiar smell of animals. She quickly scurried across the short distance to Jacob's quarters. Tapping lightly on his door, she cautiously looked back over her shoulder to make sure no one else was aware of her presence. She strained her eyes to adjust to the darkness of the night and was thankful she saw no movement other than horse tails. Rachel shivered slightly as a cool breeze tickled her bare shoulders. A thick blanket of goose pimples danced across her satin skin. The bright moonlight beamed in her eyes and her heart purred as she anxiously waited to face the man who laid her heart out in lavender.

With so many prying eyes and people milling about on the ranch, privacy was not easy to come by. One would have thought she was committing a crime or something just by falling in love with Jacob. *Well, so be it,* she thought quietly. If sneaking around late at night is what she had to do to be alone with him, then that's exactly what she'd stoop to.

The Truth about Jacob

Rachel felt explosive and yet at the same time a little tense and nervous. She held her breath in anticipation trying to imagine his reaction to her unexpected visit. She had never done anything as brazen as this before in her life. Rachel hoped Jacob wouldn't be angry with her, and most importantly, that he wouldn't disappoint her again.

Her eyes lit up when Jacob finally opened the door. His gaze met hers and they stood there staring at each other for what seemed like the longest time. It was an intimate look that made her feel more than welcomed. Within a matter of seconds she knew she had done the right thing. The electricity between them began to sizzle.

"Rachel, what a pleasant surprise. Is everything alright?"

"Of course, silly. I'm just restless tonight, that's all. I couldn't bear staying cooped up in that stuffy old house for one more minute. Father's asleep and our dinner guests have finally left, thank goodness. The Merryweathers' are about as exciting as reading a boring book for the fifth time, if you know what I mean. I just thought a nice walk in the fresh air would do me good. May I?" she asked graciously, since Jacob had for the moment forgotten his manners and neglected to invite her in.

"Oh, I'm sorry, of course, come on in. You'll have to excuse the mess. I've been a little lax with my housekeeping chores, lately."

That comment roused a playful chuckle and naturally sparked Rachel's curiosity. With wide eyes she scanned the immediate area with interest. It came as no surprise that the entire room was neat as a pin. She moved forward across the room, purposely brushing her bare arm against Jacob's naked chest.

He couldn't help but notice the provocative way she was dressed. Just watching her shapely hips sway from side to side made his heart knock beneath his breastbone. The way she moved, the manner in which she spoke, was enough to melt any man's resistance to think shameful thoughts. He could feel the fire in his face, so he quickly turned his eyes away from her.

Nothing looked out of place, Rachel thought to herself as she studied the room. It was immaculate. Even though he had a million other things to do outside, the inside chores were taken care of too. Jacob had always been much neater than any other man she knew. How he ever managed to become so well organized growing up in the middle of less-than-tidy old cowboys was beyond her.

Rachel could smell the clean scent of the Bay Rum on Jacob as she wove her way around him. He looked good in just his jeans, riding low on his hips. He was a distraction that placed her at war with her emotions that governed her wants and needs. Her heart was pumping and she could feel her body trembling. There was a fire burning beneath her feminine exterior, an unspoken desire that was bittersweet because she knew it wouldn't be morally correct to claim the deeper rewards of love until she became his wife.

Rachel couldn't believe what had come over her. She shook her head, but still felt the aftereffects of her warm embarrassment. She quickly moved further away from her naughty thoughts and back into the present. It was difficult, but she managed to turn her attention onto something else other than Jacob's raw sensuality.

She felt a jolt of sadness as her eyes once again scanned the room. She stopped dead in her tracks when she noticed all the colored canvasses displaying hand-painted pictures. There was a full array of many different descriptive scenes capturing everyday life in the Northwest. She carefully eyed each and every one of them, noting the intricate details and the stories they told.

Rachel deliberately looked up at Jacob and gave him a smile of admiration. "I knew you were an artist, but I had no idea you could work with colors like this," she marveled. "Did you paint all of these?"

The Truth about Jacob

Jacob lowered his head with a flushed face, feeling self-conscious over the fact that she couldn't drag her eyes away from the paintings. No one except himself had ever seen these particular ones before. As she stood in judgment, he suddenly found fault with every piece of artwork. He froze in fear of what she was really thinking. Maybe she was just complimenting him because she felt she had to.

"If you want to call it that, I guess you can say I play around a bit with a brush in my spare time."

Ten more steps brought Rachel directly in front of a painting that took her by surprise. The colors were exquisite. The details of his strokes told a story that drew tears in her eyes. Sadly enough, Jacob had captured an accurate account of an uncivilized method used to track and kill mountain lions. Unfortunately, it was still widely practiced even today in the West. Curiously, she studied the story it told.

"I thought you didn't like the lion hunt?"

"I don't."

"Then why would you paint it?"

"Because it exists. It's barbaric, but nonetheless a part of life and death around here."

Rachel stared hard at the figures on the canvas, which told the story vividly, without a word. Her eyes were drawn to a young boy, standing off by himself, with his head drooped to his chest and his shirt drenched in tears.

"That's you, isn't it?" she asked. "You're the little boy with the sad face." Then her eyes trailed towards another boy positioned about two feet away from a small dead dog sprawled out on the ground. "That's Billy, of course, with a big broad smile."

Rachel grazed Jacob's eyes and they answered her questions with a yes. She could also see that he was still embarrassed over her interest in his work, but that didn't stop her. She continued to examine every inch of the painting that depicted this common practice amongst all ranchers.

Tracking down mountain lions that occasionally left their usual habitat to invade the farmer's livestock made one undertake a job nobody enjoyed. Once the hounds cornered the cat they would often keep their distance, having grown a little fearful at the last moment. That's when reinforcements were brought in. A small feisty Chihuahua who knew no fear would be released right in the middle of the handful of cowardly dogs. Within minutes this gave the larger dogs instant courage. This procedure was used time and time again, usually at the expense of the small dog's life. Rarely did the gutsy little hero survive, but if it did, it would be nursed back to health only to be used the next time around.

"You're right, Jacob. That's a primitive practice that needs to be stopped. But unfortunately, until someone comes up with a better idea, this one I'm sure is here to stay."

He could not take his eyes off of Rachel as she walked a few paces past him on her way to another one of his paintings. No vision so beautiful had ever come to him, nor could he imagine one that had moved him in such a way as he felt right now. *No one I knew equals her beauty*, he quietly thought.

Rachel purposely put a cute little swing in her hips as she moseyed along. Jacob followed directly behind her, looking as though he was a young kitten seeking warmth. Her steps moved them both front and center to a portrait that absolutely took her breath away.

She was unaware that this was the way Jacob saw her. The woman staring back she knew only too well, but this was not the way she saw herself. Even though his precise strokes had transformed her still likeness into someone so beautiful, she still couldn't believe she could ever look this pretty. As Rachel moved, the figure inside the portrait also seemed to move with her. Even the woman's long, dark hair seemed to shift slightly as it gracefully cradled her bare shoulders.

"Is this how you see me, Jacob?" she asked, feeling so overwhelmingly flattered that her head was spinning.

The Truth about Jacob

Jacob didn't say anything. He just studied the floor, but of course, that was of no surprise to Rachel. Instead of waiting for an answer she returned her gaze to the portrait, unable to drag her eyes away from her likeness long enough to see, if by any chance, he had moved his head or raised his brow to answer her either way.

While Rachel continued to explore every line and color of the portrait, a sudden awareness struck her like a bolt of lightening. The dress in the portrait was the very same one she had worn the night of the annual Farmer's Festival held inside their spacious home. If she remembered correctly, however, Jacob had refused to come to that tie and collar affair. So how could he possibly paint her in that particular dress if he hadn't been there?

"That dress, Jacob. I've only worn that dress once since Kate made it for me. So how could you know? How could you paint me in that dress?" she boldly asked.

Rachel again looked into Jacob's eyes. They were dead serious, but also seriously guilty. They betrayed him and uncovered his secret. She realized he must have been watching her from afar at sometime or other during that evening. A soothing warmth moved over her body as she witnessed the color rise high in his cheeks. Before she could stop herself, Rachel threw her arms around his shoulders and pressed her lips against his.

That bold maneuver prompted him to follow suit, pulling her even closer. His hands moved across her bare back, stroking her soft skin. After a long hungry kiss he finally drew back and paused, allowing his eyes to drift slowly over every fine line of her well-crafted face. Her unblemished skin was the color of light maple syrup, with a nose as cute as a button. She had eyes that sparkled like dark stones and a glimpse of an earlobe could be seen peeking through her long flowing locks of hair, enticing his senses.

And oh that silky hair of hers, he thought silently. It was the most spectacular auburn he'd ever laid his eyes on. It reached far below the tips of her shoulders. *She always smelled like fresh flowers, as if she had slept in a bed of lilacs all night.*

His heart hammered against his chest as they mirrored each other's eyes. He moved his hand up her throat, to her jaw, tipping her head upwards with his fingers. He buried his lips softly on top of her sweet mouth in another tender kiss. They lingered there for a while. It gave them both more pleasure than they thought was possible.

When their kiss finally broke, Rachel drew her head back with only a dime size space between their lips and asked again, "Do you really see me like the painting implies?"

"I see you as you are, Rachel. No one, not even me, could ever begin to capture your beauty on canvas and clearly do you justice. Nothing I have painted has ever equaled the pleasure I experienced painting you, and I can honestly say that my love for you grew daily during that time."

The hair on her arms rose in response and chills moved across her entire body. It was so unexpected to hear such flowery words coming from Jacob. He hardly ever spoke and yet now he was speaking in soft waves with words that could melt a woman's heart. She wished this moment could last forever because anything that felt this good should never have to come to an end. Then, as she quietly thought that it couldn't get any better than this, Jacob gently pulled her even closer to him, handling her like a piece of fine china, prized and priceless. Their lips met again.

Rachel suddenly pulled away from Jacob's embrace. She spoke in a low disappointed voice. "Shush, what's that?"

"I didn't hear anything, silly girl. It's probably just my heart pounding," he teased.

Her heart sank to the pit of her stomach. She listened carefully again. Her hands were clammy with sweat, but were still clenched tightly around Jacob's back. Again she heard the same distant sound and by the look on Jacob's face she knew he had, too. They both recognized her father's voice calling her

The Truth about Jacob

name with such a high pitch that she was certain the disturbance would wake everyone else on the ranch.

Rachel's passion dissolved immediately upon hearing his third call and both the young lovers felt the same frustration by her father's untimely interruption. *There always seemed to be something standing in our way*, she thought dimly. *It was Billy, too many chores, or not enough daylight and now my father.* Of course, Rachel knew positively that he wouldn't approve of her spending even one minute alone with any man in his sleeping quarters, much less a half an hour alone with Jacob in his bungalow.

Her father had always maintained a tight rein on her with tooth and claw rules, keeping close tabs on everywhere she went and what she was doing. There were absolutely no exceptions. He expected her to live by his old-fashion principles and that made her feel as if she had lived only half of the years that her age told. He treated her like a child and that was hard to swallow at times.

The crackles of his voice calling her name came again, only this time it carried with it a wave of grave worry. No matter how disappointed she was with his intrusion, she knew she had to quickly answer his call before he discovered on his own where she was hiding. Unwillingly, Rachel broke their embrace.

"I better go before he wakes up everyone on the ranch."

Their sad eyes met and they quickly stole one last kiss. It felt bittersweet because it would have to carry them for a while.

Without hesitation, Rachel silently slipped out the door and around the other end of the barn pretending to return from a late evening stroll, all alone. Byron Baxter would never know what she had been up to and with whom. She did feel somewhat guilty about her actions, but knew in her heart that this is the way it had to be. Her father was just a little too suffocating. He left her no other choice but to sneak around behind his back and meet Jacob on the sly. And sly she felt when she greeted her father with a smile as he slipped his arm around her shoulder to escort her safely back inside their house.

Rachel had loved Jacob her whole life and she would let no one stand in the way of marrying the man of her choosing. She now saw her future in a different light. And because of it, was full of renewed courage. The time was getting closer to share those facts with her father.

There was a set of envious eyes lurking in the night air that took a slightly different view than Rachel did on tonight's rendezvous. Having been aroused by Baxter's voice calling his daughter's name, Billy had quietly slipped outside into the darkness just in time to catch sight of Rachel sneaking out of Jacob's quarters. He carefully eased his way back inside the bunkhouse and stood beside the murky window watching her tiptoe by. Peering out cautiously, he was all eyes. Billy didn't move a muscle. A flash of gunpowder went off in his head as her undefined silhouette passed before him. Hatred turned into something uglier for he was sure he knew exactly what she had been up to in that room with Jacob. He could just imagine all that had taken place there.

For most of his life he had known that he and Rachel made a good team and would eventually wed. But as of late, Jacob seemed to be causing a great deal of interference in all his plans to capture her heart. Tonight's events would leave him scrambling to find another way to win Rachel over. He just couldn't figure out why an unsightly, scarred man like Jacob could have such a strong hold on a woman as lovely as Rachel. With all her beauty she could have just about any man of her choosing.

Billy was sick and tired of being pushed aside by the likes of Jacob, he thought critically. He decided it was time to put a stop to this meddling fool. He was ready to act on his first impulse and that was to get rid of Jacob for good. He knew he'd have to move fast, because if he didn't, Jacob just might beat him to the punch and ask Rachel to marry him before he had the chance to

The Truth about Jacob

convince her that he could make her much happier. Turning back towards the center of the room, he tried to adjust his eyes to the inky blackness. He stood there with his fingers pressed to his temples. He rubbed softly as he carefully thought the situation over.

It was survival of the fittest and under those circumstances. Billy was counting on his good sense of timing to get things rolling back in his direction. He'd wiggled out of tougher jams than this before. He figured it shouldn't be too tough to kick up a little dirt in order to damage Jacob's squeaky-clean image once and for all.

That ought to open Rachel's eyes to the truth as to who's the better man for her. If she didn't come around to his way of thinking, then old man Baxter might have a few things to say about it. Once he found out Jacob had been caught red-handed seducing his daughter right under his very nose, Billy was quite certain he'd have quite a lot to say about their relationship.

Seeing Rachel slyly slipping out of Jacob's place gave Billy a real motive to get even. He certainly wasn't about to keep a lid on what he saw here tonight. There were many ways to discredit a man without being found out. That idea lifted his bad mood somewhat.

Two men reaching for the same star was a back-and-forth battle he was tired of playing. It was time to use his head instead of allowing his heart to take a constant beating over matters that, so far, he hadn't been able to do anything about. There were even better ways to eliminate the competition altogether and he had a few underhanded resources at his fingertips that could easily bump Jacob right out of the race for good.

Chapter 7

Jacob rarely rode into town, but when he did, he usually arrived early and only stayed long enough to get what he had to get done. There were a few old timers around town who were not particularly fond of him because of an incident that had taken place at Tatum's Mercantile when he was a boy. That was the dreadful day he and his entire family were ordered to leave town after having only arrived just a few minutes earlier. Because he was wrongfully accused of stealing, the people considered him and his family to be nothing but trash.

His past grievances with them also played heavily on his mind because if they hadn't threatened to arrest his father, then he truly believed that he and his family would still be together today. Deep down he knew it was useless resentment, but he couldn't seem to conquer his long struggle to understand why a so-called God fearing community could be so cruel to a starving family of four that happened to be down on their luck.

But now, thirteen years later, he had gained a grown man's perspective and had long since quit blaming Billy for all the trouble his family experienced that day. Billy was just a young boy playing a malicious prank when he managed to frame Jacob for stealing candy that he himself had actually taken.

The Truth about Jacob

The mail was delivered to Johnson's Flat by stagecoach. There had been quite a delay in trying to hire a new driver after armed robbers killed the last two; therefore, Rachel's birthday gift that her father had ordered two months earlier arrived three weeks late. Baxter had given him the impression that the mystery gift was quite costly, so he trusted only Jacob to pick it up and safely deliver it back home.

However, Jacob knew otherwise. He suspected his real reason for asking him to tend to this particular matter was merely to prove a point to a few narrow-minded people who still resided in Johnson's Flat. These were the folks who had nothing better to do with their time than to drift to various spots around town during the day just waiting for some hot gossip to come along.

Among these healthy tongue-waggers was Dortha Mae, the widow of old man Tatum. She would station herself with her nose glued to the store's front window, hoping to gather some juicy, off-colored news. It seemed to be her one calling in life to know all movements in and out of town. Needless to say, Baxter was in hopes that his trust in Jacob would one day rub off on a few of these doubting Thomas's who still believed Jacob was nothing more than a common thief.

There were a few people Jacob considered to be his good friends. He was forever grateful for the kindhearted gift the lady without legs had bestowed upon him when he was a boy. And although he seldom saw her these days, out of respect for her generosity, he'd drop in on her once in a great while to check up on her well-being. She always made him feel welcomed. He'd never forget the first time he laid eyes on her. That was the day his good friend Doc was delivering him to the Baxter ranch to live until his family returned to reclaim him.

Jacob was pleasantly surprised that old man Tatum's eldest son, Homer, hadn't rejected him at school. The two of them had remained friends over the years. Quite close, actually, until his good buddy moved up north along the Coastal Range where the weather was more agreeable with his wife's acute breathing problems.

Actually, many of his peers he had chummed with back in those days seemed to accept him as he was, scar faced and wrongfully tagged as a boy with sticky fingers. Of course, as he grew into a man's way of thinking, he came to realize that Rachel had played a crucial part in securing him with his privileged treatment. Since everyone wanted to be her friend, her influence alone guaranteed him a solid position in the so-called popular group.

The coolness of the morning was long gone when Jacob pulled up short of Tatum's Mercantile, which was now run by his youngest son, Cecil. The young man had done so ever since his old man had dropped dead from a massive stroke ten years ago while throwing one of his many, agitated fits. That particular tantrum had ultimately caused his demise. It was brought on by a standoff in the middle of the street involving the father of a local boy who had accidentally cracked one of Tatums' front windows while tossing rocks at flies. It wasn't as if it was a physical confrontation or anything, but a verbal argument has its way of making things seem twice as bad as they really are. *At least the old man went out in a fashion that was so fitting him,* Jacob reasoned.

Jacob noticed that an unusually large number of people seemed to be roaming the dusty streets this morning. Of course, it was Saturday and anyone within riding distance of this two bit pile of planks was milling about trying to gather the items they needed to tide them over through the next three or four weeks.

To Jacob's delight, a pleasant sight caught his eye from afar. It was a rare treat to see the lady without legs out and about these days. He had heard through the grapevine that she seldom came to town since the market for her fresh eggs had fallen flat. Most people by now had quit feeling sorry for her and started using their own poultry goods. However, young Cecil did purchase every horse blanket she made, which gave her just enough money to get through the months when the weather turned bad. Canning everything she grew in her garden gave her a good food supply all year long.

Evidently, Cecil was still somewhat sympathetic to the poor woman's struggle to independently make it on her own. He had, many times over the years, openly cursed how the cruel hand of fate dealt her an infirmity a dirty dog didn't deserve.

As Jacob sat tall in the saddle he watched her scoot her legless body towards the saloon. Faint trails of dust circled around behind her. The wheels fastened to the flat board still squeaked like a violin out of tune. On a quiet day a blind man could follow her snail's pace right up to the saloon door that she was about to enter.

It was common knowledge that on days she did venture into town after taking care of her business, she'd head straight to the doggery for one shot of whiskey. After her jolt of spirits, and purchasing a bottle for the road, she would return back home to a small, one-room shack about two miles southeast of town. She repeated this ritual once a month without fail. Jacob was kept well informed of her habits over the years because Kate was kind enough to keep good tabs on her. Jacob made it a point to always ask.

As the lady without legs approached the swinging doors of the saloon, they suddenly flew open, thumping her face first like a hard fist. The force of the blow knocked her over sideways onto the boarded walkway.

With that, Jacob leapt from his horse just as Billy pranced out of the saloon into the fresh air. He looked straight out across the street at Jacob with a wry smile on his face. He showed no inclination to help her back up, and in fact, went on about his way as if he hadn't noticed her at all.

At a distance, Jacob could see she was in plenty of trouble and needed some help. She seemed to be somewhat dazed as she shook her head slightly from side to side. He ran as fast as he could, and the minute he got there, knelt down on one knee. He reached out to lift the lady and her board back into an upright position. It was obvious that she wasn't looking for any help, judging by the way she jerked her shoulder free from Jacob's grasp before she realized it was him. It seemed to take a minute or so for her to get her bearings and adjust her eyes to Jacob's face.

"Are you alright? That was quite a blow you just took," he asked in a concerned voice.

"Oh fiddlesticks! I've taken a worse lickin' than that from a damned old chicken who thinks he rules the roost around my place."

Jacob laughed at her joke as he looked down into eyes that sparkled with amusement. At that point she allowed him to help her upright. He paused a moment and gave her a smile and helped to straighten her ruffled dress. Tipping his hat he bid her good day and then turned to go on about his business.

"No boy, you come with me. Least I can do to repay your kindness is to buy you a drink."

"Sorry, ma'am, but I don't drink."

"You do today," she said, refusing to take no for an answer.

Jacob set foot and followed her into the saloon like an obedient pup. He casually sat down on a bar stool beside the one she chose for herself. He glanced around, inspecting the premises in order to give her time enough to hoist her legless body up onto her seat. He figured she certainly didn't need any more eyes watching her every move since they both had already attracted a full audience the minute they entered the room. Silence grew deep amongst a few muffled snickers.

All eyes in the busy establishment were now glued tight to the odd couple. Jacob could feel their stares. He was sure that their mutual infirmities were in part responsible for that. Of course the thought struck him that there was the distinct possibility that the very fact she was keeping company with someone other than one friendly old barkeeper also played a big role in the sudden profound silence sweeping the room.

The Truth about Jacob

The lady without legs acted as if she hadn't noticed what was going on around her. But in a few short minutes she laid that theory to rest as she blurted her thoughts out loud. "Don't pay them no mind, Jacob. Looks like the hollow heads showed up in droves today. Damned fools!"

Jacob chuckled at her humor and whispered. "I'm used to it. I tend to draw a bit of attention of my own with this face of mine."

Since his appearance hadn't improved much from the time he was a boy, Jacob hardly expected things to change. He had accepted that fact long before now.

She carefully examined him from one side of his head to the other without bothering to hide her curiosity. After closely inspecting the numerous lengthy, irregular gashes and creases across the right side of his cheek, she just shook her head and said, "What a cryin' shame."

The lady gingerly slid her torso closer to the bar, holding a finger in the air in order to catch the attention of the barkeeper. There was no indication by her expression that Jacob's scars made her feel out of sorts, quite the contrary in fact. She began to shower him with flattery.

"You're still a good lookin' young chap. Scars don't make a man any less a man, you know. You had a rough road ahead of you, Jacob, I knew that from the very first time I laid eyes on you, and for a time, that gave me cause for concern. But judging from the talks I've had with Kate, I quit worrying about you after a while. She was real good about keeping me posted on your progress. A good woman, she is," the lady declared with a stern grin.

"Some of us have to learn the hard way, Jacob. Now I know those early years taught you a lot, but learnin' those lessons the hard way ain't likely to ever leave ya." The lady raised a brow and grinned slyly at Jacob and added. "You surely didn't forget what that old sow was tryin' to tell ya, now, did ya?"

"No, ma'am. Don't guess I'll be forgettin' that day for a long time to come," he said with conviction. "She cured that young boy's foolish curiosity and made this grown man respect a sow's space."

The legless lady nodded in agreement as she downed her first shot of whiskey. Tipping her glass towards Jacob she ordered him to do the same. "Don't be shy. Drink up!" Then she quickly polished off another two full shots to Jacob's one, and by doing so, killed any rumors that she couldn't handle any more than one small glass of whiskey.

The lady then waved her hand at Packy Pete, insisting he leave the half empty bottle on his way out of their turf. He was known to do a little eavesdropping and then stretch the truth a tad bit when he told the story the second time around.

Jacob watched her swirl her whiskey around in her glass. Her thoughts seemed to be miles away. Slowly but surely her tongue began to loosen, and as she talked on about all the many things that had happened to both of them over the years, she surprisingly enough, started to talk without allowing him the opportunity to join in on the conversation.

"Wasn't your fault, you know? Six-year-old youngin' don't recognize danger when he's starin' it right in the face. Any scared young kid who had just hiked two miles into a strange town that hadn't exactly thrown out the welcome mat the day before is bound to be a little skittish about what to do and what not to do. I'm sure I would have been a little confused myself, if I was being chased by two big mean old hombres yelling at me."

After setting the record straight regarding her opinion about that day, her smile disappeared and suddenly her thoughts took a plunge to the sadder side of her own life.

"A fifteen-year-old girl should be smarter than to go runnin' along side a movin' train, tryin' to keep up with her beau. He was just sixteen, you know, and ever bit as strappin' as you. But he wasn't near strong enough to hoist his girl up onto that train.

The Truth about Jacob

They were runnin' like there was no tomorrow. Runnin' away from folks who refused to let them marry."

She sighed and gulped down another mouthful of the liquid bravery and bitter tears began to flood her cold eyes. She swallowed again, only more slowly this time. She was obviously caught up in her sorrow.

"Well, nobody got their way that day. That girl lost her legs and her fellar lost his life. They took that poor innocent boy out and strung him up. Didn't even give him a chance to defend himself. That girl's old man slipped the rope around his neck and laughed in his face while he gasped out his last breath. I heard later that my poor Ben begged for his life, but my father spit in his face and told him one bad turn deserved another. Well, he was right about one thing. One bad turn does deserve another, cause that old man's fate wasn't any better. All I can say is, he got just what was comin' to him."

With her eyes of stone she looked directly at Jacob and added, "Bitterness can eat ya alive, boy, but it keeps ya goin'."

She turned her haunted glare to the shot glass she held with trembling hands and flushed down another large swallow without batting an eye. "There was a baby born that year no one ever knew about. For reasons she'll keep private, she gave that baby to some folks that didn't do no better a job raisin' it than she could have done for herself."

The teary-eyed lady thought silently to herself about all she had been through. It was the longest four months of her life from the time of her accident to the joyous day she finally escaped that hellhole. Her hometown was full of hate and she no longer held any permanent ties to anyone there, so she settled in this valley in the fall of 1851.

Jacob continued to keep a good pace with her shots. He was too afraid to offend her since she already had so much anger built up inside her. The tragic story he had just heard suddenly made his own sad one sound like child's play. He felt as though he should reach out and console the poor woman. But he feared an attempt to make any physical contact would be rejected, especially since he knew she was a self-reliant woman who didn't particularly like men. He decided he better not push his luck with this little spitfire.

Somehow or other she had survived on her own without anyone else's help all these years. *So why would right now be any different*, he reasoned. Jacob would respect this tough little lady's wishes by keeping his silence and his hands to himself.

Their talk had gone quiet within that short moment while he was thinking seriously. When she began to speak again she had, for some reason, moved the topic of conversation off of her own troubles onto something entirely different.

"Best watch your backside around Billy Roberts. He'll kill you the first chance he gets. Ain't nothin' wrong with my eyes, you know, and I hear far more than what's meant to be heard around this town," she relayed.

"Can't trust a man with such a hard edge on him. His meanness goes beyond skin deep. Can't help but think he's just mean clear through. Who's to say, maybe life dealt him a heavy load, too, but that's no cause to take it out on anyone of his choosin'," she spoke with heat.

Jacob couldn't help but notice how angry she seemed. There was so much about this mysterious lady that he didn't understand. One thing was her profound hatred for Billy, and another was why she was so concerned over his welfare. He seemed to be missing something here. Why on earth she had remained so interested in what had taken place in his life out at the Baxter Ranch was beyond anything he could figure out. By the way she talked today, she had spent a lot of time checking up on his development over the years.

Her eyes suddenly grew more serious as she continued to speak. "And by the way, Billy talks around town like there's no love lost between you two and he's ready to do something about

The Truth about Jacob

it any day now. He talks as if there might be some gunplay between the two of you."

"That's his biggest problem, he talks too much." Jacob declared. "He's just full of hot air, that's all. So don't let him rile you none. He's a restless snake who can't seem to find that one perfect little hole to crawl into. Don't get all worried about what he says. I won't make it easy for him to outsmart me."

"That so, huh? Trouble is, those are the kind of snakes you gotta watch out for. He's sneaky, Jacob, and that boy's proved himself with a gun. He don't think twice about usin' it either! Just don't underestimate what drives a man like that. You just keep in mind if he can't get what he wants fair and square, then you can be rest assured he'll take it any way he can!"

The lady dropped her eyes to her glass, having said more than a mouthful and bathed her throat again.

Jacob could see that she was truly concerned about his welfare and appreciated that fact. He also took notice of the pronounced changes in her appearance that had taken place over the many years. Worry lines surrounded her speckled green eyes. Her hair was no longer shiny and lustrous, but had now lost its glow. The former locks of flaming red tresses that once cradled her shoulders had thinned out considerably. It was no longer the color of crimson, but had faded to a rusty gray.

Again the thought crossed his mind about how partial she seemed to be regarding his well being. That made him grin a bit. He had to admit it felt kind of nice to come across an old friend who still cared about him. In a strange way it made him feel sort of special. In fact, special, was the very word good old Doc used to explain to him how he should feel about himself the day the lady without legs gave him the bag of candy when he was just a boy.

Suddenly, she shifted her stare from her glass to Jacob's hip and heaved a weighty sigh. "You still don't pack a gun, I see."

"No, ma'am, still don't like guns much. Once saw a man shoot his own foot off just gettin' on his horse. Figured right then and there I'd do just as well without one. No reason to change my mind now."

"Like I said, do yourself a favor. You just watch your back!" she said again.

A gentle smile was Jacob's best response to her word of warning.

With those final words, two grunting noises surged from her in rapid succession and with one big swish, her torso was back down on her board. Expertly grabbing her straps, she fastened herself tightly and wheeled towards the door, a little wobbly to say the least. Leaving Jacob behind still pondering over her urgent advice, he watched her slowly disappear outside the door.

Feeling flushed and dizzy himself, he decided he, too, needed some fresh air. He tried to stand up. His head felt heavy on his shoulders and his legs refused to do what they were told. Holding onto the bar for dear life, his vision blurred and he felt a hair close to passing out as he staggered backwards.

He was dimly aware of laughter coming from a short distance away. He turned to see what was so funny, but in the process, slipped and vaulted forward, falling face down on all fours. Within seconds his head was spinning out of control. He felt a strong tug beneath each armpit. All at once Jacobs's body swished upwards. His entire body barreled forward, dragging his disobedient legs behind him. His stomach churned angrily as his legs flipped flopped over what felt like endless bumps. The harder he tried to focus his cloudy eyes the dizzier he got. With a sour taste of bile backing up in his throat he felt the overwhelming desire to heave. He swallowed a rush of bitter saliva, trying to avoid his body's own urgency to vomit. Then, all at once, he heard the distinct sound of a door creaking and he thought for sure he could hear a woman's faint voice. He was quite sure he recognized the clink-clink of coins scattering across some sort of hard surface as his head bashed against something that felt soft and feathery.

The Truth about Jacob

"Take good care of him, Sadie Lu," Billy laughed. "And you know exactly what I mean!"

A vindictive smile broke across Billy's face. Half crazy with revenge, all that he could think about right now was how good getting even with Jacob was already beginning to feel. "Won't this self-righteous little town be shocked when they find out that one of their own was riding something other than his horse?" he whispered contemptuously.

And best of all, Jacob had set his own trap and all he had to do was just wait long enough for him to step into it with both feet. When the word gets out about where Jacob is spending the night, his goody-two-shoes reputation will be ruined for sure. Right about now the spoils of a personal victory over Jacob made Billy want to buy a round of drinks for the whole house. And that he would. When the door had closed behind him, he knew good times were the order of the evening for him and his former competition.

Jacob felt completely out of sorts and struggled feverishly to open his eyes the next morning. Waking up in a room he was unfamiliar with put a knot in his stomach and a real scare into him. A woman he certainly hadn't seen before showing more skin than a baldhead, lay huddled next to him, tenderly stroking his naked chest. Blowing soft whispers in his ears, she repeatedly twisted the curly brown hairs on his chest around her fingertips.

Jacob could remember many nights he had dreamed about waking up in the morning with a beautiful woman lying next to him. Time and again that woman would be Rachel as his wife. Definitely not some stranger—and an old one at that! His head felt like he'd been kicked by a mule, but that throbbing pain couldn't compare to the discomfort of his embarrassment waking up next to this scantily clad harlot that he'd never laid eyes on before. Jacob was mystified as to how he ended up here with this big buxom gal who was old enough to be his mother.

Cautious of whom he was dealing with, Jacob edged his way farther over to his side of the bed, feeling awkward as all get out.

Acting boldly, even though he felt stripped of all his honor, Jacob finally managed to ask her a puzzling question. "How'd I get here?"

With fake lashes long enough to dust all the caked-on powder off her cheeks, she smiled ever so sweetly, puckered her lips, and blew him a big kiss.

"A couple of my regulars brought you here, honey," she informed him, her gravelly voice matching her gravelly exterior.

Jacob's eyes popped wide open; he could hardly believe his ears. Who would pull such an awful trick on a man who wasn't thinking with a clear head? His eyes nearly bulged out of their sockets when the bold Jezebel propped one leg up high enough to reveal that her bottom was bare. To make matters even more humiliating, she was urging him with her forefinger to squeeze in a little closer to her puckering lips that were smeared with lipstick and looked as if they could swallow the moon. That gesture he took to mean she was suggesting something of a wicked nature he had no intentions of obliging. Not now. Not ever.

Quite tickled over his obvious inexperience and naivety, Little Lu Lu quickly came to the conclusion that this was his first time with a woman. He looked so bubble-eyed and baffled over what was taking place or what was expected of him. Sure of herself and experienced at her trade, she began to coax him along again. And since she was quite certain what she had said to Jacob so far was as clear as mud, she elaborated as point blank as she could. "You know my customers pay me well for my services! You do know what I mean, don't you, sweetie?"

Jacob's face raged red as he sucked in a deep breath. You could count every rib around his torso. He shuddered at the thought of what a humiliating picture the two of them made lying side by side on a feather bed in a house of ill repute.

She was obviously in her declining years, overripe for Jacob's taste and wrinkled as a road map. Everything on her body that

The Truth about Jacob

should be facing north had now gone south. Her breasts had long since seen their heyday, way past the budding stage. No longer perky, one huddled somewhere down between her shrunken navel and the last layer of saggy skin around her midriff and the other caressing the sheet beneath her. In a different time and a different place, Jacob was sure she was once quite a looker. But at sixty some years old, she really needed to wear something else besides a sheer black lace chemise with dangling straps to cover her ancient birthday suit.

"My, my! Aren't we the shy one! You've been hiding your head in the sand for much too long, I see. Maybe you should let Little Lu Lu take those blinders off your eyes. You're old enough now, you know."

Jacob decided to put an end to all this insanity and quickly took his eyes off the antique relic with black bouffant hair piled in big curls on top of her head. Her fluffy eyelashes, batting furiously, were making him dizzy, anyway.

His face flushed royally, but with a heightened sense of curiosity, he managed to ask her again, "Who brought me here? What are their names?"

"Braggin' Billy and Winter Jones!" she giggled. The lady of the evening moved closer to Jacob, wiggling slightly and allowing her wrinkled shoulder to shed the thin strap that held her chemise in place.

Jacob tried to camouflage his shock. "Oh, my God," he gasped. He'd just seen more skin on this woman than on his own mother at the tender age of four while he was still nursing. It occurred to him that this was his cue to find the fastest way out of this place and do it quickly. And that might have happened if it weren't for the fact that when he glanced downwards he realized that he, too, was showing plenty of skin.

He felt a sudden surge of shame, just fearing the idea of anyone walking into the room to discover he was laying stark naked under a thin sheet that left nothing to the imagination. That thought sliced his heart like a knife *because what if that someone were Rachel?*

He knew this whole scene was not an accident. It was staged with one purpose in mind — to discredit him. And since it turned out to be Billy who managed to pull off this despicable stunt, Jacob knew for sure he was ornery enough to go one step further. It would not be too outrageous to think that he might have Rachel conveniently waiting outside the door because of some concocted story he told her. He himself, of course, would be hiding around another corner just so he could witness the fireworks when it started.

Jacob gathered the sheet about him to cover himself, his whole body shuddering in shame.

"What happened here last night?" He demanded.

"Nothing, unfortunately," she grinned, "But the offer's still open. I was paid more than enough for two nights of good sporting, but I'm afraid you weren't a very willing partner last night, sweetie pie. I'm saying you definitely weren't in any shape to lift a little finger, much less, well, you know… anything else," she giggled.

"S'pose I could tell a few juicy secrets about your life, though, if someone were to pay me enough money. When a man's full of whiskey his private thoughts just come pouring out. You were all talk last night, sweetie. Why you just rattled on and on like you were the town crier or something. And whoever Rachel is, she's one lucky lady to catch the heart of such a fine young man like you. But don't worry yourself none. I won't breathe a word to anyone. I was just kidding about the money part. I swear on my mother's grave I won't let out a peep about your love life," she declared with mischief in her eyes. " I'll keep mum about your lady love and all the rest of your little secrets."

Jacob felt compelled to apologize for his less than proper behavior, so he launched a series of apologies. While doing so, he looked around the room, searching for his clothes. He spotted them piled in a heap beside the bed and reached down to pick up his pants.

The Truth about Jacob

With great difficulty, he tugged and pulled, trying to get them up over his bare bottom. He struggled to do so while still hiding beneath the convenient cover of the thin satin sheets. As Jacob continued to fully dress himself, Little Lu Lu did her best to convince Jacob to change his mind about leaving. She crooned in soft whispers with words he'd be embarrassed to repeat to a tree.

"Billy paid me more than enough, so anytime you feel the urge, honey, you know where you can find me. I can do some amazing things to satisfy a man's wildest desires." She gave him a wink with a seductive smile on her wrinkled face

Blushing bright red, Jacob politely excused himself. He left the old gal without as much as even the slightest impression that he would be back to collect on any of her services at a later date. He didn't doubt one bit that she was quite good at her profession, but he sure wasn't going to hang around long enough to find out.

Jacob decided to slip out of the brothel by using the backstairs. He was no stranger by now to Billy's dirty games and even if Rachel wasn't stationed outside the door, there might be someone else he planted down below in the saloon drinking his breakfast just waiting for him to pop his head around the corner. Naturally, anyone would assume the worst.

Once back at the ranch, Jacob located Billy standing amongst a half dozen men grouped together. By the way they were all snickering, he knew immediately that Billy had already spilled the beans about what happened back in town. There was little doubt that he had filled them in on exactly where Jacob had spent the night. No telling how big his story had grown by now. Judging by the look on their faces he could just imagine what they were thinking.

Jacob's cheeks burned when he saw a slow smile curve Billy's lips upwards. Their eyes met. They both understood their hatred for one another.

"How was she, Jacob? As good as Rachel?" Billy asked sarcastically, his words heavily clumped with suggestive overtones.

Billy stood leaning up against the side of the corral with one leg resting across the other, grinning from ear to ear. Holding the last remnants of a cigarette between his fingers, he puckered his lips and took a long drag. He paused, holding his breath, then finally began to blow small smoke rings into the air.

Jacob's patience was spent. He was sick and tired of Billy running his mouth off, especially when it concerned Rachel, giving every man here the impression that she was an easy woman was more than he could handle. His natural instinct was to first pop him in the mouth, then force the little weasel to set the record straight.

Showing no fear, Jacob secured Rachel's gift to his saddle horn and quickly jumped from his leather, digging his heels in the dirt as he raced towards Billy. The only thought in his head was that nothing mattered right now except his woman's good name. By the time he got finished with Billy he'd be screaming for mercy.

There was a depth of anger in Jacob's eyes, which up until now, no man on this ranch had ever witnessed before. He let out a mighty grunt and threw his full body weight on top of Billy. Once on the ground he drove several hard punches right into Billy's ribs. Then he cocked his right fist up and landed three quick socks right between his eyes. Jacob was all over the bald-faced liar like a hungry flea on a mangy mutt.

The fight erupted so quickly that Billy was taken off guard, plus the wind was knocked out of him the moment his body was thrust against the dirt, struggling to break free of Jacob's grasp.

To Jacob's disappointment, before he had the chance to knock some sense into Billy, he was overpowered by some of the other bystanders. It took three able-bodied ranch hands to peel Jacob off of Billy and drag him backwards onto his feet. They held a tight grasp on his arms, preventing him from picking up where he had left off.

Purdy and Toby helped Billy back to his feet. His face was puffy, blood dripping from his nose and lips. He rubbed his mouth with the sleeve of his shirt and spit some blood out, along with one false tooth that had been loosened during the scuffle. With one sharp jerk, he managed to free himself from the hands that held him and then made an aggressive charge towards Jacob.

The crowd of men that had gathered around was cautious, knowing that more sparks might fly between the two. Two other men stepped forward, grabbing Billy from behind, preventing him from making a lunge at Jacob.

Billy cocked both of his fists upwards in Jacob's direction, which only made him look stupid. "You're gonna regret this, Scarface!" Billy threatened, a bloody scowl on his face.

Jacob's expression was cold. The fight was over as far as he was concerned. Even the rest of the crowd had begun to disperse.

Someone in the group yelled, "Let it be, Billy, you made your point!"

Jacob could tell that nothing he had done here was going to change anything.

Billy truly believed that Rachel was his property and he would continue to use every dirty trick in the book to get what he wanted.

One thing for sure, Jacob thought dryly, *Billy's aware that I am the one man standing in his way.* Even though he had no way of being certain when Billy would make his next move against him, he was certain that with his demented mind, it would be sometime soon.

Chapter 8

Shortly after rising out of bed, Spud headed for the corral. Toughened by a lifelong struggle with sleep deprivation, he believed there was no end to what a man could get done, if he started early enough.

In an hour or so, the rest of the cowhands would wake and head straight for the chow room to satisfy their hungry appetites. He'd join them at that time for his usual: four cups of coffee on the dark side, hash browns fried just right with two eggs on top, and most important of all, his turn to spin the yarn. He was a master of many words who thrived on talking and could easily live up to his reputation by immediately controlling the conversation in the room. Spud was tagged with his odd nickname because of his unusual liking for potatoes. It was told that he had eaten practically nothing but potatoes every day of his life since the age of two.

He was a slight man with a hunched back and a nose bent over like an owl's beak. No one paid any mind to the fact he was a might strange looking. He had a way with words that could take a man, who hadn't traveled more than fifty miles from his own front porch, clear across the country without actually

The Truth about Jacob

taking a step. The Baxter Ranch became a much bigger place with this natural-born storyteller around.

Now that breakfast was behind them, the ranch was alive with workers. Spud the early bird, had his own way of doing things. And when it came to keeping record of the exact number of horses on the ranch, he did so during the separation process. Twice a year the healthy horses were separated from the ones that needed a little tending to. Today, as he counted one by one, he was a bit surprised it had been such a productive year all the way around. He had no idea so many mares had already foaled. He'd been a little under the weather for the past eight months or so with a reoccurrence of dysentery, that condition had kept him pretty much housebound for the better part of that entire time.

His face was wrinkled with a ruddy complexion. It was drawn tight as he puckered his lips to take one last drag on his cigarette. Discarding the tiny butt on the ground, he moved about at a snail's pace, counting with his fingers and then scratching the correct numbers on a piece of paper he carried in his shirt pocket.

His attention was drawn to a handsome sorrel right in the midst of a big yawn. The horse displayed a full set of teeth, which reminded him of a funny story he had told more times than he could count on ten toes. He couldn't resist repeating it again.

Spud Reeder loved to get a rise out of Billy. And since Billy was the butt of the joke, he hotfooted it over closer to Jacob so he and the rest of the crew could listen as he poked some fun at him.

"Hey, Jacob, did I ever tell you about the time Billy's folks took him clear down to the Mexicano border when he was just a little tyke? Well, you see, they had met up with some half-breed Americano who was famous for makin' them thar false teeth. Fit Billy here with some mighty fine lookin' choppers. Why that boy could chew through rawhide with them thar teeth if'n he took a mind to. Only trouble was poor kid came back home speakin' Spanish."

Spud nearly split a gut cutting loose with laughter over Billy's ugly false teeth. When he laughed the left side of his face stayed motionless. This was due to a stroke he had suffered a good number of years ago. So unbeknownst to him, he actually looked pretty ridiculous himself, with his left eye and the left side of his mouth sagging south and as stiff as a board, while the right side twitched northward. So if anyone was laughing, it was most likely at him, not with him.

Slim and Toby, who were also working the horses nearby, weren't making a sound. They were even less enthusiastic than Jacob was to hear that same old stupid story they'd heard a hundred times before. Right about now the two of them had their minds on their work and avoiding any possible trouble with Billy.

Jacob made an honest attempt to hush the old man before Billy caught wind of what he was saying. But unfortunately, the old fool couldn't hear any better than he could take a hint. Whether meant in a good-hearted way or not, Billy took offense to Spud running off at the mouth about things he'd rather forget had ever happened. Everyone and their dog knew he had experienced an unhappy upbringing. He didn't care if the old geezer did practically have one foot in the grave, his ribbing wasn't one bit funny and was beginning to leave a bad taste in his mouth.

"Oh constipate that diarrhea mouth of yours old man! It's startin' to draw more flies than usual! Now I'm warning ya, you're just about one notch away from me thumpin' your ugly mug, so you better button it up!"

Because Billy was much younger and stronger and a little unpredictable, Spud lowered his head and limped towards the north end of the corral. He quickly ducked behind a group of horses to wait for the smoke to clear. Fuming, Billy marched back to the south side. He tossed a saddle onto the back of his stallion and angrily cinched it on. Neither man made eye contact again.

The Truth about Jacob

In the meantime, Jacob, who had pretty much kept to himself, watched from afar. He didn't say anything, but stood guard just in case the two men did come to blows. There had been times when Billy had lost his temper with Spud, but as of yet he hadn't actually physically hurt the old man. He usually resorted to shouting a few threats and insults. However, in Billy's present frame of mind, one never knew what he was capable of doing. So if the worst-case scenario did happen to come into play, Jacob would be ready to put a stop to an altercation that would be highly one-sided.

Standing along the sidelines, however, Jacob couldn't help but feel a little sorry for even the likes of Billy. For anyone, even as rotten to the core as Billy was, to have ended up being stuck with a set of brown, corroded teeth much too small for his mouth would be extremely humiliating.

As the day wore on, everything pretty much returned to normal. Jacob fanned his hand a few times to swat the horse flies away from his face and he finally dropped thoughts of Billy altogether. He had been working furiously removing the clumps of dirt and rocks packed tightly in the crevices of the horse's hooves.

There was no shortage of admiration on Jacob's part when it came to horses. He'd work endless, backbreaking hours with his own horses long after his day was done as far as Baxter's chores were concerned. Fact was, he enjoyed working with horses so much that, had he not been offered this particular job, he would have paid Baxter to let him take care of his horses instead of the other way around.

Jacob's sights were set on building a large herd of his own. One day, maybe his herd would be twice the size of Baxter's. He knew that was stretching his imagination a bit, but what horse hunting he had done throughout the years had already netted him a pretty hefty herd. At least there was enough to brag about if he took a mind to.

Just last week he sold five of his finer studs, giving him a tidy sum of cash. Thanks to Baxter, not one man working for him was required to reimburse him for grazing any of his own stock on his land. He was kind enough to allow any one of his ranch-hands that owned their own horses the right to graze them along with his, providing they were properly branded. A good man like Byron Baxter was hard to come by and every cowboy who worked for him was of the same mind.

Fall was definitely beginning to nudge its way in. The recent mild disturbances in the skies over the past few days were a good indication that winter was just around the corner. So it was high time to take care of all Baxter's livestock before winter settled in for good.

Today and the next day would be totally devoted to the horses' immediate needs and to make sure that all brands were legible. The rest of the week every man on Baxter's ranch would be rounding up cattle that were spread out across every nook and cranny of the surrounding hillsides. That would be the last official chore of the fall season. All of Baxter's livestock needed to be brought down to lower pastures to graze once the snow covered the higher ground it would close off the mountain range.

Today, within the dusty circle of the corral, this group of horses looked to be in fairly good shape. Looks could be deceiving, so Jacob would still perform the time-consuming task of checking each and every horse for any signs of hoof or leg injuries that may have gone undetected. This maintenance program was an ongoing ritual throughout the year, just not as painstaking as this one. It was one that Jacob thoroughly enjoyed. As usual, he went the extra mile making sure each horse was properly branded.

On this particularly crisp day in late September the sun was now two hours away from high noon. Jacob, along with a large number of other men, had been laboring for hours mingling amongst the shifting hooves. He was wrestling with a rowdy

The Truth about Jacob

pack of horses jammed into a small space in the left-hand corner of the corral. The thick dust was making it difficult to examine them from any distance, so he cordoned them off one by one.

Suddenly, something unusual caught his eye. He turned his head for a second look and shaded his eyes from the sun with his hand pressed to his forehead. There was something that was definitely out of the ordinary on a horse with significant splashy pinto markings. An eyeful soon emerged and it sure did stick out like a sore thumb. It was an odd looking brand he had never seen before on this ranch, or anywhere for that fact.

He didn't say anything. He just stood there staring at that one spot for at least another minute or so.

The letter B was burned unusually deep into the hide. There was an extra speck of lettering exposed above that letter that looked curious enough to give a man a good reason to believe there might possibly be another brand hidden just below. The quarter inch line protruding outward from the top right circular portion of the letter B. Jacob knew positively was not part of Billy's original brand. It looked more like an F. An F just about the same type and size as was on his own brand.

Jacob didn't move as he stared at the brand for a moment longer. All the chaos that had taken place earlier this morning between Billy and Spud was bad enough, *but now this*, he thought to himself. *This was the worst thing that could possibly happen on a ranch where all men were expected to be trusted.*

Upon seeing this unusual brand, Jacob realized someone among them was a horse thief. Since Billy was the only man on this ranch with the B brand, he was really the only one who had something to gain by branding over the top of his. *Who else around here would bother to stoop that low?* he questioned himself.

Jacob quickly scanned the animals in the immediate area, carefully checking the brands. There was definitely one more mare with a strikingly similar mark. Both horses looked very familiar and for that reason his mouth suddenly felt dry. It wasn't to Jacob's liking to think of Billy as a horse thief, but these horses were in all probability his and not Billy's. He still found it hard to believe that Billy was capable of plotting such an under-handed scheme to make off with his horses. How stupid could he be to think that no one on this ranch would notice the discrepancy in the brand?

Jacob now wondered how many other horses he'd stolen in the past and had already sold. Probably more than he would care to know. He shook his head in disgust. This is what Billy had finally resorted to. It's about as low as you can get to steal another man's livelihood right out from under his very nose. With growing dread he decided something had to be done about it.

Jacob rubbed the calm, along with some dust, from his face as he caught sight of Billy standing close by. He hadn't ponied up yet, but was about ready to mount his horse in order to ride out to gather more horses from the outer pastures. He placed his left boot in the stirrup in an effort to swing his other leg over the top of the horse, but Jacob's angry voice brought it back down.

"Hold up there, Billy!" he yelled.

The two men shared a brief moment of silence, understanding fully that it was the calm before the storm.

"How far you reckon changin' these brands was gonna get you, Billy?"

"What are you tryin' to say?" Billy snorted, giving a pretty good performance at playing possum. His left hand dangled freely holding his reins while his right forefinger toyed with the hammer on his six-shooter.

"I'm saying these two horses here look to be the same ones I rounded up not three weeks ago out by the Butte Creek Canyon."

"So what the hell does that got to do with me?"

"Seems like it has quite a lot to do with you since, for some odd reason, they both have your brand on them!"

Billy just shrugged his shoulders and curled his lips down at the corners that downsized a chin that was barely visible to

The Truth about Jacob

begin with. He didn't appear to be the least bit concerned about the accusation.

Jacob, on the other hand, wasn't impressed by the, "I don't know what you mean," look on his face so he wedged him a little tighter into a proverbial corner.

"Cut the innocent act, Billy. Somebody has gone to a whole lot of trouble to cover up my brand. I'm thinking that somebody is you."

At this point, Billy felt a little uneasy because he shot a glance over at Baxter and noticed that his head was cocked in their direction. It was obvious he was trying to pick up on their argument.

"You claimin' I stole those horses from you?" Billy snarled with a hard glare.

"I think the brands speak for themselves." Jacob returned.

"And I think you're talkin' out of turn. I think you think there's some kinda special sun that shines on you, don't you? Now you're a so-called expert with brands and have some kinda crystal ball that tells you who did what? Well, if you're so damn smart and know as much as you claim to, why ain't you done better for yourself? Why ain't you sportin' pockets full of money and a ranch of your own? You're just a measly old hired hand like the rest of us, Mr. High-and-Mighty."

Jacob paid no mind to Billy's criticism. He was aware that he was just trying to skirt out of the corner he was backed into.

"Quit playing games, Billy. It'll do you no good to change the subject. All the proof I need is burned right here on this horse's backside. This brand is nothing like the ones on your other horses. It doesn't even come close to looking like this one for instance," Jacob pointed out as he cornered a golden brown mustang known to be Billy's.

"That don't prove nothin'," he fired back. "Who are you anyway to go accusin' me of anything? You're nobody. Now if it were Mr. Baxter here doin' the askin' then I'd be obliged to answer. Now maybe someone did doctor up your brand, but you're barkin' up the wrong tree by lookin' in my direction. I'm an honest man and can do well for myself without stealing from the likes of you."

For a short time the two men shared icy glares and a moment of silence. Billy had regretted more than once that he hadn't settled the score between him and Jacob long ago. There was a good chance it was finally going to happen today. If nothing else, at least he was getting somewhat of a thrill out of watching Jacob squirm. Because the way he looked at it, right about now Jacob was looking like a fool trying to pin this one on him with no hard proof to go by.

"Who's to say you didn't do this yourself and now you're trying to lay the blame on me? Yeah, that's it! You probably played a hand in this one yourself. Admit it."

Jacob just shook his head. He should have known better than to think for one minute Billy would take this matter seriously. But Billy had another thing to think about if he figured he was going to play along with his stupid games and just let this matter pass. There was no way he was going to let the little weasel worm his way out of this one.

Now the air grew graveyard quiet and all eyes were drawn in their direction. Most cowpokes there knew Jacob and Billy had long been at odds with one another, so it was no surprise the two men were going at it now. It was also common knowledge that Billy wouldn't know the truth even if it crawled up beside him and said hello. Nevertheless, the other men now feared that this argument was taking a deadly turn.

When Jacob looked at Billy from under a heavy brow and advanced in his direction even Baxter realized the animosity between them had grown to the point that he would be forced to get into the thick of things. So, he moved right in-between the two ramrods with a firm hand pressed against their chests.

Without placing the blame on any one cowboy he took a full breath and spoke his opinion on the matter.

The Truth about Jacob

"I'll say this as simple as I can so every man here can understand me well. I had better not see any of these particular brands popping up around here again or I'll just simply add the horses in question to my own herd. So as you can see, it won't be worth anyone's time or trouble to repeat this kind of dirty-work."

Listening to what the old man had to say riled Billy a bit because Baxter sounded as if he didn't sympathize with him in any way. If anything, much to his dismay, the old man had administered his demand directly towards him as if he had already established his guilt. That didn't set well, Billy's sly smirk fell from his face. Now he felt betrayed.

Billy felt a deep need to speak up on his own behalf, and even a deeper need to protect his job. He was well aware that if he shied back and didn't make one attempt to maintain his innocence it would be the same as admitting his guilt.

He cocked his head and turned to face the old man. He glared at him and demanded that he clarify his statement. "You sayin' I'm a thief, too?" he challenged.

"Now just hold your horses there, Billy. Don't you go jumpin' to no crazy conclusions! I'm not making any claims here either way. I'm merely stating that there better not be any more of this kind of nonsense conducted on my ranch."

Billy knew he had to protect his interests on this ranch. In a perverse way he thought that, of course, meant being brave enough to argue his way out of the hot seat, regardless of whom it was with.

"All of a sudden you're actin' like you can't trust me just cause he says so!" Billy shouted as he pointed an angry finger at Jacob. Then he turned a furious eye back on Baxter. "You've never questioned my honor before. So what have I done to deserve it now?"

There was a slight shift in the atmosphere. Every cowboy there gasped with astonishment. They were stunned at Billy's audacity to raise his voice right up into Baxter's face.

"As in the past I'm not questioning your code of honor now," he pointed out.

Baxter felt pressured to think of a better solution to this whole mess. Why couldn't Billy just leave things be? Jacob didn't resist his judgment and he certainly had more to lose. There was no use in digging for proof of who did what because there was no hard evidence to go by. Billy wasn't caught in the act so his hands were tied as far as coming straight out and accusing him. *So why couldn't the fool kid see that*, he thought to himself.

Actually, when push came to shove, Baxter had to admit to himself that there was the possibility that Billy might be capable of stealing from Jacob. The young man had a history of problems in that area. However, the fact remained, no one here had possession of any concrete proof that he actually tried to claim these horses under false pretenses. Before he had the opportunity to address Billy again, the accused began to scream in his face.

"What do you expect me to do, just stand here and act as if he's not callin' me a horse thief?" His hardened glare was now fixed back on Baxter. "Looks to me like you're sidin' with old Scarface," he bluntly accused.

For a moment, Baxter was taken aback by Billy's unexpected barrage of angry words directed at him. He knew Billy to be the impulsive type, and he had been known to be rather trigger-happy. But right now, even that thought didn't stop him from putting a halt to all this nonsense before it did take a deadly turn. After all, there was more at stake here than just two of his best men coming to blows. There was the possibility that this might spark some sort of brawl involving his entire crew of men. Knowing that they were somewhat divided in their loyalty between Billy and Jacob, that's exactly how they would handle things.

Even the assembly of men standing nearby sighed with a breath of apprehension. They were well aware that this just wasn't another show of manhood. With great cause for concern,

The Truth about Jacob

they feared that the worst was yet to come from Billy and maybe by now there was nothing the old man could say or do to stop it. Most of them were friends with both men and to their dismay assumed at least one was about to get either fired or shot.

Baxter stood his ground, letting every man here know he still held the upper hand in this arena full with two angry bulls. "This unusual brand just didn't mysteriously appear on these two horses. Now somebody had a hand in it! I'm saying this for everyone's benefit. Whoever it was, had better not do it again! I have yet to hear or see any conclusive evidence as to who actually did this, so as you can all see, I'm pretty much in the dark here as far as laying the blame on any one man. Without conclusive proof, I have no way of knowing just who is right or wrong. Now I'm gonna say this only one more time. This particular brand had better not show up on my ranch again. Not tomorrow, not next week, not ever! I shouldn't have to put it any clearer than that."

Billy still felt that the deck was stacked against him, and for obvious reasons. He was the only man on the ranch with a brand anything remotely similar to the disfigured B. He was also the only man here that had something to gain by leaving things just as they were. Not only was his reputation at stake here, but also his chances for the old man to give him his blessing as far as he and Rachel tying the knot one day soon. And there was certainly no way Baxter would ever hand his ranch over to an accused horse thief.

If he couldn't fix things with a few angry words, then he wouldn't have to look too far to find all the help he needed. His gun could settle this matter once and for all. Now it was time to throw the spotlight back on Jacob. Billy shifted his feet and moved back around to face his accuser.

"Nobody calls me a horse thief and gets away with it! Now you better find yourself a gun, Jacob, and we'll settle this score once and for all!" His eyes were brimmed with hatred.

Billy stomped over to Spud and removed his pistol and holster from his hip and tossed it at Jacob's feet. Then he blurted, "I know what kind of tricks you're up to. You've been looking for a way to get back at me for snagging that white stallion. I'm guessin' that's exactly what your motives are in blaming me for this. You're just tryin', to get even with me, that's all. Well, I'm gonna give you more than you bargained for. Now belt up!"

At first Jacob wasn't quite certain how serious Billy really was, but as he tilted his head to take a closer look at his aggressor's hardened eyes, he didn't like what he saw.

Billy was flushed pink and his eyes were evil. He was acting like an absolute lunatic, prancing around in the dirt like he had hot feet. It was obvious to Jacob that Billy had looked forward to this very moment for a long time. He was acting more than anxious right now to put some lead right between his eyes.

But even a fool wouldn't face certain death against Billy's quick draw, and no man had ever called Jacob Fowler a foolish man. He knew first-hand that he was in no way a fair match for Billy, especially since he had never as much as held a gun in his hands, much less aim and fire one with any accuracy. He didn't take kindly to coming off looking like a coward, but it stood to reason that even a brave dead man is still dead.

"You're talkin', crazy Billy. This is just your way of trying to shut me up for good."

"And you're hiding behind Baxter's apron strings, runnin' scared like a scalded dog!" Billy accused. "You made your claim, now back it up like a man."

Billy kept his eye on Jacob and Jacob kept his eye on Billy's gun.

Baxter never moved his eyes away from either man. He stepped right into the line of fire. Only this time he knew he had even a bigger job ahead of him because Billy had his hand on his gun looking like he was ready to shoot the whole lot of them if he had to.

The Truth about Jacob

"Just hold up there, Billy!" Baxter demanded. "There's not going to be any gunplay here. Killing one another over this certainly isn't going to settle it. Now what's done is done and we can't change it. Simple as that! Now if I have to knock some sense into both you boys, then that's just what I'll do," he warned.

Billy grit his teeth and wiped the sweat from his brow. His fingers toyed with the handle of his gun. "That's easy for you to say, Mr. Baxter. Your honor's not at stake here. Old windbag here just turns around and walks away from this smellin' like a rose. And me, I leave smellin' like a horse thief! So don't you even try to pretend that he hasn't raised some doubt in your mind," Billy snarled. "I've got no quarrel with you, so just step aside and let us handle this like men."

In the back of Billy's mind he worried that Baxter would call his bluff. He knew he couldn't push the old man too far, but he couldn't just lie down and play dead, either. It wasn't that he was afraid of the old fart or anything like that. It was because he valued everything he'd worked so hard to gain, his job and Rachel. After all, he had played the part of the loyal subordinate for too many years to risk losing it all. That meant he had to toe the line with the old geezer, at least until after he had taken Rachel as his wife.

Baxter hated to think that he would be forced to fire Billy and just run him off his ranch, but if that's what it was going to take to shut him up, then so be it. He'd just have to forget that he ever promised Billy's dying mother the young man would always have a place to call home.

But as he glanced from one angry face to the other, a light suddenly came on in his head; he was reminded of a famous chapter right out of the Bible. King Solomon was once faced with a problem quite similar to this one and he had cleverly come up with a great idea that quickly solved his dilemma. Fortunately for Baxter he didn't have to suggest splitting a horse in half to settle this dispute. There was plenty enough goods to go around. He would give one horse to Jacob and the other to Billy.

"This is my final word on this matter," he stated. "Jacob, you take the bay and, Billy, you can have the pinto." Then, he rested casually back on one foot more than the other and waited for the icy glares to melt.

To his dismay neither man seemed pleased. Jacob said nothing. He just stood there staring at the ground. Billy, on the other hand, began to pace back and forth, kicking the dirt a few times as he stomped. He took his hat between his fingers and then thrust it against the ground. "The hell you will!" he yelled. "That don't sound like no deal to me! Sounds like you're just trying to pacify two kids in a squabble. Now this is more than just a squabble. My reputations at stake here."

Baxter had never seen Billy act like this. He'd heard of him throwing such tantrums, but until now he'd never actually witnessed one for himself. He began to spit profanity like it was tobacco and stomped the ground below his feet to dust. Then he picked up his hat and threw it in Jacob's face.

Job or no job, Billy wasn't going to just stand here and let Baxter cater to Jacob's every whim. Oblivious to the consequences, he moved within a few inches of Jacob and started cursing again. "You son of a backstabber! I'd rather put a bullet through their heads than give even one of these damn horses to you!" Then he circled around to face Baxter and blurted, "I've worked just as hard as anyone else around here to get where I am today and I ain't gonna let nobody take away what's rightfully mine! He's tryin' to make me look bad, can't you see that?"

He whirled back around without a warning and threw a sucker punch at Jacob. Billy's fist caught Jacob square on his right jawbone. With the element of surprise on his side, he had managed to land a good solid hit.

Jacob was normally quicker than the buzz of a fly, but Billy had gained the edge by hitting him while his guard was down.

The Truth about Jacob

The blunt force of the punch was so fierce it slammed Jacob straight to the dirt, sending him crawling on all fours trying to scramble back to his feet.

That underhanded maneuver didn't set well with Mr. Baxter, or with Weckles, who was standing nearby. Billy's aggressive move towards Jacob prompted the dog to latch onto his arm. The fur flew as his teeth drew a gush of blood through Billy's shirt from six deep puncture wounds in his right forearm. It was at least sixty seconds before he could beat the canine off with the heel of his boot.

Even though the faithful dog was forced to release his grip on Billy's arm, Weckles stationed himself as close to Jacob as he could get, as if he expected his services might be needed again.

Billy hated that mangy mutt and if Baxter weren't standing beside him he would have shot his fool head right off. He'd despised that mongrel from day one anyway, if for no other reason than because he had taken such a liking to Jacob even as a pup. Besides, that inbred mixed conglomeration of every breed that ever resided on this ranch was constantly licking himself in his favorite spot every time he looked at him, which turned Billy's stomach.

Meanwhile, Baxter and Spud stepped over to help Jacob back to his feet. That allowed the head honcho time to think about what had just happened. Infuriated at Billy, he stepped beside him and thumped him hard on top of the head with his big hat. With a glare that could kill, he then pushed him three feet from where he stood. "You ever pull a stunt like that again, Billy, you'll be looking for another job!" he shouted.

Billy got the message loud and clear and gathered it was time to back off. Whether he liked it or not, Jacob was no longer fair game.

Weckles didn't beat around the bush either. He again raised his hairy lips exposing the same sharp teeth that Billy had come to know only too well. All the while, the dog growled every time Billy tried to make a move. Even when he shifted his fingers, trying to hold tight to his bleeding arm, the dog continued to show teeth.

It was all Billy could do to keep from kicking that dog's hind end to town and back. A deep sense of resentment rushed through him. He not only had to pay strict attention to how Baxter was reacting, but he had to keep a watchful eye on that stupid dog. Still, no matter how badly he wanted to strike back at Jacob again because of all that had taken place, he was forced to walk away keeping his tongue still.

Billy was aware he'd almost pushed the old man too far. Baxter's words had indicated that not thirty seconds ago. He sure didn't understand why the old man got so bent out of shape. Since it didn't have anything to do with him, why should he care if he poked Jacob in the face? It certainly wasn't the first time he and Jacob had exchanged a difference of opinion, and it wouldn't be the last.

"Guess a man can't even speak his own mind around here anytime he takes a notion," Billy mumbled as he moped towards his horse.

There was really plenty of time to take this matter up again with Jacob at a later date, he thought with contempt. *One thing for certain, it wouldn't be where there was a full audience of eyes, one big angry boss, or a smelly old dog with sharp teeth lurking around.*

As for Baxter, he was skeptical that this argument would end here. It would most likely fester back up sometime, somewhere down the road. His biggest fear was, that if it did, it would happen without a warning and with no one around to stop it. He was also sure as he was tall that if it came to pass, then one of them wouldn't walk away to tell about it.

Jacob absolutely despised Billy. He didn't have any reason to think that Billy felt any differently about him. Physically showing him the road off the ranch would be a pleasure. If he happened to meet up with an untimely end out there on that road somewhere it sure wouldn't cause him to shed a tear. He

The Truth about Jacob

would only pity the poor man that had to waste a bullet on the big lummox.

Billy reckoned Jacob had one thing coming to him, retaliation in full measure. He'd never give up the idea of finding some way to discredit Jacob in the eyes of Mr. Baxter. If that didn't come to pass, then he could think of other ways. Maybe he'd disappear into thin air like his folks had years ago. Today he'd just have to settle for the small satisfaction he was feeling right now, because as to date, he had successfully stolen six fine healthy mares from Jacob's herd and had already sold them for top dollar.

Chapter 9

With winter well on the way and already unseasonably late, most of the horses were finally taken care of. Now the day had arrived to gather up the cattle that were spread out around the foothills before the bad weather really started calling the shots.

Rachel always rode right along with the rest of the crew doing her part to help tie up all the loose ends. It was her responsibility to help guide the livestock back down where there were greener pastures to forge in. The valley floor had a good supply of fodder and other necessary provisions to see them through the cold winter months ahead.

Rachel saddled up at daybreak. She rode with style and grace. Her skin was as silky and natural as the science that had created it. Her well-defined curves were obvious beneath the blue shirt she wore tucked neatly under tan pants with a black belt cinched tightly at her tiny waist. As usual the attention she drew went unnoticed by her. Her thoughts were elsewhere.

This would be a good a day, she thought. Today she'd take a chance on a long shot. She would watch Jacob's every move and as soon as the first opportunity arose she would lure him off alone.

The Truth about Jacob

Even as she conjured this idea in her head she worried somewhat about her father. *What would he say,* she thought, *if he found out what she had planned?* Knowing what she was up against if someone was to tattle on her nearly spoiled her good mood. She took a deep breath and sighed, trying very hard to push that ugly thought out of her head.

But then she whispered to herself, "It's no one's business what I do, especially not Father's." She was old enough to take care of her own affairs. As long as he didn't know what was going on, everything would be okay. Then they could keep the peace between them. Every now and then throughout the day she'd make a point to look over her shoulder to make sure no one was aware of her movements.

Rachel knew, that just as sure as a horse comes to water, Jacob would be more than willing to come to her aid. That's the excuse she planned to use to draw him away from the herd and the other cowpokes. She had carefully formulated everything last night while attempting to capture some sleep, sleep that never met her tired eyes. But it was worth it because today she would fall into the arms of the man she loved.

Late in the day, after most of the cows had been gathered and were well on their way back to the ranch, Rachel broke rank and the rules of the day. No lady in her right mind would follow a cowboy back into the thick brush not knowing for sure what nature of business he was tending to, but she'd already shed all her shyness when it came to Jacob.

Allowing him only enough time to quickly finish matters at hand, Rachel turned her horse away from the others and approached cautiously in his direction. She had a quick eye and browsed the area around her making sure no one saw her. She carefully led her horse away from the bulk of busy hooves and advanced into an area covered with tall trees and brush as thick as grass. She came to rest in a small clearing just thirty feet from the border of trees and away from the moving herd.

Although she was feeling a bit nervous, she prepared herself for a well-rehearsed performance. Rachel cleared her leather and stooped down on one knee pretending to remove a stone from the hoof of her horse. Jacob returned about that same time back through the very trail he had entered to find her struggling with the steed's heavy leg.

"Got a problem, Rachel?"

"Not one I can't handle. I just picked up a stray rock," she returned with some real theatrical value attached to her words. "I think I got it all out." Giving him a sad eye that was quite convincing she added, "I've exhausted my canteen Jacob, could I bother you for a drink out of yours?"

Her efforts paid off big time judging by the broad smile on his face. You'd have thought she just gave him the world. Without haste, he scurried towards his horse that was tied to a tree and removed the canteen from his saddle and returned to her side. He handed her the cool drink and stepped back a bit allowing her more room to lift it to her thirsty mouth.

Rachel licked her lips and then lifted the cold metal to her mouth taking a huge swallow. A considerable amount of water sloshed down onto the front of her blouse. It felt cool and refreshing as well as exciting because she knew very well Jacob was watching her movements the full time. His eyes devoured her indisputable beauty as she drank the water. Her tender throat rolled in short sequences as she swallowed hard, large drops of the crystal clear liquid splattering across her chest.

Jacob didn't know for sure if she had purposely orchestrated this whole scene in order to be alone with him, but if she had, he wasn't complaining. He was already deeply entangled in her web of tricks and laughed to himself each time she came up with a new one. If he were a bolder man, he'd a thought of a few of his own.

The air had a romantic feel to it, and Jacob was acutely aware of his strong longing to take Rachel into his arms. He could hear nothing but the sound of his own heart pounding. There was a

The Truth about Jacob

relaxed sense of tranquility just in knowing there wasn't even one set of eyes watching their every move. It meant so much to Jacob to enjoy her loveliness all by himself.

Sunlight shimmered onto her hair like a stroke of his brush across the very canvas he used to paint her image. Deep, dark eyes against clear-bronzed skin, hair the color of chocolate swirled with streaks of reddish gold. *So beautiful, so very beautiful,* he thought to himself. And now he wanted to pick up where they had left off the last time, his heart felt like melted butter in his chest

Rachel thought for a moment of how romantic this felt. Years of frustrations and insecurities seemed to disappear. She had dreamed about this very day for so long and found herself experiencing all and more of the wonderful emotions she only encountered before in her mind.

She smiled coyly and asked. "Could we rest a spell, Jacob? I really am quite out of breath."

Most eager to oblige her, he cleared away some sticks and gently helped to nestle her down on a soft mound of leaves he had scooped together with his hands. Then he eased down next to her snuggling as close to her warm body as he could. Jacob sat as still as a church mouse and waited for her to make the first move.

Rachel calmly leaned forward, pressing her temples gently against his soft lips in a touch that sent her blood rushing. Caught up in the moment, she drew back gazing into his eyes. During that short span of time she continued to lather him with her sweet smiles.

All Jacob wanted to do was pull her closer to him and kiss her. No sooner had that thought escaped him, than Rachel moved forward aiming her lips upwards, giving him the invitation he was waiting for. Jacob leaned down and softly placed his lips on hers. Rachel kissed him like a woman sure of what she wanted. Jacob poured himself into that kiss with no resistance.

"I could stay this way forever," he murmured. "This must be what heaven feels like."

"It doesn't have to end, Jacob. Forever is of our own choosing. No one can stand in our way if we want to be together," she added. "And frankly, I truly believe we are meant to be together." A smile grew on her face when she realized her comment seemed to please Jacob immensely.

Jacob stared at her button nose. He couldn't help but notice how cute it was. He had known how much she hated it. That's what made every other part of her all the more beautiful and all that much easier to appreciate because of the fact that she harbored no conceit. It was as if every time he looked at her he could see all the way through to her soul, a soul so pure and innocent. She was an exquisite creature, so full of goodness and kindness and with so much love to give, that she was ready to explode.

Jacob felt comfortable. Their bodies molded together like they were born to belong. On bended knees they rose upwards simultaneously with little space between their shoulders, kissing long and hard again. When they broke away for a brief moment he pressed his lips to her hair. It smelled as fresh as a new day.

Their minds floated freely and uninhibited for the very first time. In broad daylight, they took the maiden voyage one step further. Venturing beyond a passionate kiss, they slowly eased back down upon the crumpled leaves, allowing their passion to grow and flourish. Like newborn pups not really knowing for sure what would happen next, they explored new boundaries that had never been crossed before.

His fingers stroked and kneaded her back, just above her tiny waist. He couldn't hold her tight enough. He gave her something she needed. She gave him something he never had. Rachel's fingers walked up and down his back before burrowing in tight under his shoulder blades. Their passion drove them to new heights. They were sprawled out on the

The Truth about Jacob

ground driven by the desire to physically declare their love for one another. Up until now they were forced to keep their true feelings all bottled up and now, suddenly, with courage beyond belief, their love for one another was finally unleashed.

While emotions were running wild, unbeknownst to the preoccupied couple, they had attracted an unwanted guest. Billy had silently crept in behind Rachel from the very instant she had first entered the thicket. His eyes were green with envy and hate as he stood alone in the shadows of the forest listening to their soft murmurs, watching what he could only dream about.

"Who are they kidding," he whispered sarcastically. "Did they really think their sudden disappearance would go unnoticed?"

Like a hawk hidden in the trees, he watched their hungry lips explore new horizons, hardly taking the time to come up for air. Together they created the kind of passion Billy had only experienced in his dreams with Rachel, or any other woman for that fact.

He continued to watch for a while, hunkered down like a cat ready to pounce on the prowl. He was suffering like he'd never suffered before. To only suspect an affair going on between Jacob and Rachel was one thing, but to see it actually played out before his eyes carried with it incredible pain.

Outraged with jealousy, he angrily wiggled his way back out the same way he crawled in. His mind had simply snapped and was now a graveyard of decay as his hate for Jacob grew. He was tired of messing around with this freak face. It was high time he got him out of the picture for good. Then he could get on with his life, with the woman of his choice. Rachel was his gal and that's all there was to it.

Billy didn't give the dust time to settle below his feet before he hoofed it back to the ranch and scurried right up under old man Baxter's nose. He planned on being a real package of information, there was no need to wrestle with a lot of words.

He'd just deliver the bad news exactly as he saw it. And if he slaughtered the truth a bit, then thumbs up for him, he figured.

Baxter was busy cinching his saddle into place on a chestnut mustang Billy had just finished breaking the day before. He tried to ignore Billy for a moment giving him the opportunity to start the conversation. The big boss figured that whatever he had on his mind had better be a good enough reason to explain why he wasn't where he was supposed to be. If it wasn't, then he would remind him of the fact that he should be back with the herd doing his part. If his reasons really fell short of his approval, then he'd be getting more than just a few things off his chest.

Baxter's stall for time didn't work. Even after Billy dismounted from his horse he stood not two feet away staring like a big mute. Billy's silence finally forced him to speak up first. "Why aren't you with the herd? You taking the rest of the day off or something?"

Billy wiped the sweat from his mouth with the sleeve of his soiled shirt. His eyes filled with a strange sparkle and his mouth curled up at the corners.

"Maybe it's something of a more important nature."

"Don't play word games with me, Billy spit it out! What are you up to now?"

"Maybe you should be asking Jacob and Rachel that same question." At that point Billy could see the irritation on his face.

Baxter swallowed hard. "Spell it out, Billy. What are you tryin' to say?"

"May sound a little hard to believe, but I saw what I saw."

"And just what did you see?"

Sly-eyed, Billy looked down at his boots and away from Baxter's steady glare. "I saw Jacob and Rachel rollin' around like a couple of old hung dogs out in the woods!"

They both fell silent in a dead stare at one another. Billy's ugly words were cruel, slicing Baxter's heart like a knife. This was not the daughter he knew. An ache too heavy for one heart to bear

The Truth about Jacob

made it impossible for him to shelter his pain. He widened his eyes in anger, but held back his urge to belt Billy in the kisser. He needed to know exactly what Billy meant by the nature of his words. "You suggesting what I think you are?"

Billy turned to his horse and stepped up into his saddle. No matter what came to pass, he decided he wasn't saying another word. He straightened his look directly at Baxter and waited for all hell to break loose. Baxter mistakenly concluded by his silence that even Billy was too embarrassed to explain further. He couldn't argue that point and did appreciate what he believed to be the young man's obvious respect for his feelings.

Billy knew he'd done enough damage for one day just by the way the old man's mouth was nervously twitching. It was obvious that with such a sober look on his face Baxter's imagination was, by now, running away with itself. The old man could run as far as he wanted and fill in all the rest of the dirty details any way he saw fit for all Billy cared.

Baxter's hurt seemed to shut down his good thinking. Under normal circumstances, he would have insisted on more information from Billy to back up his claims. At least he would have asked why he happened to be spying on Rachel in the first place. But his mind was miles away worrying about his daughter.

Baxter thought carefully. He knew he would never again look upon Jacob in the same way as before. He had no idea Jacob was capable of doing something this disgraceful, and certainly wasn't aware of his devious dark side.

He had let his guard down and was buffaloed into thinking his daughter was safe in his hands. But when it came down to it he turned out to be as sneaky as a wily coyote. *At least you knew where you stood with a dirty dog staring you in the face*, he thought. Now, come to find out right under his very own nose he ignorantly allowed his sweet little flesh and blood to be taken advantage of by a man that couldn't be trusted. And for that very reason, he would never forgive him.

Worry lines creased his face as he focused on a much broader spectrum. His thoughts quickly raced back to Rachel, reminding him of the most serious problem to consider right now. He sank down on a sawhorse, which was positioned up against the corral and then the questions began to pour out. *How am I supposed to handle this delicate matter with my daughter? How could Jacob act out in such a dishonorable way purely for his own satisfaction? Should I just go there, confront them now and ask straight out what had taken place? Or should I sit here and gradually become dark and morose, thinking the worst?*

Baxter sat there, consumed by his thoughts, not knowing which way to turn. He wiped the sweat from his brow with the back of his forearm thinking about one thing he did know for sure. He felt a deep sense of betrayal from a boy he took in when no one else would give him the time of day. *A boy he had always loved like his very own son. But obviously the little worm had forgotten all about that. Or maybe he simply took it for granted. Why else would he do such a horrible thing?* Baxter asked himself.

His pain moved him to tears because that young man had added so much meaning to his life. "And Rachel," he whimpered beneath his breath. "My poor sweet little girl. What kind of a mess has she gotten herself into?"

If Jacob had just approached Rachel in a proper manner, more fitting of today's traditional courtship practices, he would have gladly given them his blessings despite that fact that she was a little young. At least he'd like to think he would have. Instead, Jacob had done all he could do to destroy Rachel's reputation and possibly ruin her chances to ever regain any respect around this community. Worry over what would become of his daughter tore at his heart. If news of this ever got out she'd be known as a common hussy for the rest of her life.

Baxter looked up at Billy and raked his tortured eyes carefully over his undisturbed expression. A sheen of perspiration on his face glistened in the sun.

The Truth about Jacob

He had a history of coating his stories, but even a dimwit like Billy couldn't hold such a straight face and lie about something this serious. Baxter convinced himself that the sweat drenching the rest of his soiled body must have been caused by his hearty ride back to the ranch during the hottest part of the day, rather than worry over what he was reporting and whether it was true or not.

"You keep hush about this, you hear! I don't want a scandal on my hands. Now get on back to the herd before they notice you're gone." he demanded. He lowered his head, as his brown eyes broke free from Billy's freckled face. His pain pounded him hard as tears welled again in his eyes.

Billy tipped his hat and headed his horse back towards the herd. He smiled big once Baxter could no longer see his face. If he got real lucky, it was possible to move right into Jacob's shoes in more ways than one, maybe even as soon as tomorrow. His mind was full of big ideas like a fancy wedding and a foreman's position.

Baxter was still studying matters of the heart when, not two hours after hearing what Jacob and Rachel had been up to out in the woods, his daughter came prancing through the front door shining like a new penny. She looked calm and cool as ever, almost convincingly innocent of any bad behavior. She sailed across the floor humming like a saintly butterfly with a smile.

But he knew better and was outraged by her proud, smug manner. Her tangled hair hung to her shoulders. The back of her wrinkled shirt was smudged with patches of dirt and bits of crumpled leaves. He could only imagine what she must have been doing earlier to show up here now with such an unkempt appearance. Baxter moved aggressively towards her. He stepped out in front of his daughter to halt her flighty steps with a grim face and fists clenched tight.

Rachel was startled by her father's angry glare. She knew immediately something was seriously wrong. As he advanced closer and still did not take his steady stare away, she began to feel that it was she that had done something to disturb him. Even his graying temples were pulsating. The walls surrounding them seemed to move suffocatingly close. She'd never forget the brief silence they shared as long as she lived.

"Have you no shame, girl? What did you do, throw your good morals out the back door as you left the house this morning?" His voice rose as his words became more heated. "Do you fancy yourself a loose lady now with no standards to live by? How can you even look at yourself in the mirror after what you've done?"

There was a stillness that fell upon them again that was cold and distant, a shadow of gloom hung over their heads as if it were pitch dark in the room. Rachel squared her shoulders and loosened the scarf below her chin. She pulled her eyes away and suspended them out into midair somewhere and then stood for an instant thinking. Extremely puzzled, she tried to figure out what he was so mad about without swallowing her pride and asking. As she stood there, she realized that this moment of silence between them was far worse than the angry snarl of his voice.

Contrary to what he obviously thought, she had no idea what his words meant. So with her pride dangling from her tongue, she cleared her throat, found her voice and came right back at him. "What are you talking about, I have no morals?"

"You of all people should know very well what I mean."

"Well, I don't know what you mean. If I'm being reprimanded for something I've done wrong, then you need to clarify what it is. I can accept that, but don't think I'm going to stand here and let you yell at me for something you think I've done wrong or maybe you suspect I'm involved in. So what is it? What's happened that's so terrible that you find it necessary to talk to me in such a hateful manner?"

His expression hardened and his eyes narrowed to dark thin slits as his words began to erupt again. "I trusted you and obviously that means nothing to you. Seems as if you haven't

The Truth about Jacob

learned one thing I've tried to teach you all these years. I just don't understand what's come over you, young lady. Or maybe that's the problem here. You don't know how to act like a lady!"

Rachel placed her hands upon her hips and moved towards him. Her own anger began to soar. Coming from anyone else maybe these same exact words wouldn't have hurt so much, but hearing them from her father felt they were like a sharp jab in the heart.

Her face changed every shade of red and she blurted, "Excuse me, I'm not going to stand here any longer and let you accuse me of such a horrible thing! Must I remind you that this is your daughter you're talking to?" They both stood for an instant and stared with daggers in their eyes.

Rachel quickly found some more courage and—with nothing more than a handful of sketchy clues to go on—she put the shoe on the other foot. She began to interrogate him. Her breath trembled and her tongue felt much too big for her mouth as she shouted, "Just what in 'tarnation are you talking about, Father? Who's been filling you full of a bunch of lies?" She stared hard at her father, wondering what on earth had given him cause to speak to her in such a demeaning way.

She just couldn't believe what she was hearing or what she was seeing. The hurt in his eyes was alarming. His face was stone cold and he seemed to age right before her eyes. Baxter took a heavy breath, recalling only too well the horrible secret revealed to him earlier today. Once more his anger boiled. He was so upset over her seedy actions with Jacob that he ignored her claims that she did not understand what this whole argument was about. He believed she knew very well what this matter pertained to.

Rage rode on his words as he raised his voice to her again. "That's enough, don't play possum with me, young lady! You know perfectly well what I'm talking about. Billy filled me in on all the filthy details of your escapades out in the woods today with that son of a lizard, Jacob. Evidently you both put on quite a show from what I hear. What must I do, watch every move you make to be sure you mind your manners? Is it still necessary to chaperone you at your age? And at all times, I might add!" he practically screamed.

Rachel could understand why it had come down to this angry discussion in view of the lies Billy was capable of concocting. She could only imagine what kind of a lurid picture he drew for her father, for she too had on more than one occasion caught him coating the truth. But the fact that her father had chosen to believe anything Billy had to say disappointed her greatly. It also angered her to think that he would swallow this sort of trash.

Rachel did not like what she had just heard here and definitely was not inclined to let anyone, not even her father, talk to her like she was a cheap floozy. Without waiting to hear even one more word about what she had or had not done, she decided to interrupt him before he had the opportunity to cast a few more stones since he had already accused her of practically every sin in the Good Book.

She rooted herself right up under his nose and rebuked his charges. "First and foremost, Father, I can assure you that I can take care of myself. And secondly, when you decide to come down off that high horse of yours and clean the filth out of your ears that Billy's been feeding you, I might, just might, talk further on this matter! Then maybe we can skip the mudslinging and talk this out like mature adults.

"Must I remind you of what a liar Billy has always been? I'm absolutely crushed to think that you would believe anything he would have to say about me. I have absolutely nothing to hide! My life has always been pretty much an open book. Open enough for every cowboy on this ranch who takes a mind to—to stick his nose in it."

Rachel coughed slightly and cleared her throat and adjusted her hands on her hips. But by the time she was ready to throw a

The Truth about Jacob

few more choice things in his face, he took advantage of the pause in her words and fired back.

"You mind your manners, young lady! Your mother would turn over in her grave if she heard such disrespect coming from you!"

"You're the one that needs to hush, Father, before you say something we will both regret. And for your information, if Mother were here right now, it would be you who would be on the receiving end of her wrath. I'm glad she's been spared this indignity. You have separated yourself from your good judgment, and what makes it even worse is that you believed the biggest liar this side of Virginia City! That alone I'm sure would be a big disappointment to her—and as far as me, you have hurt me deeply. So until you decide to take those blinders off your eyes, I'll be waiting in my room for your apology."

Given the high level of anger her father had just displayed, Rachel could only imagine what kind of blarney Billy must have fed him. Now that she had let her father know exactly how she felt about this matter, she turned away from him. The sound of her stifled sobs followed her as she stomped her way up the staircase out of his sight.

However, in the silence that followed, Baxter could only hear the echo of Billy's words. From where he was standing he could only see the two people he loved the most rolling in the weeds acting like a couple of wild animals. They ran the risk of getting caught in the act without one thought of what would come of it if they had. Now he had deeper things to think about. What if she were to come into the family way?

Baxter's eyes suddenly filled with fury. Unable to catch his breath, he straightened his back. He couldn't bottle his pain and leave well enough alone. His only recourse now was to beat it out of the house in Jacob's direction. With his anger still on the rise he had only one thing on his mind. He would do more than just bend his ears. He had more in mind, like breaking every bone in his body.

Baxter charged down the walkway in a fit of rage to confront the young man who had just dismounted his horse. There was a battle going on in his head, but the real battle was about to begin. Byron slapped a hand on Jacob's shoulder and pulled him around to confront him face to face. With no real proof or tangible evidence to really stand on other than Billy's say so, Baxter proceeded to give Jacob a tongue-lashing loud enough for the next county to hear.

"Didn't ever figure you to be the kind of man that would take a starving man's last biscuit. She's all I have and you know that. All that's left of the memory of her mother, and you go sneaking around behind my back dragging her good name through the mud! You've made her out to be nothing more than some common floozy!"

By now the two men standing nose to nose had drawn a crowd.

"You play real dirty, boy! I'd never guessed you to be the one to end up packing such bad bones!"

Jacob was stunned to say the least. He stood by silently taking a verbal licking without lifting as much as one finger to defend himself. Baxter's voice continued to cut through the crisp air while Jacob watched in horror. In twenty years of living in the same yard with this man, he'd never once seen this side of him. His eyes were full of hate. His face was hard and cold. Jacob didn't know this man who was wrapped up in so much anger.

He saw clearly that this wasn't a matter that could be resolved with a few heated words passed back and forth. He was also aware of Baxter's unwillingness to hear anything that he might have to say right now in his own defense. The old man was much too busy drilling an angry finger into his chest. There was certainly nothing that Jacob could do right now except listen to the old man continue to vent his rage.

Whatever was to happen now would just have to happen, Jacob reasoned. It's not like he took kindly to being treated this way, quite the contrary in fact. It caught him wrong, but Baxter had been good to him in the past, so he could only hope that the old man would soon stop his lip long enough to consciously think better of what he was screaming about.

One thing became apparent, his ears hadn't deceived him earlier. The raised voices he had heard coming from inside the house screaming loud enough to wake the dead must have been Rachel and her father. And even in the face of all his immediate problems, her welfare was also one of grave concern to him at this time. He had every reason to believe that quite possibly their exchange of angry words had something to do with him.

The air fell deathly quiet. Baxter stood unblinking with his eyes glued to Jacob. His hands were gripped into tight fists. Staring at each other, he waited for Jacob's response to his accusations against him. When he offered no word in his own defense, Baxter plainly took his silence as an admission of guilt.

With that point in mind, he narrowed his eyes and coldly cut the ties between them. "Well, I've washed my hands of the likes of you! Billy was right about you all along. Under the surface of your soul beats the heart of a calculating menace to everything that's good and decent. I have no need for a man of your caliber on this ranch!"

Jacob could do nothing but stare in disbelief as Baxter stared past him as though he was deeply troubled over what he had just said. And yet he had just as much as told him he had worn out his welcome. Regardless of what the old man's face was communicating, his words revealed something entirely different.

Baxter tried to detach himself from Jacob. He figured he would be less troubled by his decision to get rid of him if he appeared unmoved and did not allow anyone to read the pain he was experiencing right off his face.

The death of their close relationship disturbed him greatly because he had always been quite fond of this young man. He had, almost from the beginning, thought of Jacob like the son he never had and found it difficult not to look upon him in any other way. However, Jacob had made it quite clear by his cold, calculating actions and the horrid way he carried them out that he certainly didn't feel the same way about him.

Jacob stood quietly with a saddened heart. Truth was, he was devoted to Baxter and thought of him almost like a father. But now it was as if he was looking into the eyes of a complete stranger, a man moved by hatred, who had no interest in finding the truth, and seeking revenge without looking further.

Jacob cried inside because of the apparent death of a long-time friendship. He saw nothing right now in this man's eyes that even remotely resembled the kind, gentle man who had personally nurtured him into adulthood. Baxter had always been there for him no matter what and now there was no sense in being disillusioned. This dear old friend no longer wanted anything to do with him and had already handed him his walking papers.

With the sun on his back, sweating profusely, Baxter raised his right hand in the air and pointed it towards town. Their eyes met for only a split second. Baxter's face was blood red. His eyes were cold, empty and unforgiving. Nothing about him resembled a Bible toting man.

"You just turn your rotten hide around and walk out of here the same way you came in! With nothing! With nothing, do you understand?"

Jacob didn't doubt for a second that Baxter meant every word he said. He looked down the barren road. His eyes squinted as the wind blew dust in his face. He ran his dry tongue over his gritty chapped lips. He turned around and with very little light left in the day walked away as quietly as he had come in when he was just five years old; with nothing but the shirt on his back.

Jacob didn't know for sure who was behind this plot to get rid of him, but if he were a betting man he'd lay seven to one odds Billy had a hand in it. He clearly saw a smirky grin on his face as he watched from a distance. Right then and there Jacob smelled trouble and figured he was at least involved in some small way.

The Truth about Jacob

Revenge never tasted so sweet, Billy marveled to himself. As Jacob turned to walk down the long dusty road stretched out before him he stayed put, deeply amused by what had just taken place. He had never expected all this to play out so easily. He could not say for sure which part of today's adventures had given him more pleasure, listening to the entire argument between Jacob and the old man, or telling the gullible old fart a big pack of lies that he swallowed with such ease.

Billy had watched the entire scolding from a short distance away, while leaning against the railing of the corral, keeping a very low profile, just biding his time. He listened carefully, and thoroughly enjoyed his involvement since it was some of the best play acting he had ever done, if he did say so himself.

Triumph over Jacob had been a long time in coming. And since Baxter had done most of the footwork for him he was able to stand back and eat it all up with the patience of Job. There was nothing left for him to do now but sit in the shade with a smooth expression on his face and just wait for Rachel to come crawling back to him. She'd forget all about Jacob after a short spell of mourning. It might take some time, but eventually she'd declare her love for him and beg for his forgiveness. *We were destined to be together*, he thought quietly. Although he wasn't much in the line of being a patient man, in her case he'd make an exception.

Baxter felt no pleasure in what he had just done. Lost in his thoughts, he could still see the shock in Jacob's eyes. Upon his slow return to the house he tried not to dwell on that young man's pain because he still had matters of his own to deal with. A problem that was much more important to worry about now because he still had to tend with Rachel, an undertaking he didn't look forward to.

The confrontation by the corral wouldn't be the last heated discussion her father would be involved in today. Rachel had had enough time to think things over and was determined, more than ever, to get to the bottom of this whole mess once and for all. From her opened bedroom window she had heard every word her father had screamed in Jacob's face. That alone tempered her anger, shifting her focus on protecting Jacob's reputation as well as her own.

Not only was she ashamed of her father's hasty actions, but she was terribly sorry she hadn't run down there long before he made an absolute fool out of himself and hurt Jacob in the process. Unfortunately, his verbal attack was nearly over by the time she realized what was really taking place. She certainly never dreamed her father would take such drastic measures against any man, especially Jacob, purely on the word of a habitual liar like Billy.

By now her temper was as thin as piecrust and she was ready to give her father a firm piece of her mind. The minute he entered the doorway she charged towards him with an accusing finger pointed at his face.

"You've got more cows than common sense, Father! Just who told you that Jacob and I have done anything inappropriate?"

Baxter stopped abruptly, blinking in surprise. He ran his fingers through his hair.

"I heard it from the horse's mouth!" he blurted. "Billy saw you two with his very own eyes!"

"You mean you heard it from the mouth of a jackass! When have you ever heard one ounce of truth come out of Billy's mouth? He doesn't know the meaning of the word and you know it!"

She's usually right, he cautiously thought to himself. He paused. "What would Billy have to gain by making up a story like that?"

"Are you really that blind? It's me he wants, Father. I can't believe you've just ignored the obvious all these years. Everybody on this ranch knows what he's after! Me, and all the trimmings that go along with that package! Everything you have worked so hard for, that's what he wants and he'll do anything in his power to get it. He doesn't care who gets hurt in the process. You, me, Jacob, it doesn't matter, don't you realize that by now? Billy figures with Jacob out of the way, you'll just hand it all over to him, no questions asked."

Rachel continued to smear a few other truths in his face, sparing absolutely none of the unpleasantries.

Baxter had always considered himself a just man, but right now he didn't feel much like a man, and least of all a fair-minded one. What Rachel had just said to him made a lot of sense and hit him hard. His thoughts again returned to the scene between he and Jacob and to every cruel accusation he'd thrown in the young man's face. He wished he could take it all back.

His eyes began to show what was really behind the door of his soul. He was a man who for one brief moment lost control of his better judgment. Feeling regret over his actions, he slumped down in a chair beside the doorway letting out a big sigh, and retreated into deep silence.

Rachel had a score to settle with her father and if the truth moved him to tears, then so be it. She wasn't finished slinging the truth in his face, she had a thing or two yet to tell him.

"And furthermore, Father, for your information, not that it's any of your business, mind you, but I would like to point out that it was me who pursued Jacob and not the other way around! He's everything any man could wish for his daughter, he's fine and decent. Regardless of how you think you see him now, I love him and nothing you can say or do will change that!"

"Why do you suppose he stood there allowing you to rake him over the coals like a worthless dog, knowing full well he hadn't done one thing wrong? Well, I'll tell you why! Just to save your face in front of all your men who think the sun rises and sets on their esteemed majesty!"

Byron sat still, slumped further down in his chair like a whipped pup, staring at his boots.

"And since we're airing the dirty laundry, I want to clear my conscience free of any hidden truths. I would have gone as far as Jacob wanted me to, just because I love him that much! But it was he who exemplified proper restraint by not moving beyond the boundaries of respectability.

"He's a gentleman in every sense of the word, just like I still believe you are. You taught him well. Now maybe it's time for you to practice what you preach. From here on out, when you want the truth, I suggest you go to someone who can at least pronounce the word!"

Byron's face was the epitome of repentance. He knew he deserved the verbal licking she had just given him. He also knew that he'd said enough for one day and there was no way he could even begin to make up for all the wrong he had done, at least right now.

Now that Rachel had set her father straight, it was time to put Billy in his place. He was responsible for everything that had happened here today and now she had a good reason to get rid of him once and for all. She felt no loyalty towards him in any way and believed by now her father had finally taken his head out of the clouds and saw him for what he really was, a disgraceful, bald-faced liar.

In less than a heartbeat she was out the door and down the pathway standing not six inches away from Billy. She had him firmly pinned to the border of the corral with a finger buried against his breastbone.

"How could you stand there and deliberately deceive my father? You know, you not only have all the earmarks of a lying skunk, but you smell like one, too! Most men have a few shortcomings, but you beat 'em all, Billy. You're just plain treacherous!"

Billy couldn't back up any further with the corral gate already pressing a crease across his shoulder blades. Sidestepping a bit did him no good, either. She just followed suit. He scarcely had the time to think twice about what was happening before she had crawled right up into his face and continued to bite his head off.

The Truth about Jacob

He kept his quiet. His eyes did not move away from her mouth. The cigarette that dangled from his lips nearly slipped from his grip when she produced another stiff finger and drilled it deeper into his chest. She acted as if she were on the verge of hysteria as she began to yell and scream every cruel remark you could imagine.

For several seconds he stood and just listened to what she had to say. Once it was clear to him that she was not going to give him any breathing room, he took it upon himself to cut her words short in order to rebuff the roar of her words. But, unfortunately, that fatal slip of the tongue opened a whole new can of worms.

"C'mon Rachel, give me a break! Jacob was no good for you. He's gone now and believe me, that's nothing to cry about. You're too good for him anyway. Besides, you know I always thought you and I would get together someday. Jacob was standing in the way of that dream. Well, he's long gone now and the looks of the place have improved already, if I say so myself!" he bragged.

It was at that point Rachel realized just how stupid he really was. Until this very moment there was no man known to her that could not outsmart a chicken. But now she could say with certainty that she was staring into the eyes of one who couldn't.

"No, I don't know anything about you and me ever getting together. And if that's what you thought, then you thought wrong! I was never your girl and never will be! After what you pulled here today, I don't ever intend to speak to you again! You know, that's been part of your problem your whole life. You have always tried to take what wasn't yours for the taking. Fact is, I've always believed that if given half a chance, you'd steal Christ right off the cross if you thought there was a profit in it!" Rachel glared at him and kicked dirt on his boots.

"Well, I've got news for you! Today you're gonna get a good taste of your own medicine. You're gonna find out what it's like to get caught up in your own evil schemes. Some people never seem to learn until it's too late!" she added. "And as for you, firing your sorry butt is long overdue!"

Then she coldly stared right through him as if he weren't even there. "You're finished around here! You've dug your last hole with your lies and Father's finally seen how your evil mind works. He's flat tired of covering up for you and has washed his hands of this whole matter."

Billy's eyes squeezed tight into little black beads and his face sucked in, in a few more places. "That's plumb crazy, Rachel! You're carrying things a little too far," he insisted. "Come on, Rachel, you're not givin' me a fair shake!" he pleaded. "We've got a good many years behind us. You just can't throw it all away like this!"

Rachel had grown impatient with Billy. "Yeah, and most of those years I'd like to forget!" she clarified. Still wide-eyed and staring at him, she added, "You made your own misery and have no one else to blame but yourself. So maybe you oughta go tell your troubles to someone who gives a hoot, 'cause I sure don't! You're wasting your time whining to me. So, I'll say it again, you're all washed up around here, Billy. Now take what belongs to you and get off my land!"

His jaw dropped with his pride now lying at his feet. Pondering over the matter for a minute he wondered just how much control on this ranch she was allowed to exert.

"What right do you have to fire me? From what I remember, your father gives the orders around here!" he protested.

In a flash of anger, Rachel blurted, "There you go trying to think on your own again. Haven't you learned your lesson yet? Apparently thinking is too dangerous for you."

Then Rachel thought hard for a moment about what he had said. Maybe it wasn't such a bad idea to let Billy see the situation at a closer hand. *Why not,* she thought to herself, *He deserves it. That would suit me just fine to see him prance into the house and get a piece of Father's mind.*

The Truth about Jacob

"Feeling real brave today are we, Billy?" Rachel barked. "Then by all means be my guest, don't let me stop you. Why don't you just march yourself right up into that house and face that old bull you just helped to turn into a jackass! You can just plead your case till the cows come home for all I care! But if I were you, I'd be thinking of one little fact you obviously overlooked. If you're in such good standings with my father, then why isn't he out here right now trying to rescue your lying hide? Or could it be he's a little tied up right now himself trying to lick his own wounds?" she taunted.

Billy felt trapped. He knew every move he made now must be made with caution, because maybe there was some truth in her words. He swallowed hard, feeling humiliated. By now he feared he was the laughing stock of this ranch because every man here just witnessed him being scolded by a woman. But he had no desire to press his luck further. She was too hot under the collar, so he kept his silence. Right now it seemed like the smartest thing to do was to leave quietly, on his own accord.

Then a fresh thought came to him. *Once they both had some time to settle down and think things over they'd surely change their minds. Besides, old man Baxter held more weight around here than she did. Hopefully he wouldn't be so willing to write him off as easily as Rachel was claiming. Tomorrow they would see things in a different light.* Rachel just shook her head in disgust as Billy awkwardly walked away sulking and muttering to himself. There were no fanfares, only a silent cheer within her as he left.

Now that she'd wiped the slate clean of the likes of Billy, another troubling question rose in her mind. What should she do about Jacob? Should she run after him and try to bring him back, or should she just give him some time to think the situation over? Then she wondered what Jacob would want her to do, instead of what her heart was telling her. She was torn with mixed feelings. After chewing on these thoughts for a minute, she decided to seek outside help and knew right where to turn. Spud could give her a definite answer, one way or the other.

Rachel made her way across a twenty foot patch of dirt and stood in front of the new top dog, now that Jacob and Billy had both been fired. Spud knew all these men on the ranch better than anyone else. She was confident he could steer her in the right direction.

Rachel paused a moment looking down at Spud. She blushed, feeling a bit awkward about what she was going to ask him, but she had no other choice because there was no other man on this ranch that was more in tune to a man's way of thinking. Nothing in his daily experiences went unobserved. Most men she knew put a great deal of stock in what he had to say, and often times had put themselves in his hands as far as getting advice went.

Rachel couldn't help but notice the spindly paths of wrinkles on his face. He was a small sized man with a nice new hat that rode comfortably on his head. Squatting down close to the ground he was tending to a horse that was almost too old to worry about. *The two of them made a good pair*, she thought.

Spud felt her presence and shot Rachel a glance. "What's on your mind, missy?" he asked. Taking into account all that had just happened he could give a pretty good guess as to what it might be.

Rachel finally found her voice so she came straight to the point. "Should I go after Jacob and bring him back?"

Spud stared back down at the ground for a moment. He hesitated before giving her his honest opinion because he feared that what he should say, she wouldn't want to hear. But putting his apprehension aside, he finally decided to be straightforward. After all, that's what she had asked for in the first place.

"All I can say is if it were me, missy, I'd want some time to myself to think. Showing back up around here so soon might look to be a sign of weakness. No man wants to come across looking like he's begging for his job back, especially from a woman," he clarified.

The Truth about Jacob

"You know, your father made it quite clear that his job weren't his for the keeping. And I can tell you one thing more for sure, Jacob's not the kind of man to come crawlin' back where he's not wanted. It's not you that Jacob's worried about and it can't be you to be the one to ask him back. Maybe it's best you give him the chance to think on what he wants to do and give that father of yours the opportunity to change his position on the matter. Time is what's needed here, little gal," he confirmed, shaking his head up and down. "So you just give it some more time and things will work out the way they're supposed to."

Rachel knew he was right. The fool notion of running after Jacob was not a good one. It would only cause him more humiliation. Even she had to admit that to herself and in her heart she knew Jacob had endured enough embarrassment for one day. It still galled her, however, to surrender to logic rather than follow her own womanly intuition. But for now, she would let age and wisdom prevail over youth and a lovesick heart.

Rachel smiled modestly and thanked Spud for his time. She then slowly turned around and headed for the house. When last she saw her father, he was visibly shaken. No doubt, right about now, he too, needed some real consoling. She was aware that he was as vulnerable as any other man and prone to make a few mistakes. Besides, she was quite certain that by now Kate had given him her two cents worth, too.

Rachel giggled to herself. That's one battle she'd kind of like to have witnessed.

Chapter 10

During the first leg of his travels, Jacob was forced to comb the surrounding area in search of a safe place to hold up for the night. He was just shy of an hour into his journey towards town when darkness fell upon him.

As he was prowling about he caught the faint scent of smoke along with the fresh aroma of coffee in the air. Jacob headed off in the same direction from which the smell seemed to be coming from. He cautiously closed in on the muffled sound of voices just ahead in a thicket of oak trees. Taking a careful look around, he moved in closer, trying to peer through the dry brush and prickly shrubbery.

Several seconds had passed with neither sound nor movement. Confident he was going in the right direction, he started forward again weaving his way through the under brush emerging into a small clearing. He poked his head up over a large, hairy branch and suddenly, to his surprise, he found himself staring down the barrel of a shotgun.

Jacob's body stiffened. He was leery of provoking the strange little man with a stone face. He had two big hairy moles on his chin and a gun that looked much too eager to speak for him.

The Truth about Jacob

Jacob had had his fill of trouble today and the possibility of bloodshed was not what he was looking for. Especially not his own, he thought reverently.

"Where you headin', boy?" the man grunted.

Jacob had a little trouble finding his voice and when he did, he stuttered.

"Ah, ah, wherever I can bed down for the night."

"What brings you way out here in the middle of nowhere sneakin' around in the dark? You got company out there with you?" he asked, stretching his neck out peering around both sides of Jacob. When he was confident that Jacob was alone, he continued to rattle off a few more questions.

"Where's your horse and gear?" His eyes quickly dropped to Jacob's hips. "Why you ain't even wearin' a gun! You crazy or something?"

"No, sir, I'm alone and I ain't crazy. I just never had a need for a gun, that's all."

Then Jacob decided to tighten his lip because there was no point in repeating his story a half dozen times. He was near certain that wherever the cowboy was escorting him, there would surely be others waiting with a long string of similar questions.

Curtis Monroe thought Jacob was about as cracked in the noggin as a man could get, so he kept a close eye on him. Since he wasn't in a position to decide what to do with him, he'd have to take him to somebody who was.

"Just you keep walkin' straight ahead, real careful like, so's I can get a better look at what sneaks around in the dark like a damn fool!"

Both men walked with synchronized steps further into the thickest part of the oak trees. Once they crossed through, they emerged into another clearing where three other men were huddled around a blazing campfire. All heads bobbed up taking a quick inventory of everything Jacob had and didn't have.

"Caught this kid here wandering around just over yonder," informed Curtis. "Fool boy don't even pack a gun! Ain't got no bedroll or horse neither."

The big, burly man, with more whiskers than face, seemed to be the one in charge and looked Jacob over real good. Then, when the mood finally struck, he took the floor.

"What might your business be, young feller?"

"Ran into a little trouble back up the road a bit. I had to leave rather sudden like, so I didn't get the chance to grab my belongings." Jacob's mouth felt dry after a short pause in the interrogation process.

With a few sour looks they all began to give him the once over again. Uncertain as to why all the scrutiny, it worried Jacob a little about what they had planned for him. And although there was a certain deceptive stillness in his face, the main man finally said, "Take a seat on the ground where you stand, boy."

The inspection resumed again once Jacob knelt to the ground and settled back against a tree. Thoughtfully he examined the leaves and dirt around him for any unwanted predators.

Intermittently the men began to pass around a little small talk amongst themselves. When they weren't whispering and snickering low to each other, they continued to glance over every so often at Jacob.

The stocky man seated nearest to the man in charge looked to be the closest to Jacob's age. He couldn't have been more than seven or eight years his senior. He seemed to be the least interested in what brought Jacob to their camp so late in the evening. He asked very few questions.

The other man was a wiry fellow and hardly held still for more than two seconds. He was constantly looking over his shoulder in the direction of every little sound. He must have gotten up at least a half dozen times in less than ten minutes to either relieve himself or check on the horses. His stature was stunted and his tangly blonde hair, that looked like it hadn't seen a comb in a week, hung over his ears

The Truth about Jacob

As pleasantly as possible, the boss man explained to Jacob. "You can grab yourself a little grub and hold up here for the night if you take a hankerin' to. But we're pullin' up stakes in the mornin', and that don't include you," he declared.

"Lefty," he barked, "get the kid a cup so he can grab some of that coffee, if that's what you wanna call it, and some grub."

Jacob was conscious of their stares, but tried to ignore them as he ate. What they were looking for, he sure didn't know. He continued to spoon beans into his mouth. They tasted pretty good with the stale bread Lefty had given him. He flushed it all down with coffee that tasted more like charcoal. When he was finished with his meal, he thought it best to at least thank them for their hospitality.

"I'm beholden to you men 'till you're better paid," he said. Then Jacob waited for some sort of response. When not one word came back in his direction, he quietly picked up a sturdy stick off the ground and started prying off small patches of dried mud that was caked to the bottom of his old boots, boots that were worn down at the heels.

Jacob welcomed the warm blanket that the smaller man called A.D. had tossed him. Long after Jacob had nestled in for the night on a bed of leaves like the rest of the tired cowpokes, he could still hear a murmuring of voices.

It occurred to him at that time that this was quite a strange group of men he had come across. There was always at least one man awake at all times left to guard the others as they slept. No man there offered a reason why and he most assuredly wouldn't be asking. They kept watch in shifts and that seemed to work well for quite a spell. However, sometime long before daybreak, their last man on duty dozed off, leaving them unprotected and wide open for the possible trouble they were so obviously trying to avoid. The obvious happened just before the sun peeked its head above the horizon.

The snoozing comrades didn't have a chance to reach for their guns before a very angry posse crept up quietly and surrounded them. Completely at their mercy, they watched in horror as the men with badges rummaged around, searching through everything in the camp. Some of the lawmen were taking a real good check of the two-dozen or more horses that stood with their tails to the wind just ten steps beyond where they all had slept. The horses were huddled together fenced in by a makeshift corral constructed of ropes tied to a long string of close-knit trees. The lawmen were weeding through the stock, carefully examining the identifying brands burnt on their backsides.

The man with the biggest silver badge pinned to his chest gave a hardy nod to a few of the other men, who in turn, seemed to know exactly what that meant.

The clean-shaven, husky sheriff poked around some more before approaching the rest of the anxious crowd. Calmly strolling over to the large gathering of men, he confirmed, "These are part of Hanson's herd alright. Looks like we've caught ourselves some no good horse thieves, boys!"

Jacob glanced around the arena of angry faces only to see additional armed men standing between the trees, bringing the total number of men in the posse to twelve. All of the cowboys looked to be quite dusty and tired. He concluded they must have been traveling for days without much rest.

Offhand, judging by his first survey, Jacob figured that every man there had been sworn in to carry out justice and was pretty eager to get on with what had to be done. Jacob knew only too well how a just sentence was carried out. The "law of the short rope," governed the mode of living modeled in this day and age. Not necessarily the best way, but the only one practiced in the absence of organized law and order when horse thieves were captured so far away from home.

One by one, the angry men hoisted the thieves on their horses with their hands tied behind their backs. The Kangaroo Court didn't waste any time listening to the bandit's lame excuses and pleas of innocence. Then, slowly but surely, the number narrowed down to just Jacob.

Jacob could only watch in horror as the last man before him quit kicking his feet and frothing at the mouth. With the relief of A.D's bowels, he knew he was dead. It was his turn now. Jacob breathed deeply and shut his eyes and prayed.

The sheriff examined Jacob carefully as if sizing him up. His face reddened with a frown. He spoke in a tone of deep remorse, obviously getting a little something off his chest that bothered him.

"I ain't never hung a feller as young as you, boy. Leaves a real bad taste in my mouth that I gotta do this, but you're the one that made the choice to pick up with the wrong kind of friends. Bad business deal, son, real bad! The next time I talk to Hanson's widow, it will be to tell her we took care of the no goods that murdered her husband just for the hell of it."

Jacob was in no position to stall around and that meant he had to set the record straight before he, too, became buzzard bait. So with every ounce of strength he could muster, he shouted sternly at the sheriff.

"I didn't kill nobody, and I didn't even know these cowboys until last night. I swear I didn't do nothing wrong. I needed a place to stay for the night so they offered me a meal and a warm fire to bed down by."

"Well, that's as good as any lie I've ever heard"

The sheriff grunted a few times, spat on the ground and completely ignored Jacob's plea for clemency. He then turned to the man called Colby and growled, "Stretch him up, right along with the rest of this dirty lot!"

After Colby placed the noose around Jacob's neck, two other men grabbed him by the arms and tossed him on the back of a black stallion that accepted his weight with ease.

"Say your prayers, boy, cause you're about to meet your maker," the sheriff blurted.

"I'm telling you, I didn't have no hand in stealing those horses! You can ride just an hour south of here and ask at the Baxter ranch. They'll back me up and tell you the same thing."

"Could be an ambush waitin' out there and we don't like surprises. Get it over with, Colby," the sheriff ordered, turning his head away. He never liked to watch a man fight and kick like a chicken with its head cut off.

Jacob couldn't deceive himself. They were a posse bent on revenge and they weren't listening to anybody. These men meant to sift him out right along with the rest of these guys who went down pleading for mercy.

Suddenly Jacob saw his life flash before his eyes and he knew his own fate. He also had a new understanding at to why God never intended for man to know his own future. He thought reverently of God's wisdom, wishing he had used some of his own before bedding down with a bunch of horse thieves.

Jacob's palms were slick with sweat. He gave his best effort to wiggle and twist his hands free of the ropes tied snugly around his wrists. All his hopes were dashed when the skin beneath the rough twine rubbed raw and he began to feel the blood drip down his hand and onto the horse. He swallowed hard and tried to prepare himself the best he could to the same fate that befell the other men.

That might have been the case for Jacob, if it hadn't been for his guardian angel sneaking through the trees watching the whole scene unfold from a short distance away. During all the noise of the hooting and hollering of pleading horse thieves, not one man paid any mind to the large lady who snuck up silently not ten feet away with her gun aimed and loaded.

Kate didn't waste any time shooting the pinky finger right off the eager beaver jerking the rope tighter around Jacob's neck. She fired a few more shots that buffeted the heads of his pals simply to grab their undivided attention. In no time at all every eye in the place was fixed on the fat woman full of fury.

The Truth about Jacob

Kate locked an icy glare on the wounded man sucking on his bloody stub who was still standing much too close to Jacob for Kate's comfort. He foolishly reached down for his gun encased in a leather holster strapped cleverly out of sight behind his right thigh.

Kate was aware of his intentions and straightened her aim directly at his head. She questioned him angrily. "You in a big hurry to get shot again?"

He shook his head from side to side as if to say no and then brought his hand back up into her full view.

"I'm the owner of this land and let's see how good you are at gettin' out of here in record time before I decide to take the rest of your hand off, and your head too!"

The mean looking hombre, standing just to the right of the trigger-happy Colby, tried to sneak a run down his pants leg for a gun he had hidden behind his lower holster strap.

"Nuh-uh, don't even think about it! Reaching for that pistol will be your last harebrained idea!" Her voice, like her eyes, blazed with fury.

"He's a no good horse thief just like the rest of these guys!" he protested. "They killed a man stealing these horses. You're makin' a big mistake by tryin' to protect him. You're just gonna wind up in hot water yourself. Don't matter if you are a woman. If you become party to this crime, then we'll hang you, too!

"He's no more a horse thief than I'm a beauty queen! And you ain't got a rope strong enough to hang me, you old fool!"

Kate scanned the faces of all the men just waiting for their next move.

"Now when did these horses come up missin' anyway?" she asked.

"Four days ago. We've been trackin' these pistoleros ever since," the sheriff piped up.

"Is that right?" Kate shot the sheriff a snarly look. "Who's the bright one that's leading this pack of amateurs?"

The sheriff puffed his chest out and said, "I'm the sheriff!"

"Four days ago this boy was with me," she confirmed.

"I don't buy that. I don't believe one word you say," the sheriff fired back.

"You knucklehead, I really don't give a rat's ass what you believe. But you better think long and hard about this. If I hadn't spotted your campfire last night and come snoopin' around this morning to see who was squattin' on my land, then you'd a hung an innocent boy! Did any of you so-called experts by any chance take the time to count how many horses were actually carrying riders? I'm assuming of course you know how that's done!"

That question caused a healthy vein of skepticism to rise. A few doubters shrunk back into their shells along with the sheriff who had been acting high and mighty until Kate brought that question into the light. Some of the members of the posse began to question one another with their eyes.

Kate spotted the truth on at least five faces. She figured it had all boiled down to that they saw what they wanted to see.

"That's what I thought! Guess you boys aren't in the habit of piecin' all the facts together before you start handin' out neckties."

The only sound heard was the swishing of horses' hooves amongst the dried leaves. No man offered a rebuttal. Kate had seen too much in her lifetime to doubt that they'd actually hang her if given the chance, but her eyes swept over the entire group in a quick measuring of glances missing nothing. She kept her gun ready in position just in case.

"Now I didn't come here huntin' for trouble, but if that's what you want, then I can oblige you!" she explained as she lifted her rifle slightly to the left aiming straight at the sheriff's head. "If any man here don't see things my way, then he's a damned fool and sure don't give a hoot if he sees tomorrow. Now you can bet your bottom dollar that when I squeeze my trigger, I don't miss my aim. Just ask old stubby finger over there," she pointed out.

The Truth about Jacob

The sheriff offered no comment. He just stood there with a cold stare on his face.

"So whatcha say, how 'bout you boys all just back on out of here, real careful like, and take your horses with you? And take those horse thieves, too! I don't need their stinkin' carcasses smellin' up my land!"

Kate didn't want any gunplay, so she quickly reminded the sheriff again of something he shouldn't forget. "Oh, Sheriff, by the way, be sure to check those horse prints along your way back out. That should kill any doubt you may still have about this young man's innocence."

The sheriff, who was still a might suspicious of Jacob's possible involvement in the horse heist hadn't as yet made a move to leave. But the fat woman's attitude of indifference finally influenced his change of heart. After she pulled back slightly on her hammer, he reluctantly gave his order to saddle up.

He raised a brow. His face was past the pink stage when he tipped his hat at her and bellowed, "Let's get out of here, boys. We got what we came after."

Kate was well aware that one wrong move might spook the horse that Jacob was still sitting on. She quickly captured the attention of the only man left standing close to him.

"You there, small fry, come back over here and loosen the ropes around this boy's wrists. You're all makin' me and that horse there a bit nervous!" she added.

He approached Jacob with a quick nervousness in his steps. He removed a small knife from his hip pocket and with little exertion cut the rope. He stepped back and took the liberty of walking away, which pleased the female sergeant-at-arms.

Then Kate watched carefully as they all lined up like an army of ants and ambled off single file through the thick forest. She was sure the thought still crowded some of their minds that they were leaving behind one guilty man, but Kate didn't give a hoot as long as they got off her land.

She watched them snake their way through the trees, keeping a hair trigger on them all until she was sure the coast was clear before lowering her gun. After their shadows fell below the hump in the prairie floor, she finally felt safe enough to take her sights off of the group of whipped puppies.

Jacob sat stiff as a board with the rope still wrenched tight around his neck. His mouth felt parched, his voice mute. All he could think about was that he was thankful it wasn't his dead body dangling, lifeless, from one of those stolen horses.

"Well! What are you waitin' for Jacob, Christmas?" Kate asked sarcastically. "Now if I were you, I'd be getting' that necktie you're wearin' there off before that gang of angry lawmen decide to change their minds and come back after a piece of your hide!"

With trembling hands, Jacob removed the scratchy rope from around his neck. He lunged forward and gathered the reins to the black horse he was sitting on. He turned its head and followed directly behind Kate's heels, back out a short distance, where her horse and rig were tied to a tree.

Wasting no time, Kate climbed up onto her buckboard, pulling hard on the rigging. With her hands flipping the reins in the air, she circled around a few big clumps of trees and then headed straight for her homestead.

There was certainly nothing fragile about Kate, Jacob thought reverently. *She played hard and worked hard and made every moment count for something. She was no ordinary woman.* After what she had just done here today, she was his hero that was for sure.

Kate had led an almighty fast race back to her ranch because she was already late as it was. Jacob and his horse were sweating profusely by the time they got there. Jacob looked around. The place sure was a welcome sight. In fact, it was a mighty fine sight, especially since he didn't figure he'd ever see it again.

He had ridden within an eye's good view of the house on several occasions, but didn't actually stop in. Oh, he tried to

The Truth about Jacob

once, but Ma was kicking up dust all around his horse taking pot shots at him. It was a known fact that if she didn't recognize a man who was prowling around her place, then he instantly became fair game. No doubt about it, that old lady could shoot the wart off the end of a man's nose if she took a mind to. And since her eyesight had failed her somewhat over the years, there would be nothing left of the head either, Jacob figured.

Kate guided Jacob up to the front steps of her house. She was still pretty aggravated and spoke to him rather sharply. "Now if you think you can stay out of trouble long enough to get a few chores done around here, then you're more than welcome to stay with Ma and me as long as you want."

Jacob's face warmed slightly upon hearing her words. He noticed there was gladness in her eyes as she spoke, so he knew Kate was not bothered with him as much as she let on. Being a little rough around the edges, it was just her way of blowing off some steam. He was quite certain that her verbal potshots were directed more at the sheriff and the barbaric way he and the posse had handled things than they were at him.

Jacob had been run off the only home he'd known since he was six, all his belongings were confiscated, and he'd been nearly hung. All this happened within a short period of time. So right now, as he took another sweeping look around and this place, it sure did look good.

He felt beholden to Kate. He passed her a generous smile and struggled to find the right words to say. "If it weren't for you, Kate, I wouldn't be standing here right now. I sure don't know how to thank you enough for saving my life. It's awful good of you to put me up like this."

"Oh fiddlesticks!" she said. "You'd a done the same for me if the shoe had been on the other foot and you know it. Now let's not go makin' a mountain out of a molehill here. You just mend some of these broken down fences around this place and we'll call it square. Besides, having you around will take some of the load off my back."

Jacob could easily see eye to eye with Kate on the matter of her needing some extra help around here. Just about the same time he was nodding in agreement, a wrinkled lady, as old as Methuselah, crept through the open doorway onto the porch.

Ma's eyes scaled Jacob like a fish. She greeted him, "Good mornin' to ya!"

"Ma, you remember Jacob Fowler, don't ya? He's the young feller that used to keep company with Doc from time to time on his house calls. Seems he somehow played out his welcome at the Baxter ranch, so we'll be putting him up here with us for a spell."

"Of course I remember the boy!" she retorted. "I'm not deaf and blind you know! You've been boasting about this youngin' since he first showed up around these parts."

Ma's focus returned to Jacob. She was still bothered by his reasons for leaving the Baxter ranch. "What kinda trouble you in?" she asked making a real show of looking him over.

"Now, Ma, you just leave the boy be. He's answered enough questions for one day and he surely don't need more from a nosey old woman like you. You just make him feel welcome while I'm gone and don't go meddling in his affairs!" Kate warned.

"Oh, quit your complainin'!" Ma barked, as she continued to size up Jacob and ignore her daughter's demands.

Kate turned her buckboard back around in the direction of the Baxter ranch. Trying hard to make up for lost time, she barreled over the rough road with lightening speed, treating it like it was a smooth surface. Of course, her cargo of freshly ironed linens would beg to differ.

Jacob glanced around the place again. It was plain to see that the house could use a good face-lift. The barn could stand some fixing, too, with a few boards missing here and there. *Actually, the barn looked older than Ma, if that was possible,* he thought, grinning to himself. Somebody had tried to patch the well

The Truth about Jacob

house, but failed miserably and the outhouse looked beyond help.

Ma wasted no time tapping into Jacob's personal affairs again. "You don't look old enough to be out on your own. How old are you?" she pried.

"You don't look old enough to be Kate's ma," he quickly returned.

"I'm well past my prime and feeling every bit of it," she blurted. "Now you listen here, baby face! If you think payin' me a compliment is gonna get you anywhere you got another thing to think about!" she said, trying not to smile.

"Sorry, ma'am, I didn't mean to offend you. I tend to say things as I see 'em." Jacob's face split into a sly grin. He was aware that Ma was trying to camouflage her flattered smile. He also remembered all too well just how Doc used to handle this tough old bird.

"Where's your belongings, you fool boy? Nobody roams these parts without a good supply of food and water! And where's your bedroll?"

"I kinda got a little out of sorts with Mr. Baxter. You could say he asked me to leave rather sudden like. I didn't have much of a choice about what went with me. It was of his choosing to send me afoot without my belongings, but I'm hoping it's just a temporary setback," he added.

Ma beetled her brow. She still carried a grudge against Mr. Rich Fancy Pants, *as hot as a chili pepper*, she thought. She had little good to say about the man ever since he tried to sweet talk Kate into signing some stupid paper regarding water rights. Whether a selfish proposal or not, she was still aggravated at him over a matter that should have been water under the bridge by now.

Ma stood bent over with her hands on her hips. "Don't surprise me none. Baxter's a good man, but can be a darned fool too just like most men. Got a wild bunch working for him and there's a real scalawag leadin' that pack. I'm sure, Billy the Brat had his hands in the batter somewhere, since he's full of nothing but greed and no good!"

Fireworks seemed to burst from her eyes as she spoke his name. "He's a real rotten egg, that one is! You're better off to stay clear of that little worm. Why, if I had a face as ugly as his, I'd kill myself!"

Jacob assumed Ma knew Billy well by the way she went on about him. He was also quite certain that Kate had already informed her about what had happened at the ranch yesterday.

"Ah, don't worry about it! You're too good for the likes of that bunch, anyway!"

Jacob suspected she held something against somebody at the ranch besides Billy. He didn't have the slightest inkling who it may be and she sure wasn't about to elaborate any further. It dawned on him that Ma could be the type of stubborn lady that would hold a grudge for a lifetime, if she took a mind to.

"Well, don't just sit there on your haunches like a big bump on a log! Put your horse in the barn while I get you some grub. You ain't et this mornin', have ya?"

"No, ma'am."

"Well then get on with ya! The sooner we get you fed and those wounds on your wrists tended to, the sooner you can start earnin' your keep around here!"

With those words having been said, Ma turned around to inch her way back into the house.

Jacob made his way to the barn. Even though it was a warm day, he was relieved to discover that it was actually quite cool inside. Each stall, six total, were still lined with layers of hay leftover from last night's feeding. The walls were made of thick wood, the roof was higher than most, and there was a loft that extended from one end of the barn to the other.

Jacob stripped the leather from his horse and placed it down on a sawhorse in one of the stalls. He paused for a moment, bracing his hands against the wall, and peeked through a large

The Truth about Jacob

crack in the board. He chuckled slightly as he viewed the few animals that helped to keep this ranch up and running. Most were huddled under a cluster of trees.

There was one scraggly plow horse that looked sickly, two measly milk cows and three mighty fine looking ponies. He also counted six stray kittens scattered about and a seventh one under the porch badgering the daylights out of a mangy old dog trying to nap.

Having already removed the rest of the gear from his horse, Jacob hung the bridle on a hook along side a handful of Kate's other farm equipment. It occurred to him, after suddenly feeling the grit on his hands, that he hadn't even had the opportunity to wash the sleep from his eyes this morning. It didn't feel right to just plop down at Ma's table without first cleaning the sweat and dust from his hands and face.

He walked out of the barn and edged toward the well house. He took the initiative to pour some of the water he drew up from its depths into a large gourd bowl. He drank some of the cold water before splashing his face and dipping his hands. The well was conveniently located, not fifteen feet from the entrance of the house. It was a mere twenty-five feet from the barn and it was cold enough to freeze his day old whiskers.

Jacob's footsteps creaked the old boards on the porch as he stepped through the open doorway. He shuffled forward, peering around the corner, looking for Ma. He spotted her fussing over some fried apples in an iron skillet. He paused briefly to study the interior of the house. Everything looked real nice and clean. Nothing was done halfway, which impressed Jacob because, he felt no job was worth doing unless you did it right.

The walls were constructed by someone who obviously loved to work with wood. Each piece was dovetailed and all edges were perfectly matched. The two adjoining rooms each had a door hung by iron hinges. There was a two-inch gap under each one between the surface of the floor and the bottom edge of the door to allow for easy closure over the top of thick, hand tied rugs. Each room had at least one window with floral curtains hanging, curtains that definitely had kept one woman's hands busy for quite a spell.

Jacob felt a gurgling whirl in his empty stomach the minute he spotted the scrumptious meal Ma had placed neatly on a small, wooden table fit for four. He was quite sure the bacon, eggs and potatoes on the plate were left over from the breakfast Ma and Kate had shared together, earlier. There was certainly no way a slow moving woman such as Ma could have cooked a meal of this proportion in such a short span of time.

Warmed over food suited him just fine because, by now, he had more than just a California appetite. It was more than any hungry man could ask for, especially since earlier this morning he didn't think he'd live long enough to see another sunrise much less enjoy a breakfast this plentiful.

As Jacob entered the house, Ma could easily see that he was mighty hungry by the speed in which he sat down and pulled his chair up to the table. After giving her another grateful smile he quickly emptied his plate, and then proceeded to devour the extra portion of potatoes left on the platter in the center of the table as well.

Ma settled her weary bones down in a small chair across the room. It looked as if she had sat in that same chair for decades because of the way her tiny frame fit so nicely into its depths. *It had definitely seen some use all right*, Jacob thought to himself.

The black dress she wore was now faded to a drab gray and hung like a loose flour sack on her skinny body. The moth eaten white shawl draped across her shoulders certainly didn't provide much warmth for her aged bones. Ma's face was tanned like a leather hide with quite a collection of wrinkles. The skin on her hands looked paper thin, and there was a scar across the full length of her left wrist that Jacob was sure could tell a story of many hardships suffered over the years. Her head was adorned

The Truth about Jacob

with salt and pepper hair, pulled back in a pea-sized bun. Ma smelled of stale coffee and had traces of chew still stuck to the corners of her mouth.

She sat quietly lacing small strips of thread together, obviously quite adept at crocheting. And, of course, the old charmer continued to observe every move Jacob made as he ate with a passion, stuffing the last morsel of food into his mouth.

"My goodness sakes alive, you're tearin' into that meal like you ain't et in a week! You're as savage as a meat axe, you are."

Jacob grunted out a chuckle and continued to chew. He was sure it wasn't the first time she saw a man shovel food into his mouth so fast that he couldn't taste it.

Ma really got a big kick out of the way Jacob gobbled his food. It's not as if she hadn't watched a hungry man before, she laughed under her breath. After all, Mr. Parker, her dearly departed husband, God rest his soul, used to polish his meals off before she had a chance to take two bites.

Ma suddenly got serious as eating habits were forgotten. "How'd you come by those raw bracelets carved into your wrists? Did you have a run in with the law? Is there a problem I should know about?" she asked with her eyes glued to the rope burns exposed on his wrists.

Finishing his last sip of coffee and wiping his mouth off on the sleeve of his shirt, he thought for a minute and then offered her an explanation. "Picked up with some strangers last night that turned out to be horse thieves. Darned near got myself hung right along with them early this morning when the sheriff and his posse caught up with them. If Kate hadn't come along when she did, then I'm afraid I wouldn't be here right now eating these fine vittles."

Ma cleared her throat and grunted, "Well, that's one way to start your day."

"I sure hope I never see another day like this one."

"Tough times seem to follow you around, don't they? I guess you should thank the Good Lord for looking out for you, especially when you were a young tyke. It would have been much rougher on you if it hadn't been for Doc. He wasn't the kind of man who would stand by and watch an animal mistreated, much less a homeless little boy.

"They're a sorry lot in that town, anyway. Nothin' good comes out of those folks around there 'ceptin fightin', drinkin' and chasin' them loose women around in that sin-filled rum-hole!

"According to Doc, those numbskulls kept the gossip flyin' about you for months on end after you wandered back into town when your family disappeared. The town folks were just dead set on tryin' to pin that candy business on you. Apparently old sticky-fingers bragged about you takin' the blame for what he'd done. Only rumors, mind you, but I heard it from a good source that old Sam caught wind of what Billy did, and he beat his ornery butt right through town and back again."

"You know, Kate and I would have took you in ourselves if it hadn't been for me bein' waylaid with a real nasty bug of some kind. Took a good year or more after that just to get my strength back."

"Doc was a good man," he said. "Few men could fill his shoes, I might add. He'd spend every waking hour helping anyone in need if he had to and you'd never hear him complain. I don't know what would have become of me if he hadn't taken me in when my folks disappeared."

"Well, I want you to know we'd a put you up in the barn if we'd a had to, just in case no one else offered to help. As it turned out Doc took care of things just fine all by himself." Ma sighed and cleared her throat thinking back all those years.

Jacob could see the pain in her eyes.

"That old man had a soft heart, I don't deny him that, but he had another side to him, too; a real spunky side that could lift a weary soul. He had a way of healing what ailed you with just one of his goofy old jokes."

The Truth about Jacob

Ma stiffened a lip and quickly changed the somber mood of the moment, as if she wanted to hide her true feelings. And, quicker than she could catch her breath, she began to rib the old fellow's memory as if he were standing not two feet away from her and all ears.

"Didn't know nothin' about medicine, though! Told him so, too! Why, I was tempted to fill that old fart's britches with lead many a time just tryin' to shut him up! He was always arguin' with me about what I should and shouldn't do. Always tryin' to push his big miracle cure-alls in my face. That fancy schoolin' of his gave him the bright idea he could fix almost anything if he took a mind to. Oh, he had a right to try, but I told him that weren't no magic wand he had to work with. He had just plain old hands like the rest of us have."

"Of course, no doubt in my mind that Doc truly thought he could perform miracles. So I finally quit arguing the point, since it really didn't hurt no one for him to believe it was so. Why, my pappy knew more about healin' than most of those schooled fellows, and he never picked up a book in his life!"

Her voice cracked and she shook her head slightly. "That old fool's thinkin' cap got mighty slow there, towards the end. He looked normal enough, but I knew better. It was difficult for him to even make his way outdoors to get a bit of fresh air, much less take care of even his most basic of needs. He never mentioned a word about his problems. Not once did he complain. Things he'd normally done with ease had finally become near impossible. Caused, I supposed, by a stroke or some such thing. He just slowly wasted away, strapped to his bed."

It was only when Ma caught her breath for a second time that Jacob noticed her tears. Her eyes looked past him with a look that seemed to say her great loss was still hurting more than she cared to admit.

"Miss the old poop, I do. Thought that old man would live forever! Guess nobody lives forever 'ceptin me. He passed on not long after you went to live at the Baxter Ranch, you know."

Jacob nodded his head, but their eyes never met. His sadness went unnoticed by Ma, since she was seized by her own fond memories of the man she cared more about than most people knew. Jacob began to wonder if their connection was stronger than just a lifelong friendship.

"He was right all along for not keepin' me," Jacob admitted. "I'm inclined to believe that he had a good idea his days were numbered. I also think he knew it long before he made all the arrangements with Baxter to take me in," he relayed.

Ma nodded her head in agreement.

"I never paid much attention to it at the time, but he did rub his head a lot as if it bothered him in a bad way. He took quite a large number of little white pills. I asked him once, if they were candy. He just laughed and said it was special medicine for old men who were too old to grow hair on their heads. He even went as far as letting me feel the tiny stubbles on top of his, that he adamantly claimed were starting to sprout up," Jacob let out a hearty laugh. "Why that head was as bald as a baby's butt, but I was too young not to believe every word he said."

Jacob lowered his head and sighed. "I believe Doc knew all along that he'd end up passin' on before I was old enough to fend for myself. That was one of the roughest years of my life. After that, I found myself getting used to the idea of expecting disappointments, but I'd have to admit losing Doc for good was one of the hardest to accept."

"Something real bad went wrong inside his stubborn skull. He just chose not to share it with anyone, not even me," she declared.

It occurred to Jacob that Ma was not a particularly good actress. He could easily see through her crusty exterior. She had just talked a blue streak about a man she claimed was just a close friend. Never once did she mention the man she partnered with for more than half of her life. Her devotion to Doc was more than skin deep. Her words and actions seemed to support his suspicions that maybe they had been in love.

The Truth about Jacob

Ma's runny eyes narrowed and she licked her dry lips. "You best be makin' some tracks outside and start earnin' that meal you just swallowed whole before Kathryn gets back. She runs a pretty tight ship around here you'll sure find that out soon enough! Now I'm no spring chicken anymore, you know, with these bum legs of mine, so I'm not much help with the chores." Ma cocked one eyebrow to an upside down V on her forehead and added. "But I'm still plenty able to bark out a few orders with the best of em! So you get! Ya hear?"

"Don't you worry none, ma'am, about the chores. They're as good as done," he smiled and said in response.

"Folks around here call me Widow Parker," she said with her head held high in pride. "My friends call me Ma. It'll be Ma to you."

Jacob was touched by the honor she had just bestowed upon him. With that thought in mind, he calmly rose from his chair and walked over to the strange little bird and pecked her on the cheek with a soft kiss.

That kind gesture caught her by surprise and blushed her rosy. She rubbed her eyebrows and blinked several times trying to conceal her quiet embarrassment, but Jacob could tell she still loved every minute of it.

"I'm truly beholden to you, Ma," he said gently.

"Oh, for pity sakes alive! Get on with ya before you have us both bawlin' our eyes out!"

"You can trust that I'll do my best to please both you and Kate," he promised.

"I don't doubt that a bit." she added softly, in spite of herself.

As Jacob turned around and headed for the door he was thankful in thought. He considered himself a mite lucky to be standing here. For that major miracle he gave half the credit to Ma for raising such a smart daughter. A daughter, who in a very short amount of time, had saved his life, gave him a place to hang his hat, and just pure and simply made his life a whole lot better. Especially since earlier this very day it wasn't worth any more than the price of the rope it would take to hang him with.

No job was too big or too small for Jacob. So with duty calling, he walked briskly out through the doorway to do what he could with what little time was left in the day.

Chapter 11

Over the course of the ensuing weeks Jacob had taken care of most of the chores he considered to be pressing. The corral gate which was barely hanging by a thread was now fixed and working properly. The fencing around the barn had been completely rebuilt. He removed the rusted wire holding the well house intact and replaced it with some decorative rockwork.

The days were getting shorter. Most of the trees in the surrounding area had already begun to shed their leaves. The weather was changing, and fall was doomed to an early death.

From the first day he set foot on this ranch Jacob had worked long, hard hours trying to accomplish the goals he set for himself. His body paid a high price for all his efforts through aching muscles that screamed with pain, but in the end it was worth all the sacrifice. Before long, he had this ranch looking better than it had in thirty years.

Some of his time was spent in another capacity. On Sundays, when Kate was home all day long, getting to know the two ladies on a more personal basis was something that just happened naturally. Both women quickly became a very important part of his life, each in a very different way.

He often found himself piddling around inside the house doing frivolous things he'd never dreamed he'd be doing, but amazingly enough discovered them to be quite rewarding. Of course, he'd never breathe a word to a soul that he actually crocheted a potholder all by himself.

Jacob had his early morning chores behind him before the daylight had a chance to fully peak its head over the hillside. As the streaks of sunlight grew more visible, all he wanted to do now was to tear into the breakfast Kate had been working on for nearly an hour.

From one pan to the next she scrambled eggs, fried potatoes and tossed pancakes. She was capable of turning three-day old table scraps into a well-manicured banquet that would send a river of saliva flowing down his throat.

Once seated at the table, Jacob began to stuff his mouth with some crisp fried potatoes, cooked just the way he liked them, with their jackets still on. Right off the bat, a heated discussion ensued. Jacob hunkered down in his little corner of the table and continued to attack his food, ignoring the word slinging.

Ma and Kate would argue over everything, from too much salt on the spuds to who snored the loudest last night. At the present time Ma was complaining about breakfast being late.

"The pancakes are too cold!" Ma said.

"Then blow some of your hot air on them!" Kate returned.

"Only a fool would say something that stupid."

"Only an old fool would complain about cold hotcakes."

"Mind your manners, young lady!" Ma demanded.

"Mind your own business. Just eat up and quit spinnin' the yarn! Can't you see you're disturbing Jacob here. Poor boy's just barely pickin' through his food," Kate teased.

Ma cast Kate a look that could kill. Kate threw one back.

Jacob shoveled in another mouthful and silently held his chuckles to himself. His eyes never met their gaze until the storm had passed and they finally began to exchange

The Truth about Jacob

pleasantries. All the while he marveled over the fact that Ma was a small eagle with a big talent for talk.

When the breakfast mess was completely cleaned up and put away, the trio retired to the front porch like they usually did on Sunday mornings. They chatted about almost everything and of course most of the conversation shifted to Ma's corner. She lounged in a small chair whittled out of an old tree trunk that her husband of thirty-seven years had carved for her in the three years before he died.

In Homer's younger years he had been an industrious man. He had a true love for working with wood. Pa, as he was called, could whittle his way to town and back with oodles of energy to spare. Folks came from miles around to barter for some of his goods, which included everything from kitchen utensils to every size bed to fit every size body, even Kate's. In return for his wood products, Pa would swap for horses, cows, pigs and anything else of value.

The chair he carved for himself, which sat for thirty-seven years on this very porch, Ma had buried along with him and his faithful dog, Brodie, who passed on just two days after he did.

Pa was seventeen years her senior and was the only man to ever share her bed. She couldn't remember a day without perfect harmony in their marriage. She claimed his problem with stuttering offered a great deal of assistance in those amiable years. He couldn't speak fast enough to keep up with her.

As the morning sun was easing slowly behind a large number of clouds trying to formulate, Jacob opened his first bit of conversation." What a view you have from here. I can see everything clearly as far as the wind blows," he marveled.

"Yeah, it's just a helluva thrill!" Ma concluded sarcastically, looking directly at the old outhouse.

Jacob squished a mosquito flat to his arm with a rapid slap of his palm. Picking it off, he flicked it aside. "Dang, these long-legged blood suckers you grow out here carry quite a grudge, don't they?"

"They're a little on the hungry side all right," Kate agreed laughingly as one buzzed at her ear. She flipped it away with her hand and continued to work her nimble fingers unwinding a fresh spool of yarn.

Staring out over the large expanse of countryside, Jacob soaked in the breathtaking view. His thoughts settled on Rachel because she, too, possessed that same kind of delicate balance in her beauty. He missed her so much and truly hoped that they would one day have the opportunity to iron out all their problems.

Deep within his stomach there emerged a bit of a monster. His belly began to grumble, so he switched his position several times in his chair trying to coax it to settle down. When that effort failed to ease his discomfort, he loosened his belt a notch or two. It occurred to him then that he had simply eaten too much.

Ma took a full sweep of Jacob's face and saw the pained expression he carried, which juggled her curiosity. She pulled her eyes completely away from the overalls she was mending for Jacob and began to interrogate him.

"What you thinkin' about, boy?" Ma pried. "Something's sure got you stirred up! Looks like you're sittin' in the anxious seat or do you just have ants in your pants?"

Much to Ma's dismay, Kate turned a sharp eye towards her and promptly scolded her. "Ma, it ain't proper to ask a man what he's thinking! Now leave him to his own thoughts!"

Ma ignored Kate's remark. She took in a heavy breath, leaned over her spittoon and spat into its depth. She wiped her mouth with her hanky and then scoured Jacob's face again.

"He looks like a young pup still wet behind the ears to me!" she pointed out.

"You better put your eye specks back on, Ma. Jacob's no longer a little boy. Why, he's well past eighteen now. Don't let that baby face fool ya. Now mind your manners and quit being so meddlesome!"

The Truth about Jacob

Ma squinted her beady eyes to examine him even more closely to see if he actually could grow a beard. Of course she was at a slight disadvantage because her glasses were still lying on top of her nightstand. Most of the time Ma refused to wear her glasses simply because they irritated the fragile tissues on the bridge of her nose. She concluded that her glasses did more justice to her nightstand anyway.

Ma was not willing to lose an argument now, or anytime, no matter how trivial. So with that in mind she snapped right back at Kate. "Oh, hornswaggle! This whipper-snapper still looks green under the collar and I'll bet a rat's ass he ain't even matured enough to snag himself a gal!"

Ma knew darn well Jacob and Rachel had quite a thing for one another. This was just her sneaky way of getting him to open up a little and enlighten them on the status quo of their relationship. Kate had kept her completely informed over the years about their fond affection for each other. Digging around in his intimate affairs was of great interest to her, so she again pressed the issue.

"Well, you gotta gal? Speak up, don't be playin' shy!"

"Ma, I've told you before that ain't none of your business!" argued Kate.

"Now he either has one or he don't!" Ma stated. "How hard is that to fess up to? And for your information, young lady, everything on this ranch is my business and don't you forget it!"

Jacob sat cross-legged, astonished by all the many different ways Ma found to pick an argument with Kate. He could see that they were both very ill at ease with each other, so he allowed his thoughts to drift elsewhere.

Thoughts of Rachel consumed nearly every waking moment of his day. Not knowing for sure just how things stood between them anymore had caused him a great deal of concern since he was run off her ranch. Although he hadn't seen or spoken to her since that time, she was still fresh in his mind.

On days like this he could almost hear her sweet voice like a lullaby in the breeze. His only recourse was to go through the motions of daily living trying hard not to think about her too much. Of course that was nearly impossible since she was a part of the very fabric of his existence.

In a simple approach to avoid the subject of his love life, Jacob cleverly diverted the focus of their conversation elsewhere. "I'm thinking I'm one lucky man to be keeping company with two of the prettiest ladies this side of the bluffs."

Outspoken as usual, Ma blurted, "You know very well we're the only women this side of the bluffs, you big oaf! And don't you even try to pretend you weren't aware of that."

Ma could see she was getting nowhere fast with this conversation. So she quit speaking directly to Jacob and began idly babbling about a few other matters that were of no interest to anyone but her. Ma pointed out her opinion on everything from how to boil water properly to the best month to plant carrots.

She was boring them both to no end, but Jacob was happy nonetheless because she had finally stopped prying into his love life. Ma finally lost Kate's interest altogether. Even Jacob thought it was a phony excuse for her to get away from it all by quietly shuffling off towards the outdoor privy.

Kate had long ago made her opinion known about her disapproval of the position of the outhouse. "It created an infraction on the sanctity of privacy," she claimed.

It had been placed much too close to the front side of the house without near enough seclusion to her liking, but of course, the reason behind its unusual location came into being way back when her Pa was still alive. His arthritis had become so debilitating it was much too difficult for him to use a chamber pot or walk any extended distance, especially in the dead of night.

Doc had suggested that a warmer climate would have worked wonders for his stiff joints, but Ma wouldn't hear of it.

The Truth about Jacob

"This is our home and we're stayin' put, arthritis or not!" she adamantly repeated many times over the years.

Ma watched closely as her hefty daughter got at least five feet from the door when she let loose with a shocking comment that flushed the faces of both Jacob and Kate.

"Careful of those worn out boards, buffalo butt! I've told you time and again they need fixin'."

Kate could have just died of embarrassment on the spot. Jacob wanted to crawl into a hole for a week. Ma just split a gut laughing her head off and slapping her leg silly. Then she quickly covered her mouth with her hands to keep from sprinkling Jacob's face with any more chewing tobacco.

By the time Kate returned the air was a mite cool between the two ladies. Jacob knew they wouldn't sleep on their anger tonight. They would take care of this unfinished business later on, after he was clear out of the picture, maybe out in the south forty somewhere. Jacob had been around long enough to know exactly what was in store. They'd toss around a few more heated words. Ma might feel guilty, but wouldn't openly admit it. And then Kate would feel bad and would say so. Ma would, in the end, come out of the argument smelling like a rose like she always did, as if the whole incident was Kate's fault to begin with.

Kate continued to crochet on Ma's new shawl all the while giving her the cold shoulder. Right about now, she felt more like strangling her with it. The thought had crossed her mind to forget about it entirely after what her mother had just pulled, but Kate knew that by the time this day had drawn to a close, so would their anger.

Ma kept minding everyone else's business like a spectator with a thousand eyes.

Jacob was once again lost in his thoughts about Rachel. His eyes grew troubled showing some of his sheltered pain. The tension between he and Baxter felt bad enough, but the fear of losing Rachel forever was ten times worse. He tried to steer clear of any thoughts of Billy, but at times they'd butt heads in his mind anyway.

Then, just about the time Jacob's thoughts practically had him in tears, out of the south, he noticed a tiny puff of dust lift, grow, and become a fast-running horse with a rider. The other two porch squatters realized it was Rachel about the same time he did.

In a matter of minutes Rachel pulled up, her sweat soaked sorrel rearing with the sudden stop. She had a troubled look on her face.

At first, all Jacob could do was stare in disbelief that Rachel was actually here within an arms length. Her image shimmered like a heat wave, with the sun's glow for a background. He could hardly wait to reach up and touch her. Unable to compose himself, his hands quivered as he stepped towards her, fighting back three weeks of mounting questions.

Jacob positioned himself between Rachel and the two eagle eyes on the porch. By doing so he avoided a thousand and one questions from Ma. Jacob wasn't too concerned over what Kate might have to say, but Ma was another matter altogether.

Jacob lifted his hands upwards, grasping Rachel around the waist, swiftly assisting her dismount. "Ma, Kate," he politely said, "We're gonna take a walk." The two young lovers disappeared behind the barn and away from Ma's catchall eyes before her interrogation had a chance to start.

Once isolated from the others, they turned and faced each other. Jacob could tell by the pain in her eyes he wasn't the only one who had been suffering. They couldn't find each other's lips fast enough. That first kiss put an end to more than three weeks of torturous loneliness. With the first soft touch it was as if they had never been apart. It was then that they knew they would never be apart again.

With a shredded heart she backed up three paces, took a deep breath and asked, "For heaven sakes, Jacob, why didn't you let

The Truth about Jacob

me know you were here? I was so worried about you. I didn't even know if you were alive or dead."

"I'm sorry. It's just that I wasn't sure how you felt about me anymore. I was afraid you wouldn't even want to speak to me again after what had happened."

"What put a fool idea like that in your head? How could you doubt my love for you, Jacob? Besides, what did it have to do with how we felt about each other? I would have been at your side the very next day had I known where you were. I still don't understand why Kate kept it such a big secret for so long."

Jacob released a coy little smile knowing that Kate was just trying to honor his wishes. He had privately asked her not to breathe a word of his whereabouts to anyone. Now he realized that was a big mistake.

"What about your father?"

"What about him? I'm not bothered by his stupidity nor should you be. His pride is the only thing that's kept him from crawling over here on hands and knees to beg for your forgiveness. When Kate did finally tell us of your whereabouts, he actually asked me what he should do. I believe he's a little leery of saying anything to upset you further."

"What did you tell him?"

"I ribbed him a bit of course. I told him he owed you an apology, but that he needed to do that in person. I sure wasn't going to deliver the message for him. He really is sorry for fallin' for Billy's big pack of lies about us."

"So it was Billy who caused all this ruckus?"

"Who else but the biggest mud mouth around? He told Father some cockeyed story about seeing you and me out in the woods that day. Well, you can just imagine what he said. He loaded my father up with enough ammunition to start another Civil War. But if I know him the way I think I do, he'll be bending over backwards trying to make it up to you."

Rachel paused long enough to allow her next thought time to come together. Gathering strength in her voice, she gave Jacob a serious look and snuggled closer to him. "I don't suppose you'd consider coming back home with me, would you? For good, I mean."

He gave her a sincere answer with his eyes and, as sure as the sun sets at dusk, she knew it wasn't a yes. Rachel lowered her head in disappointment. "I didn't think so. Silly of me to ask, huh? For a lack of a better way to put it, I don't guess I'd care to show my face back where my self-respect was run through the mud," she declared being more understanding than hurt by his response.

"Thanks for asking anyway and it's not such a silly question. It's one that I would have addressed if it had been you instead of me."

"Actually, to be honest with you, I kinda like it here with Ma and Kate. They're quite a pair, you know. Not a dull moment around here with those two characters. Speaking of the odd couple, we'd best be getting back over there before they come looking for us."

Leading the way like a lone wolf amongst the feline population, Jacob slipped his hand into the curve of her arm, guiding her back in front of the two women who were obviously growing mighty restless with many questions. Their talk died for a moment as they approached.

Kate politely turned her eyes away. Ma, of course, didn't intend to miss one thing, so she held her stare. Kate kicked Ma's foot and scolded her with a frown trying to break her intense concentration. No doubt she was contemplating saying something that would raise a few brows. And sure enough, Ma didn't disappoint anyone.

"Looks like we'll be seeing warmer temperatures today, judging by the way you twos' faces are all flushed. S'posin' by now there's no frost left on the pumpkins out back of the barn either! Speakin' of the barn, with all that sparkin' goin' on, s'pose we better check it for fire, Kate?"

The Truth about Jacob

Kate groaned, "Ma, now cut that out! Can't you see your embarrassin' the youngins'?"

"Shouldn't be, unless they've gone and done something to redden them faces!"

Ma offered a little sneer and held her ground, showing a real interest in pursuing this matter further. As if she expected them to tell her everything she asked, "You do understand what the scriptures say about that sort of thing, don't you?"

Kate's face got blood red. She quickly prayed for a miracle, like maybe something big enough within reach to gag the old lady with. She in no way wanted Ma to ruin this day for Jacob and Rachel.

In an attempt to change the subject, Rachel abruptly asked Ma a question. "The winds are starting to pick up a little, aren't they? Do you suppose maybe we're in for more than just a few sprinkles? By the looks of those black clouds moving in overhead, something of a more serious nature might be brewing."

"You've called a spade a spade there, youngin', cause it'll be coming down in sheets before noon!"

Rachel turned again to look at the little weather whiz. Ma could not conceal her delight that Rachel had asked for her expert opinion. Her face was all smiles.

Having her initial suspicions confirmed, Rachel decided that her long ride back home had better start right away. "I've got to beat this storm home, Jacob," she said, moving ever so close to him. "And since we don't have anything to hide from these two fine ladies, I guess we'll just exchange our good-byes right here." She looked into his sweet face for a moment before planting a soft kiss on his lips.

Kate quickly turned her stare away from the young couple and flushed pink. Jacob turned red and Ma just squirmed in her seat and went right on talking.

"Yep, just like I was sayin' before, she's a girl after my own heart! Better hold on tight to this one, Jacob. You'd be workin' with half a noggin if you let her get away."

The fact that Ma had changed her tune to a happier note certainly set well with Rachel. From what she remembered over the years, Ma was really quite harmless. She was just a butterfly full of fun as long as you stayed in her good graces.

"Good day, ladies," she said as she winked at Jacob.

He helped Rachel back onto her horse, thinking the whole time how much he dreaded to let her out of his sight again for even one minute.

Ma had wandered off into a world of her own, buried deep in thought. More and more lately her thoughts had been about Rachel. She had missed seeing her over an extended period of time. Visits to this house had been few and far between over the past ten years. She figured Baxter deliberately discouraged the young girl from coming here because of the bad blood between the two of them.

"Come back again real soon, young lady, when you can stay a while longer, ya hear?" Ma exclaimed. "You know it's been a while, so let's not be strangers now."

"Thank you, Ma, it would be my pleasure, I assure you." Unlike her ride over here, the ride back home would be a pleasurable one free of any uncertainties of where she fit into Jacob's life. As Rachel lifted her reins and settled in her saddle, Jacob finally caught hold of his senses. He waved his hand to halt her horse.

"Hold up a minute, Rachel! Give me a minute to rig up my horse and I'll ride with you as far as the east road forks into your ranch."

Ma was privy to Jacob's true mind. But she had private matters of her own to take up with him. This had to be done when no one else was around to hear what she had to say. Right now was a good time, she quickly decided, while it was still heavy on her heart.

The Truth about Jacob

It had occurred to Ma that she needed to provide Jacob with a legitimate reason for it to be Kate, rather than him, that accompanied Rachel part way back home.

"Kate, don't you think this would be a good opportunity for you to discuss your plans for the banquet you're puttin' together for Rachel's father?"

Kate smiled with a gleam in her eye. The dinner that the elders of the church were planning in his honor for donating some of his property for a new schoolhouse certainly needed a few more kinks ironed out. Besides, a moment to herself with Rachel without being sidetracked by work and a thousand and one other interruptions at the same time sounded like a good idea.

Hopelessly out-matched by Ma's stubbornness, Jacob gave her a weak smile and conceded to her wishes with a certain degree of reluctance. His face mirrored his disappointment. He stood beside Rachel's horse, rubbing the back of her calves with the tips of his fingers. Rachel in turn stroked the side of his face in an affectionate manner, apparently reading his thoughts and feeling the same disappointment he was. The two of them exchanged some more small talk while waiting for Kate to saddle up. When she returned, they bid their good-byes and rode away.

The two onlookers left behind could feel the full strength of the wind beating dust particles against their faces as they silently watched the women disappear into mere dots in the distance. Once they had vanished completely out of their sight, it was Ma who opened their conversation.

"I'm not getting' any younger, Jacob. Ya know, there are times when you find it necessary to go against your own grain…times when there's a need to open doors that you'd just as soon stay closed, but it's my time to make peace with God."

Jacob was startled by Ma's serious tone of voice and feared something bad had happened. He had never heard her talk in such a disturbing manner before. He didn't look directly into

Ma's eyes; he just studied her pained expression as a whole, concerned, and wanted to hear more of what she had on her mind.

"I never told anyone this before 'cause I figured it weren't nobody's business. No, I never breathed a word to a soul," she said shaking her head, "But now the time has come and I feel I must."

"Doc and I were mighty close. More like kin, you could say. Not a finer man ever walked this earth 'ceptin' our good Lord. There was a time when we shared most everything together. That man sure could keep a secret, even from me. Why, he wouldn't whisper a word about something that was private in nature if his life depended on it. He didn't say one word to me about this matter until that night on his deathbed."

Ma's muscles moved nervously, twitching her wrinkled cheek. She shut her misty eyes briefly.

Jacob could see she still missed her dear old friend, as pain completely gathered her up. She obviously had taken Doc's passing much harder than he thought, and that made the moment very moving for him. He knew it took a considerable amount of courage to confess whatever it was that was weighing heavy on her mind. By now she wasn't even looking at him and seemed quite detached from his presence. Her voice grew quiet as she looked out into the air as if trying to find her next words.

Jacob felt sorry for her. Yet there was nothing he could do to help her. He waited patiently until she began to speak again.

"One of Doc's last requests was to see me all alone. Well, I went to his house and through his shallow breaths, he began to unload the weight of the world from his shoulders. Guess I gave him quite a shock though, cause I weren't quite as surprised as he figured me to be with what he had to tell me."

Ma stared straight at Jacob, her eyes perplexed. Now, seated back in her chair she worked hard to draw him a clear mental picture of everything that had taken place long before he was even a gleam in his own mother's eye.

"A woman knows of such things without being told. I always could read a face like a book. I knew darn well that hateful, high-class woman weren't full with child. Why, that bag of bones was as thin and frail as an old dog come of age, ready to take that one-way walk away from home alone. Besides, Kate had already told me Miz Baxter had flat out refused to give her husband any children. There were times when she had overheard quarrels between the two of them on that subject."

Jacob stood there in silence, giving Ma the opportunity to unload her burdens. He could see that they all had suffered so much because of this woman.

"That snooty woman was selfish in herself. Even a fool could tell she was the type that wouldn't want her trim figure all misshaped in such a way. She certainly wasn't much to look at, but she sure thought she was. That's what a man gets when he comes back home from the big city, totin' one of them thar so-called debutantes! Expectin' that highfalutin' city gal to take to country life like we homegrown women do was a crazy notion on his part in the first place!" she declared.

"Well, that fancy woman didn't have the wool pulled over my eyes. She smelled like a smokestack and drank like a fish and didn't eat enough food to keep a bird alive, much less a child within her well nourished!" Ma explained.

Ma's eyes slowly disappeared under her lids with a new sense of nervous tension on her face. He could tell she was done talking about Mrs. Baxter and a new subject was about to emerge. Jacob felt uneasy not knowing what was coming next. He figured as nervous as she was acting it must be pretty bad. Judging by the way she twisted her fingers together in little knots, he was fretful that it concerned someone she loved very much.

Ma's stomach tightened as she confessed. "Was my Kate who gave birth to that sweet little baby girl! She paid a mighty high price for her one night of sin. Baxter shared his heartbreak with Doc during one of his weaker moments. He told of how he and

Kate had poured that drunken old wife of his into her bed one night, after she had passed out on the kitchen floor. Fool woman split her head wide open just above the brow. Kate tended to her wound, and it was during the hours that followed that she tried to comfort him. That's when they uh...uh..." Ma's voice stuttered with obvious embarrassment and she curved her hand along her cheek as if the gesture gave her a sense of security.

"That's the night it happened. Baxter begged Kate to marry him, not just to give the baby a name, but because he loved her, and had for years. She wouldn't even consider his proposal even though she loved him, too! She said the shame the child would have to endure over such a scandal would be too much to bear," Ma confided.

"He asked Miz Baxter to give him a divorce anyway, but she refused, of course. She told him she wasn't about to give up her prominent position as his wife and all the wealth that went along with it." Ma beetled her brow and gave a sigh of disgust before continuing.

"But no, that wicked witch wasn't about to oblige him in any way. Hadn't been what you call a real wife to that poor man since six months after they wed. She did, however, agree to assume the identity as the child's mother. Baxter more or less forced that issue. If she hadn't gone along with the scheme, he threatened to openly expose the love affair she had going on with her whiskey bottle. She didn't have difficulty reconciling to the idea because she claimed that she wouldn't be lifting one finger to take care of that illegitimate bastard. Those were her very words! Shame on her for callin' our sweet little Rachel such an awful name," she shouted.

Ma braced her hands against the armrests on her chair. She looked at nothing in particular without much of an expression and began to speak again. "I knew all along my little girl was the one heavy with child. Kate never said a word about it to me and I sure didn't let on I knew." Ma wiped away her tears and blew

The Truth about Jacob

her nose on a small lacy handkerchief she removed from her dress pocket.

"When the time came, Kate gave birth to Rachel right there in that house with just Doc by her side. But that devil of a woman had a plan of her own. Just as that sweet little baby was pushin' her way through Kate's legs, that drunkard stumbled her way into the birthing room, totin' a gun pointed directly at Kate and Rachel. She'd a taken both their lives if it hadn't been for Baxter grabbing her from behind. During the struggle that followed, the gun went off. The bullet tore through Miz Baxter's temple. Seemed, at the time, to solve everyone's problems. Was Doc's idea to lie about the way she had died. As far as I was concerned, it couldn't have turned out better if I'd a planned it myself."

Ma's stare stayed level out into thin air. She groaned as she shook her head again. "But all didn't go as well as you'd expect. Even in death that no good, selfish woman managed to ruin everything for Kate. My poor girl just couldn't bear the guilt of her sin. Maxine may have sealed her own fate with her own hand, but at the same time, she closed the door to any possible happiness between Kate and Baxter, even though he continued to show an interest in her and practically begged her to marry him," she revealed.

"Kate, however, did stay on at the ranch night and day to nurse and care for Rachel until she reached the age that her father could manage on his own. Kate tortured herself over the way things turned out, and, because of it, she still refused to marry Baxter, even after all these years." She again wiped her tears away with her hankie.

It was obvious to Jacob that Ma felt somewhat better having unloaded these secrets that she had kept suppressed for so long. But despite all she had just told him, he could tell there was still something else bothering her. Something she prolonged for a few more minutes behind a worried face.

After a while, Ma finally broke her dreadful stare out into nowhere and once again settled her serious eyes on Jacob. She drew in a long breath. "I want my granddaughter to know I loved her, Jacob. I myself want to be sure that someday she'll be aware that she was always close to my heart and in my daily thoughts."

"Have you ever thought about telling Kate you know the truth? And maybe it's time to share that truth with Rachel."

"Don't talk foolish, Jacob! If Kate wanted her to know, she'd a told her a long time ago! I just don't want to leave this life knowing my only grandchild never knew how I felt about her. Even worse than that, it would be a cryin' shame for her to never know just how much her mother loved her, and why she chose her daughter's well-being over her own happiness."

"Would Mr. Baxter ever consider telling Rachel?"

"Absolutely not!" she exclaimed shaking her head. "He would never betray Kate! She swore him to secrecy that very night and he'll stand by his word till the day he dies. I can guarantee you that!" she confirmed.

"Promise me something, Jacob. When we're all long gone and only a memory left behind in your hearts, will you tell Rachel the truth about what really happened? You tell her she was loved by her real mother and grandmother. You promise me that, will you?"

Jacob was so moved by Ma's devotion to Rachel and her loyalty to Kate that he was subdued and speechless. *Her deep love for Kate and Rachel was her real worth*, he determined. *It seemed as though she wasn't the tough old bird she tried to portray. Beneath that rough exterior of hers lies the fragile heart of a soft-spoken grandmother who was subject to the same imperfections as everyone else.* How beautiful she looked at this moment in this new role.

Jacob knew Ma was anxiously waiting for his answer. He moved in her direction, knelt down on one knee and surrounded her smallness within his arms. He patted her bony little back with the palm of his hand trying to give her some comfort.

The Truth about Jacob

"I won't disappoint you, Ma. When the time is right, I'll explain to Rachel just how much she was loved. I'll tell her all about the kind of unconditional love that was bestowed upon her that most people would give anything to have. I'll tell her how both you and Kate watched every step she took into becoming the fine woman she is today. That's real love, Ma, and I'm most certain she feels the same way about you two, even without the knowledge of your true kinship."

A placid expression broke across Ma's face. The sheen of sweat on her brow glistened in the sun. She felt free at last from her burdens. She craned her neck to look up at Jacob in order to thank him. "Much obliged, Jacob. I knew I could depend on you."

Ma silently whispered to herself. "Now this departure from life will not be a sorrowful one." Having just crossed the last T and closed but yet another chapter in her life that had been lived to the fullest, her soul stirred with a great peacefulness.

After two days had elapsed since Rachel had her reunion with Jacob, Baxter finally got his nerve up to get things ironed out with him. On his ride over to the Parker Ranch, he nervously rehearsed the words he intended to say to Jacob once they were face to face. Upon his arrival at the last bend in the road that led up to the house, he halted his horse for a brief moment to make sure it was Jacob who was pounding the fence post into the ground about a hundred feet from the house. He was relieved to see that the young man was all alone.

By the time Jacob spotted Baxter not five feet away, sitting on his horse staring at him, a thousand quick thoughts went through his head. He swung his head upwards in a whirl. "Oh, Mr. Baxter, I didn't hear you ride up."

"Hope I didn't startle you."

"No, it's just that I didn't expect to see you all the way out here so late in the day."

The air was filled with the distant chirping of birds and the baffles of water flowing over the protruding rocks in the creek alongside the road.

The old man eased down off of his leather. "Look here, Jacob, I've been meaning to come over here and apologize to you long before this, but it hasn't been easy for me to come to terms with all the damage that's been done by my stupidity. Of course, the wrath of an angry daughter can tend to make a man think long and hard before he puts himself in that kind of an awkward position again."

Jacob let out a chuckle. "I can sympathize with you on that truth. I've had Rachel mad at me a time or two."

"I feel as though I really need to explain to you why I've allowed Billy to get away with so much for so long. Of course, it was still my own stupidity that allowed him to flat pull the wool over my eyes concerning you and Rachel that day out in the woods. Only I can take the blame for that."

"Look, Mr. Baxter, you don't owe me a thing. I know you feel bad about what's happened, Rachel's filled me in on that fact. I look at it this way, you've given me far more than any other man has other than Doc and I'm not inclined to forget that."

"I'm sorry, Jacob. I truly am." Quietly, he added, "I feel like a complete nincompoop for handling myself the way I did. Only a fool counts his chickens before they're hatched. I should have at least given you the benefit of the doubt. At least I should have given you the opportunity to explain your actions in private, without the whole kittenkaboodle at the ranch watching us."

"It's okay," Jacob replied. "Let's just put it behind us and forget it ever happened. Whatcha say, friends again?" he asked as he stretched out an open hand.

Baxter smiled broadly. Grasping Jacob's hand in a hearty shake, he said, "You're a bigger man than I."

Stepping backwards, the lines around his eyes deepened as he frowned. Byron could hear the crackle in his own voice. Trying to compose himself, he asked, "It sure would give me a great deal of pleasure if you'd consider coming back home with me, Jacob. I know Rachel would be more than happy and all the boys at the ranch say it's just not the same without you. I've had to keep poor old Weckles tied up trying to keep him from wandering off and just starving himself to death. Poor old dog thinks you're gone for good. He's homesick for you, alright."

"I don't deny that's a real tempting offer, but right now I just can't bring myself to up and leave Kate and Ma when I don't have all the work done that I promised I'd do."

"I can understand your reasoning, just as long as you know the invitation will always stay open."

"Thanks, that's mighty nice of you." Jacob couldn't help but notice that there seemed to be something else on his mind besides where he decided to hang his hat. There was more than a moment of silence between them. He wondered what was coming next.

Baxter shook his head as he finally began to speak again with his tone serious. "Getting back to the subject of Billy, I want you to know why I put up with so much guff from him. I've always felt sorry for the boy. You can see for yourself he's not much to look at. The older boys in town used to give him a pretty bad time about his drunken pa. His ma did the best she could raisin' the boy virtually without any help from old Sam, but that did little to prevent him from growing up with a real nasty chip on his shoulder anyway. Needless to say, as you well know, I grew up without a good father figure to steer me in the right direction. I just thought by giving Billy a little extra leeway that I could help to make up for what he lacked so dearly in positive guidance. Guess I thought wrong, because all my good intentions just seem to feed his overgrown ego, and simply helped to create the egotistical monster he turned out to be."

Jacob listened carefully with his eyes glued to the old man's tortured face. He could hear the pain in his voice.

"I'd always hoped the boy could rise above his hardships," he continued to say. "I told him to go forward and not look back on what he couldn't change, but I can see that was all wishful thinking on my part."

Baxter shook his head again and tried to keep his voice steady. "Billy's not the only man with a sad story to tell. It's rare that any one person goes through life unconscious of some measure of pain. I, myself, have had my fair share, and by no means have you been spared. But life goes on. You put it behind you and make the best of things. Hard times don't lay out the rules to live by. You play according to what's best for all concerned. There's no denying that life is a tough game to play, but a smart man just gets tougher. That goes without saying for a woman, too. Kate, for instance, has practically spent half her life putting her needs and wants on hold for the sake of others. She's still waiting for the right time to fulfill her dreams."

Then, when the old man abruptly stopped talking, Jacob could see the startled look on his face, as if he spoke out of turn regarding Kate. He had a pretty good idea of exactly what he was talking about, but he wasn't about to let on that he did.

Both men swapped looks, and it was then that Jacob realized Baxter wanted to say more. He definitely wanted to get more off of his chest and he assumed it had something to do with all that Ma had already told him.

Then, without warning, Baxter began to unload years of pain. He talked, as Jacob had never heard him talk before. He told him about Maxine, he explained his undying love for Kate, he gave a clear picture of the birth of Rachel, and finally, with misty eyes, he told about the unfortunate accidental death of his wife. Jacob could see his pain grow as he kept on talking, and he learned many things about those troublesome years he hadn't known before.

"Replaying these awful memories in my mind over the years, I'm afraid, have taken their toll on me. It took all the courage I had in me to unload this all on you now. Sorry to burden you like this, but I can't say that I don't feel better. In fact, I feel darn right good."

The Truth about Jacob

"Don't be sorry on my account. It does a man good to just let it all out once in a while. Cleans the soul," Jacob replied, consolingly.

As if he hadn't heard a word Jacob had said, he spoke up again. "Kate's the finest woman I've ever known. I'll be honest with you Jacob. I'm gonna marry that stubborn woman if it's the last thing I ever do.

"I don't doubt that one bit," Jacob returned with a sly grin on his face.

Baxter smiled and then looked back over his shoulder. His voice changed, a little chirpier now. "In fact there's no better time than right now to ask her to marry me. I feel good and there's no reason not to ride back towards my ranch and catch that pretty little lady before she gets home." He took in a deep breath, ponied up, and gave his horse the rein. "That's what I'm gonna do. Stubborn or not, today she's gonna give me an answer.

A slight breeze across Jacob's face broke the stillness of the late afternoon. As he watched Baxter's faint trail of dust fade away in the distance, he felt a peaceful sense of closure. A troubled heart had driven the old man over here, but a determined one was pushing him closer to fulfilling all his fondest dreams.

Chapter 12

    Ma sure did have a way with words. Jacob had made that discovery early on in the game during the short amount of time he'd been living there. At times she talked like she was ready to kick the bucket any day with all her aches and pains. Other days she felt fit as a fiddle determined more than ever to pass the one hundred mark and then some. One thing Jacob knew for sure, she was a tough old gal and he had already made up his mind that she was nowhere near ready for the bone yard yet.

    Tonight had been no different than any other. Their dinners were always late. Even though Ma would start the vittles earlier in the evening, Kate would always finish the rest of the fixings after she got home from the Baxter's.

    They had sat together for quite a spell after dinner, enjoying what was left of this lazy evening. They shared many old tales and made up a few new ones as they went along. This had become common practice for these three musketeers who enjoyed one another's company to the fullest, despite the fact that tonight Ma had napped through nearly half of their conversation.

    Kate had been gone for the better part of ten minutes or so having quietly slipped outside just after all three had finally

The Truth about Jacob

retired to their beds. Since her departure was of a private nature, no one dared to go looking for her when she didn't return right away. Both Jacob and Ma lay silent in their beds expecting to hear her footsteps at the front door any minute.

Jacob's worries about her whereabouts were laid to rest when language, not fit for the laundry basket, filled the air outside. The best Jacob could tell, right then and there, Kate had lost her religion.

Jacob beat it over to the open kitchen window as quickly as he could to see what the yelling was all about. Ma tarried in behind him, slower than molasses in the middle of winter, and more curious than a cockroach on the breadboard after dark. For five minutes or more the two sets of eyes clad only in their sleeping garb stood still and observed everything from a distance.

Kate was ranting and raving while trying to beat the outhouse to death with a stick. There were words coming out of her mouth that could curl a deaf man's ear and cause a court jester to cry.

Kate's clothes were dripping wet with muck, and by the looks of her, she didn't come by that stinky mess easily. The space within the privy was limited, but obviously large enough for her to have fallen all the way through. Kate's temper soared as she screamed and ran around in circles trying to brush off the larger chunks of muck. Jacob and Ma still didn't know what to do. They just stood and watched in silence holding back a barrage of questions.

All of a sudden Kate stopped dead in her tracks, leaned over and threw up all over the place. Right after that all hell broke loose. In a fit of rage she ran into the barn and grabbed a heavy sledgehammer leaning against some boards. She quickly returned to the outhouse and began to bang away at the exterior. She juggled the heavy tool between her hands, swinging with all her might, making each blow count. In the shadows of the moonlit night the outdated privy eventually fell into a heap of broken boards.

Ma and Jacob stood dumbfounded as they watched Kate completely demolish the structure. Leaning heavily against her metal assistant, Kate just stood there and stared.

Now at a time when silence would have been more appropriate, Ma unfortunately found her tongue. She broke a toothy grin, pushed the window open, and yelled as loud as she could.

"Must a been a devil of a drop for that buffalo butt! Did you listen to me two years ago when I tried to tell you that if you got any fatter you'd outgrow your own bed?"

Then Ma did a little foot stomping of her own and mumbled to Jacob. "Just knew by now that stubborn girl didn't have much freedom of movement in that privy! Dad gum it anyway! Now look what she's gone and done! We'll all be out in the cold answerin' nature's call. I've told her over an over again those boards needed fixin'."

"Don't worry, Ma. I've already finished the hole for the new privy out back. Kate and I can rebuild a better one in just a couple of days," Jacob explained.

Before Ma had a chance to lecture Jacob any further on how fat her daughter was, their full attention was once again pulled back in Kate's direction. She had circled around the heaping pile of what was left of the house of dirty business to gather up her lantern that sat on the ground not five feet away. In further embarrassment at having been observed and with one last burst of anger, she deliberately thrust her lantern against the dry, thirsty timbers. The smell of smoky embers filled the air.

The explosion made for a spectacular view from where Ma and Jacob stood. Bright reddish-orange flames shot high up into the cool light of the moon. It was then that Ma's eyes took a nosedive. She couldn't help but take notice of Jacob standing in his long johns with the kitchen lit up like the Fourth of July.

Now, Ma never could pass up an opportunity to rib anyone, no matter what kind of a mood she was in, and this was especially true with Jacob. Mischievously, she looked him

The Truth about Jacob

straight in the eyes and colored his face. "You've got no business, young man, froggin' around in the middle of the night dressed like that. Why, that thin piece of cheesecloth you're wearin' is no better than your birthday suit. You best be takin' my advice and get yourself covered up, there, youngin', before the bats around here make a meal out of your tassel!"

Jacob's breath caught in his throat. He quickly covered his manhood with both hands and roared barefooted back to his bedroom. Ma moseyed back into her room chuckling at her own humor. Nobody laughed harder at her jokes than she did.

Both Jacob and Ma could hear the clinking sounds of the water bucket banging against the side of the well house from where they lay in their beds. It was obvious to them both that a cold, late night bath for Kate was the last order of this evening.

Chapter 13

In this day and time it was the norm, rather than the exception that many women were capable of taking care of chores considered to be a man's work, and often performed the duties meant for the menfolk. This was especially true at the Parker ranch, where there hadn't been a man around for a good number of years. Kate was an independent frontier woman, particularly so when she was still crawling with anger and insufferably stubborn.

Late in the day, when the job was nearly complete, Jacob could hear Kate calling his name. Having constructed the new outhouse entirely from scratch without anyone's help, she finally swallowed some of her stubborn pride to ask him to run an errand.

"Jacob, run and get me that small roll of binding wire will ya? It's just inside that wooden cabinet, beside the door."

Eager to help in anyway he could, Jacob set the pail of grain he held in his hands down on the ground. He stepped around the new calf he was feeding and wasted no time getting into the house. He hustled through the doorway, chuckling to himself.

She was a special breed, one of a kind, he thought. *She always carried her own load, that was a fact. But if she deemed it necessary to ask for help, she paid them well for their service and, therefore, was beholden to no one.*

Jacob smiled quietly, admiring her as a champion amongst many other women who couldn't begin to measure up to her courage and stamina. As Ma always put it, "Her damned independence."

However, a simple task soon turned into a major chore. He was sifting through some old books, papers and small tin cans stored on the upper shelf when he brushed against a unique piece of pottery with a loose lid and accidentally knocked it over. The contents rolled out, scattering every which way across the floor.

Jacob quickly knelt down on bended knees, his arms stretched out trying to retrieve the scattered artifacts before anyone else discovered what he had done. Quietly, he scooted across the floor gathering up each piece of Kate's belongings, hoping the noise hadn't disturbed Ma. She was resting peacefully in her bed, having looked rather peaked earlier and feeling a little under the weather for the better part of a day.

Jacob stopped cold for a moment. His heart froze. Something about the relics he held in his hands looked vaguely familiar. Upon closer inspection, he understood why. He'd seen these things before many years ago. He had felt these very articles with the curious hands of a five-year-old.

Jacob held his father's rose gold pocket watch, stroking the fine crafted metal between his fingers. The sight of his mother's black and white cameo necklace that adorned her neck every Sunday for church put a large lump in his throat. Even the first tooth he had lost as a child was still in the same small black tobacco pouch that had once belonged to his Papa Perkins.

Without a word Jacob stood up, still staring at the contents in his hands. Questions welled up in his mind, crowding out the fear of waking Ma and the guilt of having knocked over Kate's possessions. *How did Ma and Kate come by his family's possessions? Why hadn't they shared them with him long before now? Most important of all, did they know the whereabouts of his family and why they left him behind?*

Jacob was both outraged and afraid of the truth at the same time. Fortunately for him, he wasn't forced to wait long before the answers to his troubling questions came waltzing boldly through the doorway with an attitude.

"For Pete's sakes, Jacob, good thing I wasn't laying out there bleeding to death waitin' for you to help me!" Kate placed him under an agitated stare until she saw what lay between his fingers and the look of wonder and betrayal that covered his face. Now she was in the spotlight instead of him. Her heart froze. She was too stunned to move.

His courage grew, spouting from the questions in his mind, and now not afraid to take the bull by the horns, Jacob broke the sudden silence. "How did you come by these things? All of this belonged to my parents!" Jacob's eyes bled with pain while he analyzed Kate's shocked expression.

Remaining quite calm and considering the enormity of the situation, Kate slowly strolled past Jacob across the room of hidden truths. She stared out the small kitchen window trying to find the right words to say, while her heart crouched in her stomach. After a long pause she began to unload the terrible secret she had kept to herself for over thirteen years.

"There's nothing like hope to keep a man going, Jacob. To have crushed your dream of finding your family one day might have killed your spirit. Even a young boy's gotta have something to hold on to. I couldn't bring myself to tell you the truth about your family. How could I do that to you, Jacob, when that's all you had to keep your family alive in your heart? I just couldn't destroy all your hopes of finding them one day," she declared looking him square in the eyes.

Kate glanced at Jacob and then looked away quickly when she saw that the hurt in his eyes had not lessened. Inwardly, Kate felt terrible about keeping the truth from Jacob, but what

The Truth about Jacob

she was about to do now felt ten times worse because she was going to literally rip his heart to pieces.

She began to explain the turn of events that led up to her having come by his family's possessions. "Actually, Jacob, I almost told you the day you and Rachel got back together. But I thought better of it. The timing just wasn't right. I finally decided that it would be easier on you to reveal the truth after you had married and had a family of your own. I figured that would help to cushion the pain of your loss."

"I had a right to know, Kate! You should have told me whatever you knew about my family long before now," he explained, judgment creeping into his voice.

Kate settled back against the cupboard and let out a sigh. She stared out the window, which by now showed signs of dusk having come and now gone.

"It was early spring. It's been over thirteen years since that day. I was trackin' a cat that had killed one of my best calves the night before. I came upon a wagon that had turned over. There was a young woman pinned beneath the heavy load with a baby wrapped in a blanket lying beside her. A young man was draped across her shoulder. All three were dead and had been for quite some time."

Kate's eyes met Jacob's briefly, hoping he didn't realize that buzzards had ravaged their bodies by that time. "It was months later before I figured them to be your folks."

Jacob's face mirrored his sudden grief. The drum of his heart was pounding as he fought back his torn emotions and his tears. His hands curled tightly around his family's trinkets because now he knew that's all he had left of their memory.

"I buried your folks where I found 'em. Took a few items of what looked to be of value and packed them away for safekeeping in case anyone came along later to lay claim to them." She paused, and in a small voice added, "Awful glad now that I did for your sake, Jacob."

Kate swallowed a deep breath and then walked over to a small bookshelf above the fireplace that housed her Holy Bible. She removed a small piece of paper hidden in the Book of John, and handed it to Jacob. "Your mother left you this letter," she revealed.

Jacob's face lit up like a lantern as he retrieved the letter from Kate's trembling hand. Kate slowly turned around. With silence surrounding her, she walked outside to tend to the last of the evening's chores now that the day had died. It was her intent to leave him alone with his mother's last words comfortably settled within his hands.

Now that the initial shock was over and he had calmed down somewhat, Jacob cautiously examined the letter with his mouth dry and his hands cold and shaking. He tried to steady his hands by wiping them on the front of his shirt, and then he carefully unfolded the old, faded paper. With fumbling fingers the young boy in him started to read his mother's final words.

Sadly enough, he could almost feel her presence there with him. It was as if it was just yesterday he last heard her angelic voice singing softly in his ears. He tried to smile in spite of knowing he'd really never see her again. He listened closely to her words, and their minds met for one last time. His face exploded with childlike excitement as he whispered the name written on the backside of the letter. " Jacob Fowler." And then he began to read.

May 10, 1859

My dearest son Jacob:
 It has been only a day since I saw you last. It seems more like an eternity. I long so to see your sweet little smile. I can still picture that inquisitive face of yours that's capable of asking a hundred questions quicker than I can find even one answer.

The Truth about Jacob

My heartbreak of leaving you behind was a loss I found so hard to bear. The injuries I have sustained cannot compare to the pain of losing you. I must face the inevitable however, I know my time is short. I fear the end is drawing near and I pray that freedom from all my pain will come soon. I pray, too, that my last words of goodbye will somehow find their way to your sweet little hands. Hands that I so long to hold again, but I know that request is impossible to grant for there is not enough time left for that kind of miracle.

But I must keep my faith. I must hold onto something, Jacob. I do believe what we did was the right thing to do. To give you up drained me of the most precious part of a mother's inner soul. I have left a trail of tears behind me. Would you, my son, open your heart to understanding? Would you open your heart to forgiving your father and me for leaving you behind? We did so out of love, not for the lack thereof.

Yesterday was the day my heart broke into a thousand pieces. We did not desert you, oh no, Jacob, please believe it was quite the contrary. We left you because we loved you deeply and you deserved a better chance at survival than what we could offer you. Even if it broke our hearts to leave you, we believed the town that had closed their doors to us as a family, would open their hearts to one small boy, all alone, in need of help.

Knowing you to be of a strong mind and full of bravery, there was no doubt that you would make your way back to the town that showed us no mercy.

Having no more food or supplies created enormous problems for us, thus forcing the difficult decision we made. Finding food enough for three hungry mouths we knew was impossible. We chose not to subject you to the pains of hunger any longer, or the dangers of the unknown in the wilderness.

As we traveled not one day from you, we were met with an unbelievable sight. A ball of rolling snakes, coiled around one another the size of which we had never seen before, spooked our team of mules, turning the wagon over.

I am pinned beneath its heavy weight. With deepest regrets I must tell you that your brother, Jeremiah, lies without breath at my side as a result of his injuries.

It is becoming increasingly difficult to breathe, but do not weep for me, my son. Even in my hour of death, God has delivered yet another cherished gift to me. Although your father now lies still beside me with shallow breaths, he managed to place Jeremiah by my side and put pen and paper in my hands, before his wounds rendered him motionless. The many snake bites he has received will take his life as well, and very soon, I fear.

I'm so thankful you were spared our fate, and for that reason alone, I know we made the right decision.

Please know for certain, my son, that your name was the last word we whispered, the last name in our prayers and with the last beat of our hearts, you were the last thought on our minds. Do not be sad. For we are going to a better place and when your time is right, you shall join us there.

There are not enough meaningful words to describe how much we love you and will miss you. I have faith that God will safely see my thoughts into your heart somehow, someday. For, Jacob, you have the right to know the truth about what has happened here. I so long to just hold you one las—

Jacob could almost picture his mother in her final moments when she was doing so poorly. With her body slowly drained of all her strength and her skin bleached of any color, she still thought of him. Even as her eyes fell into a deep sleep, her fingers continued to scratch the pen down the full length of the paper. She had stayed with him to the bitter end.

She loved him. That's what she said in her letter. She told him she was never afraid and didn't blame God one bit for their misfortunes. She actually thanked Him with her very last breath for every miracle He had ever bestowed upon her.

The Truth about Jacob

Jacob was unable to think of anything else but of how full of life she had been and how she had more love to give than this unworthy world had the right to take. His mother's last words were left unfinished, but Jacob knew what she wanted to say without reading them on paper. And even all these many years later, he found her thoughts comforting.

Having never been one to believe in miracles as a grown man, a smile gradually adorned his face because this letter had made a believer out of him. Reading about his family's tragic end written in his mother's final moments suddenly triggered many lost memories, memories that had been tucked away in the back of his mind for so long. Some were good and some were not so good, but all made him feel close to his family once again.

An avalanche of grief swept over his fractured heart. All in a short span of time, he found his family only to loose them once again, but this time for good. He wrestled with swarming emotions that came in waves. He was trying to come to terms with the reality that they were never coming back to find him like he had always believed. Along with his sense of emptiness, there was a sense of comfort as well. He realized it was nothing short of a miracle for Kate to have accidentally come across his family still in their time of need. Although they were lifeless, saving them from being ravaged by wild animals made him beholden to her, his friend now more than ever. Amongst the horror of it all, she was his hero twice over.

As Jacob stood there silently attempting to deal with his grief, something of great worth during his childhood came to his mind. Over the passage of time, he had forgotten a poem his mother used to read to him often as a little boy. At one point in time he had actually memorized it in its entirety. The words again began to take shape in his head. Only this time it held a new meaning.

Jacob whispered the sweet rhyme softly for his mother to hear him say it once again. He hoped it would give her pleasure and a sense of peace.

" If your faith is strong, let it guide you." He whispered with a cracked voice.

"If your vision is unchained, let it reach beyond God's door with power,

"Grab yourself one of his miracles —

He's expecting your prayers this very hour." He finished with a heavy, yet lightened heart.

The hunt was over, Jacob thought quietly. Now maybe he could get on with his life with some degree of normalcy. But there was one last thing he had to do. His last gesture of love would be to give his family a proper burial. Jacob would do that the first thing in the morning.

Yanking him back from his private thoughts, there was a loud commotion taking place right outside the door. Jacob could hear Kate yelling. A riot of colors captured Jacob's face when he heard fear in her voice. Immediately dropping his prized possessions to the floor, he made his way swiftly to the door. Jacob wrestled it open and burst through just in time to see Billy punch Kate in the face, knocking the hefty built woman to the ground. Jacob was unaware of the row of amused faces watching from their saddles just thirty feet away.

Anger welled within him. Before he could tell his legs what to do he bolted off the porch, flying through the air, landing them both on the ground with Jacob on top of Billy. He nailed Billy with a right cross directly between the eyes. Looking down at him with contempt he delivered three more powerful blows within seconds to the exact same spot. Jacob then poked five quick punches deep into Billy's breadbasket, causing him to lose his breath. The last punch to Billy's gut caused him to cough profusely. Unable to get up even after Jacob stood up, Billy rolled from side to side with his knees curled to his stomach trying to catch his breath.

With his heart pounding in his ears and watching Billy roll in the dirt, Jacob did not hear the rustle of boots behind him. The crushing force of a bash to the back of his head sent him sprawled out in the dirt face first. His mind went blank for a moment. Dazed, he clawed at the soil beneath him trying to get back to his feet before he could be struck again with another blind-sided blow.

By now, two other men had jumped from their leather to help Billy back to his feet. Kate had finally gathered her bearings and was also back up on her feet. With sheer anger propelling her, she ran towards Billy, hurling her heaviness on top of Billy's back pounding his head with her fists. Billy peeled her off like an onion and tossed her aside. Kate's body pole-vaulted through the air, coming to rest on the rocky ground a few feet away. After her temple had bashed into the sharp edge of the freestanding brick well house, she lay motionless. There were small traces of blood trickling onto the dust just below her lifeless body.

Billy's barbaric cutthroats were all over Jacob, like hungry fleas on a dog. They punished his body with sticks, boots and anything else they could get their hands on. Not a raw piece of flesh was left untouched. There was no leniency given, not even once that it was obvious he was already a beaten man. Their fury ceased only when they figured him for dead and let go of any worry about his return to his feet. Each man there that had taken part in the beating also had it made up in their own minds that they were the lucky one who had delivered the fatal blow.

"Hand me that torch, Purdy!" Billy demanded. He grabbed the stick full of flames that had lighted their way here. He then thrust it into the open doorway of the old house. And because it was primarily nothing but dry, thirsty timbers, it immediately burst into flames.

Billy's eyes glared with hate and triumph as he watched the house become fully engulfed. It was then that Billy made his thoughts known. "If the old battleaxe won't sell me this ranch, then nobody gets it!" He briefly looked over at Kate. "She got what she had comin' to her anyway!" he bragged.

Billy had a job to do and he did it. And as far as he was concerned it didn't bother him a bit to see this house go up in smoke, nor would he give the fat lady another conscious thought. All the water around here was now free for the taking.

"Ain't there another old woman that lives here?" asked Floyd.

"Not anymore!" laughed Billy, who thought by now he looked like a real big dog amongst his submissive pups. Being fired up with revenge gave him the courage to dispose of any witnesses left behind to report any possible evidence linking him to this crime.

The three other mean hombres that accompanied Billy on this mission of darkness remained tight-lipped with shocked looks on their faces. They were unable to disguise their own troubled thoughts about a man who would intentionally set an old woman ablaze while still alive. It was one thing to accidentally kill Kate, but Billy's choice to commit this kind of atrocious act was a different matter entirely. If Billy could actually be that inhuman, then not one of them doubted that they had more to fear than just being found out by the law. Now they feared for their own safety. If he was capable of wiping out a defenseless old woman, then three men who knew too much would be a piece of cake to eliminate.

Billy and his partners mounted their horses and hoofed it off into the protective cover of the dark night. All that was left behind of Kate's childhood was the charred remains of her home with Ma's bones buried beneath the rubble. Unbeknownst to anyone there, she had already been dead for hours, having slipped away in a peaceful sleep, without any pain.

Kate lay face down in the dirt with no more worries of her own to fuss over. Her spirit was soaring like an eagle right beside Ma's, heading straight towards their just rewards in their long-awaited heavenly kingdom.

Jacob lay still. But a faint breath of air still filtered from his body. Although he lay bleeding profusely from the mouth, nose, and various other places on his body, he held onto life.

Chapter 14

Nearly a month had passed since Rachel had found Jacob lying face down in the dirt clinging to life by a thread. She had seen to his immediate needs right there on the spot; cleaned his wounds and bound his broken ribs. Then she helped him shuffle over to Kate's buckboard with nearly all his upper weight leaning on her shoulders. She assisted him up inside and they rode off, moving at a painfully slow pace.

Jacob began to regain his strength in a matter of weeks, although his unwillingness to keep still and rest properly during that time did hinder the healing of his four broken ribs. Nothing anyone could do or say convinced him to take it easy. As his stubbornness would have it, within a week he thought himself well enough to stand on his own two feet. After some negotiating, Baxter even helped him up on his horse one week later in order to take a short ride.

And so it went, Jacob and Rachel spent more time alone than they had in all the accumulated years since Jacob first came to live at the ranch. They took long walks talking about private matters. They talked for hours as friends and as lovers, about all things good and bad. It was within this same span of time that Jacob disclosed the true identity of Rachel's biological mother.

That was the agonizing day she lay cradled in his arms as he rocked her like a baby. She sobbed for the words left unsaid to Kate and Ma, and for the things she thought were the truths of her life.

Within that significant time, they drew strength from one another and their love grew stronger. They were grateful for the love they shared, and because of it, they were able to nurture each other back to some sort of emotional normalcy.

They were fully aware that their lives as they had known them had ceased to exist. They understood each other's sorrow because both had just experienced their own devastating loss. And through it all they were able to come to terms with the tragic circumstances that had brought them to the here and now.

However, the topic of conversation eventually changed. Jacob had decided it was time to bring Billy to justice. Sheriff Morris was too afraid to hunt down any of the men who had a hand in killing Kate and Ma. Of course, that was no surprise, since the whole town seemed to lose their nerve when it came to Billy.

But as far as Jacob was concerned, whether he had a fast gun or not, Billy was through terrorizing the good folks that did care about law and order in this community.

As Jacob and Rachel discussed the matter, she begged him to let the law handle Billy. But even she knew neither the sheriff nor his deputy would take a chance against Billy's fast draw.

Jacob knew what was in store for him. Bringing Billy in wouldn't be easy. But then nothing in his life had been.

It was late afternoon when he saddled up and lifted his horse to a trot towards town. If he couldn't find Billy today, then he'd stay the night and try again early the next morning. He chose not to share his intentions with Rachel or her father. It was best they didn't know. They'd just try to discourage him and he really didn't want any interference. He especially didn't want either of them to follow him and possibly get caught in any crossfire just in case his plan failed.

The Truth about Jacob

As Jacob rode towards the enemy, thunder rumbled off in the distance. He knew rain was coming soon because the dark clouds were forming just above his head. Once he hit town, he figured on a surprise attack on Billy. Apparently he had been hanging out in his father's old house. At least that was the latest reports from town. He'd been sighted at the saloon nearly every night and had paid at least two visits to Little Lu-Lu's room.

Jacob had taken a great deal of time considering exactly how he would bring Billy in. He surmised that, by this late hour, he'd be three sheets to the wind or sporting Little Lu-Lu, and therefore, would be easy pickings. By sneaking up on him from behind, there would be no gunplay involved. There was no need for any man's blood to spill. Jacob would simply beat the daylights out of him and personally drag his no-good butt to the jailhouse.

By the time Jacob had hit the outskirts of town, it had been raining buckets. He was wringing wet when he tied his horse in front of the general mercantile.

The street was unusually still as he crept along side the saloon. He held steady and peered through the window, trying to get a glimpse of the little weasel and his pack of wolves. To his surprise, there was no sign of either. Jacob was about to turn around and head towards Sam's old house when Billy yelled from across the street.

"Huntin' for trouble, Scarface?"

Jacob stood staring at him through the dim light.

"Walk out here real slow now!" he yelled. "No use in me droppin' you where you are! I like my killin' a little more excitin' than that!"

Torn against his better judgment, Jacob walked within twenty-five feet from the man who was eager to decide his fate. He was certain that his face showed his concern.

This was not at all how he had planned it, he thought. Not at all the way it was supposed to go down, but Billy beat him to the punch and changed everything.

Jacob knew that even if he were able to get within an arms length of Billy, it still wouldn't allow him enough time to smack him in the face. So with deathly silence all around him, he began to think of a way to convince Billy to give himself up, or to at least fight like a man.

"You're crazy, Billy, to think you can get away with this! I'm unarmed and I didn't come here to shoot it out with you. If you want to fight, then why don't we just fight like men so nobody has to die? Makes even more sense if you just take your chances with the law, now, instead of running and hiding for the rest of your life like a hunted animal. Think about it, Billy. What kind of life would that be with a high price put on your head? Every man out there wanting to make a name for himself is gonna hunt you down like a dog. We can settle our score without gunplay."

But as soon as those words left his mouth, Jacob could plainly see that it was too late for talk. Billy glared at Jacob, a smirk on his face. After listening to what Jacob had to say, he was quite certain that old Scarface was as afraid of his gun as he was afraid of Jacob's fists.

"I'm not out here to prove anything to you or anybody else!" Billy laughed weakly. "Besides, this ain't no social call you're makin', Jacob. You know darn well why you're here and I know it, too! And it sure wasn't to help me get a fair shake. Do I look that stupid?"

Billy was all done talking. He certainly had no intentions of rotting away in some jail for wasting a fat woman who just happened to get in the way. It wasn't his fault she stuck her nose in where it didn't belong. And as for the little old shrimp who fried along with the house, how was he supposed to know for sure she was in there?

Furthermore, it was ludicrous to even think that one person in Johnson's Flat was going to feel sorry for him because of the fix he was in. *Never did win any popularity contest around here anyway*, he thought dimly.

The Truth about Jacob

"Might be a real good time for you to start worrying about yourself, Jacob, instead of worrying about what I do or don't do." Billy spat in the mud. Finally, after what seemed like a very long time, he tossed something across the street that landed at Jacob's feet.

"Now you just strap on that gun-belt, Scarface, or I'll drop you where you stand without one!" he demanded.

Jacob stroked the back of his neck trying to soothe the tightness in his muscles. His fingers curled against his palms in a methodical manner as he concentrated on what to do next. He kept a good eye on Billy. He didn't want to appear to be afraid, but he was afraid. Not the fear of death itself, but rather the fear of never seeing Rachel again.

Jacob knew Billy meant business. He knew this by how quickly he threw the gun-belt with a Colt forty-four slid inside at his feet. And he knew he needed to stall for time, so he could think of some way to stop this madman.

"Just out of curiosity, Billy, how'd you know I was here?"

"The same way you found out I was in town! Why else do you think I made myself so visible? I knew you'd catch wind of my whereabouts. So you see, I'm a little smarter than you gave me credit for. Now quit stallin' and buckle that belt!"

Just when Jacob thought his time had run out, he heard the sound of movement. Old man Baxter popped onto the scene from out of nowhere, sporting a troubled look and panting like a racehorse. Reluctant to see anyone get killed, especially Jacob, he briskly highstepped it straight towards Billy.

"Keep your hand off that gun, Billy!" he demanded. "Killing Jacob isn't going to solve anything. It won't give you nothing but a rope around your neck! You've got at least fifty people peering out their windows that will be witness to the fact Jacob's not packing a gun. Folks around here know he's no hand with a gun and are aware that he had no intention of using one to bring you in. Now you know you can't force a man to draw against you and then call it a fair fight. Are you that stupid to think that you can get away with it? Well, if you are, then I'm here to tell you that you won't!"

By now it was too dark to see what kind of an expression Billy had on his face. Baxter didn't care, he just kept walking in Billy's direction as he continued to lecture him.

"Now you listen up here, young man! Maybe the law will go easy on you regarding Kate and Ma, assuming of course, their deaths were an accident. Now that's something to think about, isn't it? Or do you want to be a hunted man for the rest of your life? I'm saying it's in your best interest if you just take your chances with the law."

Baxter marched towards Billy, squinting his eyes in anger because that last statement he had just made nearly burned a hole in his throat. He and Kate were so in love, and he had never given up on the idea that they would marry one day. His dreams of sharing that truth with their daughter would have come to pass just as soon as she was married and out on her own. Kate felt all along that the proper thing to do was to hold off on their marriage until after Rachel was wed. But now, in light of all that had happened, it would give him a great deal of pleasure and a sense of satisfied justice to hang the no-good killer himself for taking the life of the woman who had finally accepted his marriage proposal just a week before her death.

Underneath, he knew he couldn't act like a crazy man. If he lost control and reacted with irrational impulses like Billy always did, it would just place him in the same sinking boat along with him. That was a position he wisely reasoned he didn't want to be in.

Billy knew that everything this old sidewinder had just said was a big crock of bull simply to try and save Jacob's life. "What a liar you are!" Billy accused. "Lying to my face and trying to trick me! You've always been partial to him anyway!" he shot back. "There's no way in hell I'm gonna just step aside and hand Jacob everything I've worked so hard for! And I sure ain't gonna drop my gun and let anyone in this measly town lock me away for the rest of my life!"

The old and the young shared a moment of guarded stares. Billy released a deep sigh. The reality was, he was a man alone as he figured it. Facing the law was out of the question as far as he was concerned. What did he have to lose now by shooting Jacob? If he had to take Baxter down with him, then so be it. No man was going to stand in his way, no matter who it may be.

"Just keep your distance, old man, I ain't got no beef with you!" Billy demanded.

Baxter pushed forward, figuring Billy was just trying to spook him. Unfortunately that bold move earned him a bullet in his right leg just below the thigh. The blunt force of the lead shattering bone sent him straight to the ground groaning with pain.

Billy broke a toothy grin. "You're a fool, old man! You can't say I didn't warn you!'

Rachel, who had been just minutes behind her father, arrived in the nick of time to witness the whole incident. She jumped from her horse, ran to her father and, on bended knees, quickly began to tend to her father's wound. She ripped the red scarf from her hair and tied it just above the bullet hole in his leg. Once the tourniquet was secured she grabbed his hand placing it directly on top of the wound and instructed him to apply as much pressure as he could. When she was certain that the flow of blood had begun to subside, she turned her attention on Billy.

"I should have shot you myself for what you did to Kate and Ma! I'll see you hang if it's the last thing I ever do!" she yelled, her face red with fury.

Rachel rushed across the fifteen feet that separated her from Billy. Tears filled her eyes, aware of the fact that he deliberately shot her father and killed her mother and grandmother. And now he had every intention of taking the life of the man she loved. She wasn't about to just stand by and let him destroy her whole world. He had no right to take all she had left.

She continued to rush towards Billy not knowing what she would do once she got there. Their eyes were locked as she lunged at him trying to knock him off balance. She was hoping that Jacob could then get the drop on him.

But her efforts failed. Billy took advantage of her feminine weaknesses and overpowered her by grabbing her first. With no time to think of a better way to free herself, Rachel instinctively began to kick and scream and beat him with her fists. At first she thought her efforts to squirm away were working, but she soon discovered that his firm hold on her was actually rendering her virtually motionless except for her legs. And even that ability was the bare minimum.

Billy had placed a tight cinch around her neck with his left arm. He held his gun in his right hand and pointed it directly at her head, which abruptly brought her kicking to a halt. He then forced her to turn around and face Jacob who had tried to run towards them in an attempt to reach Billy before he could gain complete control. He stopped dead in his tracks when the gun suddenly appeared pressed firmly at her temple.

Billy garnered an eerie smile and stunned his audience with words their ears could hardly believe. "I see that you don't really have the stomach to draw against me, Jacob! Well, maybe you had just better take a good look at what's really at stake here! Is Rachel's life a good enough reason to pick up that holster and strap it on?"

Jacob was shocked to think Billy would actually use Rachel as a shield. He was even more of a coward than he ever believed him to be. But then, Billy was always one to do what a person least expected.

Now it was no longer just about he and Billy. Rachel had been dragged into this mess and his only concern was not just Billy's threat to her well being, but the fact that just one wrong move on her part could cause his gun to fire accidentally.

Irritated at Jacob's stall, Billy yelled at him again. "Pick that gun up, Jacob, and strap it on your hip nice and slow before you make me hurt this pretty little lady!"

The Truth about Jacob

Jacob studied Billy's face. He believed that Billy would actually harm Rachel just to get what he wanted. He couldn't let that happen. His whole world revolved around her, and now, even his own life no longer mattered.

Jacob slowly bent down, picked up the dripping wet holster and then securely strapped it around his hip. Staring his contender straight in the eyes with his hands draped at his sides, he stood perfectly still waiting for Billy's next move.

As precious seconds ticked away, a flurry of thoughts filled his head. He knew this confrontation was no longer about two men who hated one another. It was more about love and loyalty to the faithful women in his life, past and present. He would see this thing through to the bitter end. Jacob was willing to die for the woman he loved more than life itself.

A gun usually gave a man something of worth. But in that respect, Billy felt it didn't ring true for Jacob. He was a good judge of such things. From where he stood Jacob still looked like small game, which made him shake his head with laughter. He always thought Jacob was below his station anyway, so he took this opportunity to throw a verbal potshot at him. "You don't look like such a big man after all even with a gun on!" he snarled.

Jacob ignored his nonsense and kept his eyes focused on Billy's long barreled colt.

Billy pursed his lips. His emerald eyes glared with enthusiasm. With a show of muscle strength in his biceps, he cast Rachel back across the muddy street towards her father who still lay helpless and bleeding on the ground.

Rachel scrambled to her father's side. She began to scream at the top of her lungs for someone to help. During that time she continued to whip her head back and forth from one end of the street to the other praying for help to come quickly. But with the dark foggy conditions it was impossible to see more than fifty feet in any direction.

Rachel's eyes teared up. Her voice trailed away into the cold air as her sight began to blur even more through her tears. She knew she was helpless to stop what was going to happen and the fear of that reality was breaking her heart. With no resolve, she fell to her father's side and wept.

Total concentration kept Jacob's eyes on Billy. He even noticed his fidgeting fingers just above his gun stroke the air as if it had substance. *It was just between the two of them now*, Jacob thought quietly. There was no courageous lawman to referee, no Kate to save the day, or at the last minute one of his mother's miracles to intervene and change everything for the better. It was time to just let happen what was going to happen.

Billy's eyes were wide as he flashed a twisted grin. His right hand seductively caressed his gun. And as he looked at Jacob, he showed his proud power. He adjusted his stance in order to get a better position and elude the same stupid little rock he had stumbled on twice already.

Jacob thought the evil on Billy's face was unsettling, just as unsettling as the knowledge that the cowardly sheriff was most likely hiding in his office somewhere, and that the other spectators who were awakened by all the shouting were peaking out through closed windows. Of course, the drunks that were bellied up to the bar would get a good show regardless of which man fell.

"Say your prayers, Scarface, 'cause I don't plan on looking at that ugly mug of yours for one more minute!"

With hands in position the countdown began. Both men stared at the weapons that were ready to put at least one man in his grave.

Stationed at the side of her unconscious father, Rachel's persistent cries sliced through the chilly air. She could not bear to witness the horror of watching Jacob fall victim to Billy's fast draw. So she held her breath and one by one threw her hands up over her eyes. Painfully, she buried her face against her father's chest and continued to weep through her prayers.

Billy stood rigid. His eyes were pools of green hatred. He glared at Jacob, holding a grudge so boundless it hurt. It didn't

The Truth about Jacob

matter that he had no other reason for hating the man other than jealousy. Vengeance was only part of what he was feeling because in actuality, killing Jacob tonight was going to be just for the hell-of-it.

So it was with absolutely no regrets that his fingers clenched in excitement, eager to get rid of the man that had stood in the way of practically every dream he ever had.

Billy motioned with a quick nod of his head to initiate the challenge and then went for his gun faster than the blink of an eye. You could almost hear the wind beneath his hand. As for Jacob, there was not enough time to even search his soul much less draw a gun that was still laid to rest in his holster.

In the course of just seconds two shots rang out. And then there was dead silence. Even the wind had quieted down. Confusion gave way to mystery. The unexpected had happened and there was a sense of wildness within the mystery of whose life really lay in the balance. Slow-moving shadows were barely visible within the small hiatus between Jacob and Billy.

Time stretched out in front of Jacob as the fuzzy details of what had just taken place were being ironed out in his confused mind. By the time his whole life ceased to flash before his eyes, Billy had already hit the ground. Jacob could hear gurgling sounds coming from the prone figure stretched out face down in the mud. Then he heard one last gasping breath at the exact moment his swift footsteps brought him just ten inches short of Billy's body.

Most of the townsfolk were by now rushing out their doors and some had clustered in the street surrounding the redheaded gunfighter who lay dead at their feet. Completely bewildered, their faces revealed the conflicting story their eyes beheld. You could hear their whispered question. "How did Jacob survive the speed of Billy's draw?

Jacob stood tall, still frozen in time staring in disbelief at the gaping hole in Billy's back. After all, his gun had remained untouched during the three seconds it took to snuff out a life.

And yet Billy lay dead, embedded face down in a puddle of mud. Another stride moved Jacob closer for a better view, and his eyes were drawn to the steady flow of dark red blood, oozing from the deep wound that had laid Billy's back wide open.

At a time when few clues were coming to light, a good one creaked away into the darkness of the night on four rusty wheels.

Chapter 15

A lone breeze fanned Jacob's sweaty cheek as he stood alone in a thick growth of trees. Amongst the graves were layers of leaves that had decomposed and shed again year after year. The flattened, weather-beaten graves of his family were now barely visible. Jacob moved his eyes across the three wooden crosses examining just how brutal the elements had been over the passage of time. The crosses read: Man, Woman and Child. He would make them new ones with their birth names painted on them.

It was sad to think that this was all that was left to show of his entire family. He was thankful Kate had left behind a piece of paper with vague directions as to the whereabouts of the graves. Since they were well camouflaged from the naked eye, there was no way he would have ever been able to find their final resting spot. That information was also tucked away in her little black book that had amazingly survived the fire.

Jacob stood silent, wiping his tears. He knew his heart wouldn't heal overnight. A loss such as his would take some time getting used to. However, there was an unexplained sense of calmness. The best he could figure it was most likely due to the sudden closure of his long agonizing search for his family. At the same time, he felt such emptiness inside without Kate and Ma.

Jacob stepped back a little and worked his way twenty more steps to the crest of a small hill. He stared down at Kate and Ma's graves. The two well-rounded heaps were covered with five feet of prairie dirt and had just joined his family in this small remote graveyard about a month ago. Standing slouched, leaning against his shovel that was drenched in dirt, he prayed for his two friends in the quietness of this sanctuary. This was his first opportunity to pay his last respects to all who were buried here. At the time Baxter laid Ma and Kate to rest, he was still healing from the beating he took from Billy's boys.

Jacob searched his mind with great difficulty trying to find the right words to say at a solemn time like this. Flooded with feelings of inadequacy, it seemed next to impossible for a man like himself to give them all the dignified words they deserved. He was never much of a churchgoer, and therefore felt far from being qualified to speak on their behalf like a true man of the cloth could do. But even though he was a newcomer to this sort of thing he wasn't about to let that stop him. And because he was determined to somehow get it right, Jacob would find the proper words that were fitting and meaningful and they'd come straight from his heart.

This was the least he could do for the two women who had taken him in when he had nowhere else to go. But no matter how fond they had become of one another, he certainly was dumbfounded to discover they had generously bequeathed to him all they owned. He couldn't recollect either Ma or Kate even hinting at such a kind gesture, nor did the thought even cross his mind.

And yet now, he had in his possession many miles of acreage. That plush land included a large portion of the foothills and valley floor along with an extensive stretch of the only river vein that fed this part of the valley during the summer months.

The Truth about Jacob

Information revealing this transaction was registered at the County Seat, located in the small town of Hogsville, thirty miles to the south.

A sheet of paper stating the particulars of this document was also hidden in the same Bible that had concealed his mother's last words. Kate had dropped the little black book on the ground outside the house in the dirt during her scuffle with Billy. Amazingly enough, it had somehow gone unnoticed by everyone until Baxter spotted the dog chewing on it the day he came to dig Ma's bones out from under the ashes.

The sound of wagons came from out of nowhere taking Jacob's thoughts away from his loved ones. There was an endless herd of man-ridden horses pounding the ground off in the distance. Wagons too numerous to count were approaching in his direction led by Rachel and her father. The townsfolk were dressed in their Sunday best. Along with all the others, the local preacher clothed in a black shiny suit trotted up proudly to make his presence known. There were cowhands from miles around coming for no other reason than to pay their final respects to two highly thought of ladies and three members of a family that most had never heard of, until today.

Once their wagons slowed to a halt, Rachel stepped down to take her rightful place beside Jacob. The majority of the other people mingled a bit just briefly to shake hands and chat and then gathered around in their usual groups.

With the preacher in place and the townsfolk still taking their places, Jacob's tongue felt thick in his mouth, rendering him speechless. He had to admit to himself that this was something he never expected out of some of these folks. He wondered for a moment if he was dreaming, although Rachel was real enough tightly clutching his arm.

All he could do was breathe deep and act as cordial as possible. Any words that came to mind right now remained stuck in his throat. He didn't fully comprehend all that was taking place because everything was happening so fast. But as hard as all of this was to believe, he'd like to think that for some of the older folks here this was their way of saying they were sorry for having done nothing to help his family in their hour of need. If nothing else, this gesture of kindness would give him a more peaceful closure.

As far as Rachel was concerned, no words from Jacob were necessary. Just three days ago he had asked for her hand in marriage and that's all she needed to hear. And with that thought, she slid her arm around Jacob's waist and softly snuggled her head against his chest.

Jacob brought his right hand to his head in a self-conscious manner pretending to scratch his temple. He was visibly shaken with moisture in his eyes. Once again he felt the lazy breeze tease his beet red face. His eyes scoured the immediate area around the graves. The entire patch of dirt was lined with every man, woman and child that lived in the surrounding area of Johnson's Flat.

His heart felt heavy. A strange thing happened. He couldn't pull his eyes away from all the people. At that moment a feeling of such peace washed over him. He knew he had learned how to forgive and the wonderful grace of God captured the moment. He realized right then and there it was a good day to bury past grievances right along with his family.

Late in the day, after the last man rode off and every wagon had drifted out of sight, there were only two people left standing beside the graves. Closure set well with Jacob, Rachel could easily tell. Neither one uttered a single word, respecting one another's need for some quiet time. Both were conscious of the fact that it would take some time to heal, but they were both also aware that the healing process had already begun.

Jacob stood next to Rachel thinking about his family buried beneath thick layers of red dirt and hardpan. He could still recall in vivid detail the last time he saw them alive. It pained him to picture their smiling faces. Yet in the wake of those fond memories, he realized that things happened for a reason.

The Truth about Jacob

The events of his life had taken him on a long journey full of many experiences. Some were disappointing, but many were happy and will always be treasured. The rewards in life don't come easily. There is usually a price to pay. He would try to keep his loved ones alive in his heart. But for now, the love of his life was standing next to him and her needs took precedence over everything else, even his own pain. Jacob saw no need to burden Rachel with his thoughts. She had enough misery of her own to contend with, because her losses were just as heart wrenching as his.

At one time Rachel had thought very highly about the woman she believed to be her mother. Standing here now, beside Jacob in this graveyard, she knew one thing for sure, she'd never think kindly of her ever again. After an emotional conversation with her father, she sadly discovered that all the wonderful things she believed to be true about her were actually not true at all. Rachel came to realize that her father and Kate had fashioned Maxine's sweet, squeaky-clean image simply to protect her as a small child from the awful truth.

It was no accident that all the photos of that woman had been ripped to shreds and burned in Kate's favorite cooking range in the kitchen. Rachel saw to that little task personally. She was glad that the truth had finally been revealed after all these years. But deep inside the thought of another hidden truth brought about an ache to her heart that was bitter sweet. The reality that she hadn't recognized her own birth mother, who lived day in and day out right under her nose the entire time she was growing up, made things a little more difficult to swallow.

Her roots had begun with Kate, she knew that now. Having her as such a positive influence in her life for so many years was a blessing in disguise. Spending those years with her only as a good friend, instead of a daughter, would always weigh heavy on her mind and tear at her heart. The knowledge of their true kinship came much too late to embrace Kate as her mother face to face, but Rachel knew she would be forever grateful to have had her as the best friend any daughter could ever hope for.

It occurred to her then, how little she really knew about Ma. But since she and Kate were cut from the same pattern, Rachel found it easy to think of her as a loving grandmother. Ma had a tendency to grow on you and that made it easier to remember her with fondness.

Rachel's wide, curious eyes were drawn to a mystery that had caught her interest back when she first arrived at the burial site, even before the funeral service had begun. Separated by twenty feet or more of good earth, there were two other freshly dug graves. Unlike the others, they sadly sat beside one another all alone on top of a small knoll facing east instead of west. The dirt and rocks covering the mounds were loosely spread out in every direction and one appeared to be that of a child because of its small size.

Rachel was aware of the fact that the only graves that were ever placed facing the east were those containing the remains of some poor soul who had chosen to take their own life. And by doing so, because of the violent nature of their death, they had somehow acquired the power to cast bad luck on any other living relative left behind.

It was a foolish superstition, Rachel thought to herself, *but it was one that was taken seriously by some people.* Rachel was quite sure Jacob wouldn't uphold such a silly old wives' tale as that, so she surmised that he had placed the graves in that position for an entirely different reason.

Rachel knew he was the one who dug the graves, because his tools were still piled around the heaps of dirt and he was covered with dust from head to toe. While Jacob was busy brushing away a number of leaves that had fallen on top of Jeremiah's grave, Rachel slowly strolled towards the other fresh mounds of dirt to take a closer peek. Rachel could feel Jacob's eyes on her as she climbed the small embankment.

The Truth about Jacob

Once there, she noticed a crudely cut wooden cross twelve inches high thrust into the ground at the foot of the graves. A small wooden plaque had been propped up against a rock and was placed at the head between the two piles of dirt. Rachel advanced the short distance to the top and then stooped down on one knee to read the fine print carved on the face of the nameplate. The words she read took her breath away.

Rachel took her eyes away from the marker briefly looking over her shoulder at Jacob to see if he was paying any attention to what she was doing. Their eyes never met, thus preserving both this moment of intrigue for Rachel, and Jacob's right to privacy at what he was doing. This act of kindness had his name written all over it. If she knew anything about her man at all, it was that his heart could only beat to a compassionate drum. Yet, even so, he never ceased to amaze her, especially since this act of kindness was something of a mystery.

Rachel stood up, remaining a curious observer, yet visibly shaken. She whispered the names again under her breath, "Beloved Son: Billy Kyle Roberts Mother: Julia Mae Crawford."

The expression on her face mirrored her thoughts. Perplexed, her mind bombarded with questions, causing her to drift back in thought to two days ago. The day that dusk stood still during a gut-wrenching standoff that resulted in the death of Billy. With that event having plunged Jacob into a depressed state of mind, she couldn't imagine why he would decide to place his grave here with his family as a constant reminder of what had taken place.

Rachel was no expert at second guessing Jacob's motives, but for some reason she did understand one important thing, Billy was the least likely person she ever expected to end up in this cemetery. But the reality that he had, had demonstrated just what kind of man Jacob Fowler really was. It was no wonder why she had fallen head over heels in love with him.

If Jacob could exemplify such unimpeachable mercy towards a cold-blooded killer like Billy, then she, too, could accept the idea that Jacob had seemingly put his resentment towards Billy behind him. Even if Jacob chose not to ever confide in her, then she could live with that. In any case, even though the question had its intrigue, she wouldn't be asking Jacob why Billy and the woman whose name she didn't recognize were placed here along with their loved ones.

Jacob silently hoped Rachel would not question him about the graves she was so meticulously viewing. In a conscientious effort to honor the last request of an old friend who once gave him a bag of candy and had many years later saved his life, he wasn't talking. He vowed never to mention even one thing about her sordid story to anyone. Jacob had already burned the only evidence left behind explaining exactly what had happened in her life, and why she did what she felt she had to.

There was a letter addressed to him that he had received the very next day after Billy's death. Packy Pete delivered it in person along with a small bag of honey drops. Inside the envelope was a letter that brought Jacob to tears. It told of more heartbreak than any one woman should ever have to endure, a story of survival beyond mere self-preservation.

There had been no rules to follow where she had come from, Julia wrote. For her father to marry his very own niece thirty years his junior without her willing consent was completely acceptable in a town made up of mostly inbred rejects. Robbing his own daughter's innocence while she lay helpless with severed stumps, still raw and bleeding, placed him in a league all his own. Julia's desperate mother, who bravely put a bullet through the back of her husband's head before turning the gun on herself, set her young daughter free from the bondage of a dysfunctional life full of damnation and hatred.

The letter also explained why she, like her mother had done before her, chose the only means of escape from the constant mental torment of her despicable crime that had become more than she could bear. Unfortunately for her, having no real knowledge of God's great love, understanding, and forgiving capabilities beyond man's inner resources, suicide seemed like the only logical way for her to end her own mental suffering over what she had done.

In order to save a good man, Julia's willpower and good judgment was tested as never before. And for that reason, and that reason alone, she was forced to do the unthinkable. By taking the life of her only child she felt she had carried out an atrocity against human nature of the worst kind. She could not free herself from the haunting visions of her actions, nor could she ever imagine that one day she could actually forgive herself for this horrible thing she had done, much less a God, who teaches Thou Shall Not Kill.

Even though Billy was a by-product of incest and had been raised by the Robert's family, she still loved him, however, watching her son grow into the exact same likeness of her father over the years, carved a deep black hole inside her heart.

As the years passed by she had kept very close tabs on him. And when she saw no change for the better, she knew he would never break the ugly chain of meanness that was bred deep within his soul.

Julia and her son were strangers by all accounts especially in terms of association. Regretfully she stated that if she'd had it all to do over again, she would have done things quite differently. She would have tried to raise the boy all by herself.

She had mistakenly thought that her son would have a much better chance at a simpler life if he had all the material gains she couldn't give him. A strong family unity with both a mother and father figure to guide him, she also truly believed was in his best interest.

The beauty of that thought however had faded quickly over the years as she soon discovered that the Robert's didn't do her child any extra favors. Julia stood back behind the scenes and watched from afar to see their lives unfold into nothing more than the same dysfunctional life style she herself had escaped.

The irony of it all moved her heart further away from the beautiful concept that there were close-knit families who lived and loved to the fullest and that God and his precious love reigned as head of their households.

The truth about Jacob's family had finally been revealed. But the truth about Billy's parents would remain a secret forever, buried in a short wooden box along with the broken heart of the lady without legs.

Printed in the United States
38542LVS00005B/43-51